"A mystery fan never goes wrong when he picks up Ngaio Marsh's latest whodunit"
—*Tacoma News Tribune*

"As clever and pointed as ever"
—*The New Yorker*

"Miss Marsh puts on an ever-so-readable display of her own brilliant talents in this classical manor-house story"
—*The Detroit Sunday News*

"Peerless . . ."
—*Times-Picayune, New Orleans*

"In the best Marsh tradition . . ."
—*San Francisco Examiner-Chronicle*

"The Christmas party in which all hell and a few ornaments break loose"
—*Chicago Tribune*

"Has the Ngaio Marsh Benchmark: an inviting background and a genuine puzzle . . . had me honestly fooled"
—Thomas Lask, *New York Times*

About the Author

Ngaio Marsh has been known to mystery readers since 1933, when Roderick Alleyn strolled urbanely into his first case. Since that time Alleyn has been promoted to Superintendent, Ngaio Marsh has been made a dame of the British Empire, and novels such as *Clutch of Constables, When in Rome,* and *Dead Water* have become known worldwide as the best in mystery writing. Dame Ngaio has also spent a great deal of time in the theatre, both professional and amateur, and has worked as a producer in the British Theatre Guild. Her autobiography, *Black Beech and Honeydew,* was published in 1965.

TIED UP
IN TINSEL

Ngaio Marsh

 PYRAMID BOOKS ● NEW YORK

For
my godson,
Nicholas Dacres-Mannings,
when he grows up

Contents

Cast of Characters

HILARY BILL-TASMAN   of Halberds Manor—
Landed proprietor

Staff of Halberds

BLORE	Butler
MERVYN	Head houseman
NIGEL	Cook
COOKE ("KITTIWEE")	Second houseman
VINCENT	Gardener-chauffeur
TOM	Odd boy

Guests at Halberds

TROY ALLEYN	Celebrated painter
COLONEL F. FLEATON FORRESTER	Hilary's uncle
MRS. FORRESTER	The Colonel's wife
MR. BERT SMITH	Authority on antiques
CRESSIDA TOTTENHAM	Hilary's fiancée

The Law

MAJOR MARCHBANKS	Governor at the Vale
SUPERINTENDENT WRAYBURN	Downlow Police Force
SUPERINTENDENT RODERICK ALLEYN	C.I.D.
DETECTIVE-INSPECTOR FOX	C.I.D.
DETECTIVE-SERGEANT THOMPSON	Fingerprint expert C.I.D.
DETECTIVE-SERGEANT BAILEY	Photographer C.I.D.

Sundry guests and constables

One – Halberds

"When my sire," said Hilary Bill-Tasman, joining the tips of his fingers, "was flung into penury by the Great Slump, he commenced Scrap-Merchant. You don't mind my talking?"

"Not at all."

"Thank you. When I so describe his activities I do not indulge in *facezie*. He went into partnership in a rag-and-bone way with my Uncle Bert Smith, who was already equipped with a horse and cart and the experience of a short lifetime. 'Uncle,' by the way, is a courtesy title."

"Yes?"

"You will meet him tomorrow. My sire, who was newly widowed, paid for his partnership by enlarging the business and bringing into it such items of family property as he had contrived to hide from his ravenous creditors. They included a Meissen bowl of considerable monetary though, in my opinion, little aesthetic value. My Uncle Bert, lacking expertise in the higher reaches of his profession, would no doubt have knocked off this and other heirlooms to the nearest fence. My father, however, provided him with such written authority as to clear him of any suspicion of chicanery and sent him to Bond Street, where he drove a bargain that made him blink."

"Splendid. Could you keep your hands as they are?"

"I think so. They prospered. By the time I was five they had two carts and two horses and a tidy account in the bank. I congratulate you, by the way, upon making no allusion to Steptoe and Son. I rather judge my new acquaintances under that heading. My father developed an unsuspected flare for trade and, taking advantage of the Depression, bought in a low market and, after a period of acute anxiety, sold in a high one. There came a day when, wearing his best suit and the tie to which he had every right, he sold the last of his family possessions at an exorbitant price to King Farouk, with whom he was tolerably acquainted. It was a Venetian chandelier of unparalleled vulgarity."

"Fancy."

"This transaction led to most rewarding sequels, terminated only by His Majesty's death, at which time my father had established a shop in South Moulton Street while Uncle Bert presided over a fleet of carts and horses, maintaining his hold on the milieu that best suited him, but greatly increasing his expertise."

"And you?"

"I?" Until I was seven years old I lodged with my father and adopted uncle in a two-roomed apartment in Smalls Yard, Cheapjack Lane, E.C.4."

"Learning the business?"

"You may say so. But also learning, after admittedly a somewhat piecemeal fashion, an appreciation of English literature, objets d'art and simple arithmetic. My father ordered my education. Each morning he gave me three tasks to be executed before evening when he and Uncle Bert returned from their labours.

After supper he advanced my studies until I fell asleep."

"Poor little boy!"

"You think so? So did my Uncle and Aunt. My father's maternal connections. They are a Colonel and Mr. Forrester. You will meet them also tomorrow. They are called Frederick Fleaton and Bedelia Forrester but have always been known in the family as Uncle Flea and Aunt Bed, the facetious implication having been long forgotten."

"They intervened in your education?"

"They did, indeed. Having got wind of my father's activities they had themselves driven into the East End. Aunt Bed, then a vigorous young woman, beat on my locked door with her umbrella and when admitted gave vent to some very intemperate comments strongly but less violently seconded by her husband. They left in a rage and returned that evening with an offer."

"To take over your education?"

"And me. In toto. At first my father said he'd see them damned first but in his heart he liked them very much. Since our lodging was to be demolished as an insanitary dwelling and new premises were difficult to find he yielded eventually, influenced, I daresay, by threats of legal action and Child Welfare officers. Whatever the cause, I went, in the upshot, to live with Uncle Flea and Aunt Bed."

"Did you like it there?"

"Yes. I didn't lose touch with my father. He patched up his row with the Forresters and we exchanged frequent visits. By the time I was thirteen he was extremely affluent and able to pay for my education at his own old school at which fortunately, he had put me down at birth. This relieved us to some extent

from the burden of an overpowering obligation but I
retain the liveliest sense of gratitude to Flea and Bed."

"I look forward to meeting them."

"They are held to be eccentric. I can't see it myself,
but you shall judge."

"In what way?"

"Well—Trifling departures from normal practice
perhaps. They never travel without green-lined tropical
umbrellas of a great age. These they open when they
awake in the morning, as they prefer their vernal shade
to the direct light. And then they bring a great many
of their valuables with them. All Aunt Bed's jewels
and Uncle Flea's stocks and shares and one or two
very nice objets d'art of which I wouldn't at all mind
having the disposal. They also bring a considerable
amount of hard cash. In Uncle Flea's old uniform case.
He is on the reserve list."

"That is perhaps a little eccentric."

"You think so? You may be right. To resume. My
education, from being conventional in form, was later
expanded at my father's instance, to include an immensely thorough training in the more scholarly aspects
of the trade to which I succeeded. When he died I
was already accepted as a leading European authority
on the great period of Chinese ceramics. Uncle Bert
and I became very rich. Everything I've touched turned,
as they say, to gold. In short I was a 'have' and not
a 'have not.' To cap it all (really it was almost comi-
cal), I became a wildly successful gambler and won
two quite princely nontaxable fortunes on the Pools.
Uncle Bert inspired me in this instance."

"Lovely for you."

"Well—I like it. My wealth has enabled me to indulge my own eccentricities which you may think as
extreme as those of Uncle Flea and Aunt Bed."

"For instance?"

"For instance, this house. And its staff. Particularly, you may think, its staff. Halberds belonged from Tudor times up to the first decade of the nineteenth century, to my paternal forebears: the Bill-Tasmans. They were actually the leading family in these parts. The motto is, simply, 'Unicus,' which is as much as to say 'peerless.' My ancestors interpreted it, literally, by refusing peerages and behaving as if they were royalty. You may think me arrogant," said Hilary, "but I assure you that compared to my forebears, I am a violet by a mossy stone."

"Why did the family leave Halberds?"

"My dear, because they were ruined. They put everything they had into the West Indies and were ruined, very properly I daresay, by the emancipation of slaves. The house was sold off but owing to its situation nobody really fancied it and as the Historic Trust was then in the womb of time, it suffered the ravages of desertion and fell into a sort of premature ruin."

"You bought it back?"

"Two years ago."

"And restored it?"

"And am in process of restoring it. Yes."

"At enormous cost?"

"Indeed. But, I hope you agree, with judgment and style?"

"Certainly. I have," said Troy Alleyn, "finished for the time being."

Hilary got up and strolled round the easel to look at his portrait.

"It is, of course, extremely exciting. I'm glad you are still to some extent what I think is called a figurative painter. I wouldn't care to be reduced to a schizoid arrangement of geometrical propositions however satisfying to the abstracted eye."

"No?"

"No. The Royal Antiquarian Guild (the Rag as it is called) will no doubt think the portrait extremely avantgarde. Shall we have our drinks? It's half-past twelve, I see."

"May I clean up, first?"

"By all means. You may prefer to attend to your own tools but if not, Mervyn, who you may recollect was a signwriter before he went to gaol, would, I'm sure, be delighted to clean your brushes."

"Lovely. In that case I shall merely clean myself."

"Join me here, when you've done so."

Troy removed her smock and went upstairs and along a corridor to her deliciously warm room. She scrubbed her hands in the adjoining bathroom, and brushed her short hair, staring, as she did so, out of the window.

Beyond a piecemeal domain, still in the hands of landscape-gardeners, the moors were erected against a leaden sky. Their margins seemed to flow together under some kind of impersonal design. They bore their scrubby mantling with indifference and were, or so Troy thought, unnervingly detached. Between two dark curves the road to the prison briefly appeared. A light sleet was blown across the landscape.

"Well," she thought, "it lacks only the Hound of the Baskervilles and I wouldn't put it past him to set that up if it occurs to him to do so."

Immediately beneath her window lurched the wreckage of a conservatory that at some time had extended along the outer face of the east wing. Hilary had explained that it was soon to be demolished: at the moment it was an eyesore. The tops of seedling firs poked through shattered glass. Anonymous accumulations had silted up the interior. In one part the roof had completely fallen in. Hilary said that when next she visited Halberds she would look down upon lawns and a vista through cypress trees leading to a fountain with stone dolphins. Troy wondered just how successful these improvements would be in reducing the authority of those ominous hills.

Between the garden-to-be and the moor, on a ploughed slope, a scarecrow, that outlandish, *commedia-dell'arte*-like survival, swivelled and gesticulated in the December wind.

A man came into view down below, wheeling a barrow and tilting his head against the wind. He wore a sou'wester and an oilskin cape.

Troy thought, "That's Vincent. That's the gardener-chauffeur. And what was it about Vincent? Arsenic? Yes. And I suppose this must all be true. Or must it?"

The scarecrow rocked madly on its base and a wisp or two of straw flew away in the sleety wind.

2.

Troy had only been at Halberds for five days but already she accepted its cockeyed grandeur. After her arrival to paint his commissioned portrait, Hilary had thrown out one or two airy hints as to the bizarre nature of his staff. At first she had thought that he was going in for a not very funny kind of legpulling but she soon discovered her mistake.

At luncheon they were waited upon by Blore, to whom Hilary had referred as his chief steward, and by Nigel, the second houseman.

Blore was a baldish man of about sixty with a loud voice, big hands and downcast eyes. He performed his duties composedly as, indeed, did his assistant, but there was something watchful and at the same time colourless in their general behaviour. They didn't shuffle, but one almost expected them to do so. One felt

that it was necessary to remark that their manner was
not furtive. How far these impressions were to be at-
tributed to hindsight and how far to immediate observation, Troy was unable to determine, but she
reflected that after all it was a tricky business adapting
oneself to a domestic staff entirely composed of murderers. Blore, a headwaiter at the time, had murdered
his wife's lover, a handsome young busboy. Because of
extenuating circumstances the death sentence, Hilary
told her, had been commuted into a lifer which ex-
emplary behaviour had reduced to eight years. "He is
the most harmless of creatures," Hilary had said. "The
busboy called him a cuckold and spat in his face at
a moment when he happened to be carving a wing-rib.
He merely lashed out."

Mervyn, the head houseman, once a signwriter,
had, it emerged, been guilty of killing a burglar with
a booby-trap. "Really," Hilary said, "it was going much
too far to gaol him. He hadn't meant to *destroy* anyone, you know, only to give an intruder pause if one
should venture to break in. But he entirely misjudged
the potential of an old-fashioned flatiron balanced on
a door top. Mervyn became understandably warped
by confinement and behaved so incontinently that he
was transferred to the Vale."

Two other homicides completed the indoor staff. The
cook's name, laughably enough, was Cooke. Among
his fellows he was known as Kittiwee, being a lover
of cats.

"He actually trained as a chef. He is not," Hilary
had told Troy, "one hundred per cent he-man. He was
imprisoned under that heading but while serving his
sentence attacked a warder who approached him when
he was not in the mood. This disgusting man was
known to be a cat-hater and to have practised some
form of cruelty. Kittiwee's onslaught was therefore

doubly energetic, and most unfortunately his victim struck his head against the cell wall and was killed. He himself served a painful extension of his sentence."

Then there was the second houseman, Nigel, who in former years had been employed in the manufacture of horses for merry-go-rounds, and on the creative side of the waxworks industry until he became a religious fanatic and unreliable.

"He belonged to an extreme sect," Hilary had explained. "A monastic order of sorts with some curious overtones. What with one thing and another, the life put too heavy a strain upon Nigel. His wits turned and he murdered a person to whom he always refers as 'a sinful lady.' He was sent to Broadmoor where, believe it or not, he recovered his senses."

"I hope he doesn't think me sinful."

"No, no, I promise you. You are not at all the type and in any case he is now perfectly rational and composed except for weeping rather extravagantly when he remembers his crime. He has a gift for modelling. If we have a white Christmas I shall ask him to make a snowman for us."

Finally, Hilary had continued, there was Vincent, the gardener. Later on, when the landscape specialists had completed their operations, there would be a full complement of outside staff. In the meantime there were casual labourers and Vincent.

"And really," Hilary had said, "it is quite improper to refer to him as a homicide. There was some ridiculous misunderstanding over a fatal accident with an arsenical preparation for the control of fungi. This was followed by a gross misdirection to a more than usually idiotic jury and, after a painful interval, by a successful appeal. Vincent," he had summed up, "is a much wronged person."

"How," Troy had asked, "did you come to engage your staff?"

"Ah! A pertinent question. You see, when I bought Halberds I determined not only to restore it but to keep it up in the condition to which it had been accustomed. I had no wish to rattle dismally in Halberds with a village trot or some unpredictable Neapolitan couple who would feed me on pasta for a fortnight and then flounce off without notice. On the other hand, civilized household staff, especially in this vicinity, I found to be quite unobtainable. After some thought I made an appointment to visit my neighbour-to-be, the Governor at the Vale. He is called Major Marchbanks.

"I put my case to him. I had always understood that of all criminals, murderers are much the nicest to deal with. Murderers of a certain class, I mean. I discriminate. Thugs who shoot and bash policemen and so on are quite unsuitable and indeed would be unsafe. But your single-job man, prompted by a solitary and unprecedented upsurge of emotion under circumstances of extreme provocation, is usually well behaved. Marchbanks supported me in this theory. After some deliberation I arranged with him that as suitable persons were released I should have the first refusal. It was, from their point of view, a form of rehabilitation. And being so rich, I can pay handsomely."

"But was there a ready supply?"

"I had to wait for them, as it were, to fall in. For some time I lived very simply with only Blore and Kittiwee, in four rooms of the east wing. But gradually the supply built up: the Vale was not the only source. The Scrubs and, in Nigel's case, Broadmoor, were also productive. In passing," Hilary had then pointed out, "I remind you that there is nothing original in my arrangements. The idea was canvassed in Victorian times by no less a person than Charles Dickens, and considerably later, on a farcical level, by Sir Arthur Wing Pinero. I have merely adopted it and carried it to its logical conclusion."

"I think," Troy had said, "it's remotely possible that Rory, my husband, you know, may have been responsible for the arrest of one or even more of your staff. Would they——?"

"You need have no qualms. For one thing they don't know of the relationship and for another they wouldn't mind if they did. They bear no grudge as far as I can discern against the police. With the possible exception of Mervyn, the ex-signwriter, you recollect. He feels that since his booby-trap was directed against a class that the police are concerned to suppress, it was rather hard that he should suffer so grievous a penalty for removing one of them. But even he has taken against Counsel for the Prosecution and the jury rather than against the officers who arrested him."

"Big of him. I suppose," said Troy.

These conversations had taken place during the early sittings. Now, on the fifth day of her residence, Hilary and Troy had settled down to an oddly companionable relationship. The portrait prospered. She was working with unusual rapidity, and few misgivings. All was well.

"I'm so glad," Hilary said, "that it suits you to stay for Christmas. I do wish your husband could have joined us. He might have found my arrangements of some interest."

"He's on an extradition case in Australia."

"Your temporary loss," said Hilary neatly, "is my lasting gain. How shall we spend the afternoon? Another sitting? I am all yours."

"That would be grand. About an hour while the

light lasts and then I'll be under my own steam for a bit, I think."

Troy looked at her host who was also her subject. A very rewarding subject, she thought, and one with whom it would be fatally easy to confuse interpretation with caricature. That ovoid forehead, that crest of fuzz, those astonished, light-blue eyes and the mouth that was perpetually hitched up at the corners in a non-smile! But, Troy thought, isn't interpretation, of necessity, a form of caricature?

She found Hilary contemplating her as if she was the subject and he the scrutator.

"Look here," Troy said abruptly, "you've not by any chance been pulling my leg? About the servants and all that?"

"No."

"No?"

'I assure you. No."

"O.K. said Troy, "I'm going back to work. I'll be about ten minutes fiddling and brooding and then if you'll sit again, we'll carry on."

"But of course. I am enjoying myself," Hilary said, "inordinately."

Troy returned to the library. Her brushes as usual had been cleaned in turpentine. Today they had been set out together with a nice lump of fresh rag. Her paint-encrusted smock had been carefully disposed over a chair-back. An extra table covered with paper had been brought in to supplement a makeshift bench. Mervyn again, she thought, the booby-trap chap who used to paint signs.

And as she thought of him he came in, wary-looking and dark about the jaw.

"Excuse me," Mervyn said, and added "madam"

as if he'd just remembered to do so. "Was there anything else?"

"Thank you, very much," Troy said. "Nothing. It's all marvellous," and felt she was being unnaturally effusive.

"I thought," Mervyn mumbled, staring at the portrait, "you could do with more bench space. Like. Madam."

"Oh, rather. Yes. Thank you."

"Like you was cramped. Sort of."

"Well—not now."

He said nothing but he didn't go. He continued to look at the portrait. Troy, who never could talk easily about work in progress, began to set her palette with her back to Mervyn. When she turned round it gave her quite a shock to find him close beside her.

But he was only waiting with her smock which he held as if it were a valuable topcoat and he a trained manservant. She felt no touch of his hands as he helped her into it.

"Thank you very much," Troy repeated, and hoped she sounded definitive without being disagreeable.

"Thank you, madam," Mervyn responded, and as always when this sort of exchange cropped up, she repressed an impulse to ask, "For what?"

('For treating him like a manservant when I know he's a booby-setting manslaughterer?" thought Troy.)

Mervyn withdrew, delicately closing the door after him.

Soon after that, Hilary came in and for an hour Troy worked on his portrait. By then the light had begun to fail. Her host having remarked that he expected a long-distance call from London, she said she would go for a walk. They had, she felt, seen enough of each other for the time being.

3.

A roughish path crossed the waste that was to become something Troy supposed Hilary would think of as a pleasance. It led past the ruined conservatory to the ploughed field she had seen from her bedroom window.

Here was the scarecrow, a straw-stuffed antic goggily anchored in the hole it had enlarged with its own gyrations, lurching extravagantly in the north wind. It was clad in the wreckage of an Edwardian frock coat and a pair of black trousers. Its billycock hat had been pulled down over the stuffed bag which formed its head. It was extended in the classic cruciform gesture, and a pair of clownish gloves, tied to the ends of the crosspiece, flapped lamentably as did the wild remnants of something that might once have been an opera cloak. Troy felt that Hilary himself had had a hand in its creation.

He had explained in detail to what lengths, and at what enormous expense of time and money, he had gone in the accurate restoration of Halberds. Portraits had been hunted down and repurchased, walls rehung in silk, panelling unveiled and ceilings restored by laborious stripping. Perhaps in some collection of foxed watercolours he had found a Victorian sketch of this steep field with a gesticulating scarecrow in the middle distance.

She skirted the field and climbed a steep slope. Now she was out on the moors and here at last was the sealed road. She followed it up to where it divided the hills.

She was now high above Halberds, and looking down at it, saw it was shaped like an E without the middle stroke and splendidly proportioned. An eighteenth-century picture of it hung in the library. Remembering this, she was able to replace the desolation that surrounded the house with the terraces, walks, artificial hill, lake and vistas created, so Hilary had told her, by Capability Brown. She could make out her own room in the eastward façade with the hideous wreckage of conservatory beneath it. Smoke plumed up wildly from several of the chimneys and she caught a whiff of burning wood. In the foreground Vincent, a foreshortened pigmy, trundled his barrow. In the background a bulldozer slowly laid out preliminaries for Hilary's restorations. Troy could see where a hillock, topped by a folly and later destroyed by a bomb, had once risen beyond an elegant little lake. That was what the bulldozer was up to: scooping out a new lake and heaping the spoil into what would become a hillock. And a "Hilary's Folly" no doubt would ultimately crown the summit.

"And no doubt," Troy thought, "it will be very, very beautiful but there's an intrinsic difference between 'Here it still is' and 'This is how it was,' and all the monstrous accumulation of his super-scrap markets, high antiques and football pools won't do the trick for him."

She turned and took fifteen paces into the north wind.

It was as if a slide had clicked over in a projector and an entirely dissociated subject thrown on the screen. Troy now looked down into the Vale, as it was locally called, and her first thought was of the hopeless incongruity of this gentle word, for it stood not only for the valley but for the prison, whose dry moats, barriers, watchtowers, yards, barracks and chimney-stacks were set out down below like a scale model of themselves for her to shudder at. Her husband sometimes referred to the Vale as "Heartbreak House."

The wind was now fitfully laced with sleet and this

steel-engraving of a view was shot across with slant-wise drifts that were blown out as fast as they appeared.

Facing Troy was a road sign.

STEEP DESCENT
DANGEROUS CORNERS
ICE
CHANGE DOWN

As if to illustrate the warning a covered van laboured up the road from Halberds, stopped beside her, clanked into bottom gear, and ground its way down into the Vale. It disappeared round the first bend and was replaced by a man in a heavy mackintosh and tweed hat, climbing towards her. He looked up and she saw a reddened face, a white moustache and blue eyes.

She had already decided to turn back, but an obscure notion that it would be awkward to do so at once, made her pause. The man came up with her, raised his hat, gave her a conventional "Good evening," and then hesitated. "Coming up rough," he said. He had a pleasant voice.

"Yes," Troy said. "I'll beat a retreat, I think. I've come up from Halberds."

"Stiffish climb, isn't it, but not as stiff as mine. Please forgive me but you must be Hilary Bill-Tasman's celebrated guest, mustn't you? My name's Marchbanks."

"Oh, yes. He told me—"

"I come as far as this most evenings for the good of my wind and legs. To get out of the valley, you know."

"I can imagine."

"Yes," said Major Marchbanks, "it's rather a grim

proposition, isn't it? But I shouldn't keep you standing about in this beastly wind. We shall meet again, I hope, at the Christmas tree."

"I hope so, too," said Troy.

"Rather a rum setup at Halberds I expect you think, don't you?"

"Unusual, at least."

"Quite. Oh," Major Marchbanks said as if answering an unspoken query, "I'm all for it, you know. All for it."

He lifted his wet hat again, flourished his stick, and made off by the way he had come. Somewhere down in the prison a bell clanged.

Troy returned to Halberds. She and Hilary had tea very cosily before a cedar-wood fire in a little room which, he said, had been his five-times-great-grand-mother's boudoir. Her portrait hung above the fire: a mischievous-looking old lady with a discernible resemblance to Hilary himself. The room was hung in apple-green watered silk with rose-embroidered curtains. It contained an exquisite screen, a French ormolu desk, some elegant chairs and a certain lavishness of porcelain amoretti.

"I daresay," Hilary said through a mouthful of hot buttered muffin, "you think it an effeminate setting for a bachelor. It awaits its chatelaine."

"Really?"

"Really. She is called Cressida Tottenham and she, too, arrives tomorrow. We think of announcing our engagement."

"What is she like?" Troy asked. She had found that Hilary relished the direct approach.

"Well—let me see. If one could taste her she would be salty with a faint rumour of citron."

"You make her sound like a grilled sole."

"All I can say to that is: she doesn't look like one."

"What *does* she look like?"

"Like somebody whom I hope you will very much want to paint."

"Oh-ho," said Troy. "Sits the wind in that quarter!"

"Yes, it does and it's blowing steady and strong. Wait until you see her and then tell me if you'll accept another Bill-Tasman commission and a much more delectable one. Did you notice an empty panel in the north wall of the diningroom?"

"Yes, I did."

"Reserved for Cressida Tottenham by Agatha Troy."

"I see."

"She really is a lovely creature," Hilary said with an obvious attempt at impartial assessment. "You just wait. She's in the theatre, by the way. Well, I say *in*. She's only just in. She went to an academy of sorts and thence into something she calls Organic-Expressivism. I have tried to point out that this is a bastard and meaningless term but she doesn't seem to mind."

"What do they do?"

"As far as I can make out they take off their clothes, which in Cressida's case can do nothing but please, and cover their faces with pale green tendrils, which (again in her case) is a ludicrous waste of basic material. Harmful to the complexion."

"Puzzling."

"Unhappily Aunt Bed doesn't quite approve of Cressida, who is Uncle Flea's ward. Her father was a junior officer of Uncle Flea's and was killed in occupied Germany when saving Uncle Flea's life. So Uncle Flea felt he had an obligation and brought her up."

"I see," Troy said again.

"You know," he said, "what I like about you, apart from your genius and your looks, is your lack of superfluous ornament. You are an important piece from a very good period. If it wasn't for Cressida I should probably make advances to you myself."

"That really *would* throw me completely off my stroke," said Troy with some emphasis.

"You prefer to maintain a detached relationship with your subjects."

"Absolutely."

"I see your point, of course," said Hilary.

"Good."

He finished his muffin, damped his napkin with hot water, cleaned his fingers, and walked over to the window. The rose-embroidered curtains were closed, but he parted them and peered into the dark. "It's snowing," he said. "Uncle Flea and Aunt Bed will have a romantic passage over the moors."

"Do you mean—are they coming tonight—?"

"Ah, yes. I forgot to tell you. My long-distance call was from their housekeeper. They left before dawn and expect to arrive in time for dinner."

"A change in plans?"

"They suddenly thought they would. They prepare themselves for a visit at least three days before the appointed time and yet they dislike the feeling of impending departure. So they resolved to cut it short. I shall take a rest. What about you?"

"My walk has made me sleepy, I think. I will, too."

"That's the north wind. It has a soporific effect upon newcomers. I'll tell Nigel to call you at half-past seven, shall I? Dinner at eight-thirty and the warning bell at a quarter past. Rest well," said Hilary, opening the door for her.

As she passed him she became acutely aware of his height and also of his smell, which was partly Harris tweed and partly something much more exotic. "Rest well," he repeated and she knew he watched her as she went upstairs.

4.

She found Nigel in her bedroom. He had laid out her ruby-red silk dress and everything that went with it. Troy hoped that this ensemble had not struck him as being sinful.

He was now on his knees blowing needlessly at a brightly burning fire. Nigel was so blond that Troy was glad to see that his eyes were not pink behind their prolific white lashes. He got to his feet and in a muted voice asked her if there would be anything else. He gazed at the floor and not at Troy, who said there was nothing else.

"It's going to be a wild night," Troy remarked, trying to be natural but sounding, she feared, like a bit part in *The Corsican Brothers*.

"That is as Heaven decrees, Mrs. Alleyn," Nigel said severely and left her. She reminded herself of Hilary's assurances that Nigel had recovered his sanity.

She took a bath, seething deliciously in resinous vapours, and wondered how demoralizing this mode of living might become if prolonged. She decided (sinfully, as no doubt Nigel would have considered) that for the time being, at least, it tended to intensify her nicer ingredients. She drowsed before her fire, half aware of the hush that comes upon a house when snow falls in the world outside. At half-past seven Nigel tapped at her door and she roused herself to answer and then to dress. There was a cheval glass in her room, and she couldn't help seeing that she looked well in her ruby dress.

Distant sounds of arrival broke the quietude. A car engine. A door slam. After a considerable interval, voices in the passage and an entry into the next room. A snappish, female voice, apparently on the threshold, shouted, "Not at all. Fiddle! Who says anything about

being tired? We won't dress. I said we won't dress."
An interval and then the voice again: "You don't
want Moult, do you? Moult! The Colonel doesn't want
you. Unpack later. I said he can unpack later."

"Uncle Flea," thought Troy, "is deaf."

"And don't," shouted the voice, "keep fussing about
the beard."

A door closed. Someone walked away down the
passage.

"About the *beard?*" Troy wondered. "Could she have
said beard?"

For a minute or two nothing could be heard from
the next room. Troy concluded that either Colonel or
Mrs. Fleaton Forrester had retired into the bathroom
on the far side, a theory that was borne out by a man's
voice, coming as it were from behind Troy's wardrobe,
exclaiming: "B! About my beard!" and receiving no
audible reply.

Soon after this the Forresters could be heard to
leave their apartment.

Troy thought she would give them a little while with
Hilary before she joined them, and she was still staring
bemusedly into her fire when the warning bell, booty,
so Hilary had told her, from Henry the Eighth's sack
of the monasteries, rang out in its tower over the
stables. Troy wondered if it reminded Nigel of his con-
ventual days before he had turned a little mad.

She shook herself out of her reverie and found her
way downstairs and into the main hall where Mervyn,
on the lookout, directed her to the green boudoir.
"We are not disturbing the library," Mervyn said with
a meaningful smirk, "madam."

"How very considerate," said Troy. He opened the
boudoir door for her and she went in.

The Forresters stood in front of the fire with Hilary,
who wore a plum-coloured smoking suit and a widish

tie. Colonel Forrester was a surprised-looking old man with a pink-and-white complexion and a moustache. But no beard. He wore a hearing aid.

Mrs. Forrester looked, as she had sounded, formidable. She had a blunt face with a mouth like a spring-trap, prominent eyes fortified by pebble-lenses and thin, grey hair lugged back into a bun. Her skirt varied in length from midi to maxi and she clearly wore more than one flannel petticoat. Her top half was covered by woolen garments in varying shades of dull puce. She wore a double chain of what Troy suspected were superb natural pearls and a number of old-fashioned rings in which deposits of soap had accumulated. She carried a string bag containing a piece of anonymous knitting and her handkerchief.

Hilary performed the introductions. Colonel Forrester beamed and gave Troy a little bow. Mrs. Forrester sharply nodded.

"How do you find yourself" she said. "Cold?"

"Not at all, thank you."

"I ask because you must spend much of your time in overheated studios painting from the Altogether, I said *painting from the Altogether.*"

This habit of repetition in fortissimo, Troy discovered, was automatic with Mrs. Forrester and was practised for the benefit of her husband, who now gently indicated that he wore his hearing aid. To this she paid no attention.

"She's not painting *me* in the nude, darling Auntie," said Hilary, who was pouring drinks.

"A pretty spectacle *that* would be."

"I think perhaps you base your theories about painters on *Trilby* and *La Vie de Bohème.*"

"I saw Beerbohm Tree in *Trilby,*" Colonel Forrester remembered. "He died backwards over a table. It was awfully good."

There was a tap on the door followed by the entrance of a man with an anxious face. Not only anxious but most distressingly disfigured, Troy thought, as if by some long-distant and extensive burn. The scars ran down to the mouth and dragged it askew.

"Hullo, Moult," said Mrs. Forrester.

"I beg your pardon, sir, I'm sure," said the man to Hilary. "It was just to put the Colonel's mind at ease, sir. It's quite all right about the beard, sir."

"Oh good, Moult. Good. Good. Good," said Colonel Forrester.

"Thank you, sir," said the man and withdrew.

"What is it about your beard, Uncle Flea?" asked Hilary, to Troy's immense relief.

"*The* beard, old chap. I was afraid it might have been forgotten and then I was afraid it might have been messed up in the packing."

"Well, it hasn't, Fred. I said it hasn't."

"I know, so that's all right."

"Are you going to be Father Christmas, Colonel?" Troy ventured, and he beamed delightedly and looked shy.

"I knew you'd think so," he said. "But no. I'm a Druid. What do you make of that, now?"

"You mean—you belong—?"

"Not," Hilary intervened, "to some spurious Ancient Order wearing cotton-wool beards and making fools of themselves every second Tuesday."

"Oh, *come,* old boy," his uncle protested. "That's not fair."

"Well, perhaps not. But no," Hilary continued, addressing himself to Troy. "At Halberds, Saint Nicholas or Santa Claus or whatever you like to call the Teutonic old person, is replaced by an ancient and more authentic figure: the great precursor of the Winter Solstice observances who bequeathed—consciously or not—

so much of his lore to his Christian successors. The Druid, in fact."

"And the Vicar doesn't mind," Colonel Forrester earnestly interjected. "I promise you. The Vicar doesn't mind a bit."

"*That* doesn't surprise me," his wife observed with a cryptic snort.

"He comes to the party even. So, you see, I shall be a Druid. I have been one each year since Hilary came to Halberds. There's a tree and a kissing bough you know, and, of course, quantities of mistletoe. All the children come: the children on the place and at the Vale and in the neighbouring districts. It's a lovely party and I love doing it. Do you like dressing up."

He asked this so anxiously, like a character in *Alice,* that she hadn't the heart to give anything less than an enthusiastic assent and almost expected him to say cosily that they must dress up together one of these days.

"Uncle Flea's a brilliant performer," Hilary said, "and his beard is the *pièce de résistance*. He has it made by Wig Creations. It wouldn't disgrace King Lear. And then the wig itself! So different from the usual repellent falsity. You shall see."

"We've made some changes," said Colonel Forrester excitedly. "They've re-dressed it. The feller said he thought it was a bit on the long side and might make me look as if I'd opted out. One can't be too careful."

Hilary brought the drinks. Two of them were large and steaming and had slices of lemon in them.

"Your rum toddies, Aunt Bed," he said. "Tell me if there's not enough sugar."

Mrs. Forrester wrapped her handkerchief round her glass and sat down with it. "It seems all right," she said. "Did you put nutmeg in your uncle's?"

"No."

"Good."

"You will think," said the Colonel to Troy, "that rum toddies before dinner are funny things to drink, but we make a point of putting them forward after a journey. Usually they are nightcaps."

"They smell delicious."

"Would you like one?" Hilary asked her. "Instead of a White Lady."

"I think I'll stick to the White Lady."

"So shall I. Well, my dears," Hilary said generally. "We are a small houseparty this year. Only Cressida and Uncle Bert to come. They both arrive tomorrow."

"Are you still engaged to Cressida?" asked his aunt.

"Yes. The arrangement stands. I am in high hopes, Aunt Bed, that you will take more of a fancy to Cressida on second sight."

"It's not second sight. It's fiftieth sight. Or more."

"But you know what I mean. Second sight since we became engaged."

"What's the odds?" she replied ambiguously.

"Well, Aunt Bed, I would have thought—" Hilary broke off and rubbed his nose. "Well, anyway, Aunt Bed, considering I met her in your house."

"More's the pity. I warned your uncle. I said I warned you, Fred."

"What about, B?"

"Your gel! The Tottenham gel. Cressida."

"She's not *mine,* B. You put things so oddly, my dear."

"Well, anyway," Hilary said. "I hope you change your mind, Auntie."

"One can but hope," she rejoined and turned to Troy. "Have you met Miss Tottenham?" she asked.

"No."

"Hilary thinks she will go with the house. We're still

talking about Cressida," Mrs. Forrester bawled at her husband.

"I know you are. I heard."

After this they sipped their drinks, Mrs. Forrester making rather a noise with hers and blowing on it to cool it down.

"The arrangements for Christmas Day," Hilary began after a pause, "are, I think, an improvement on last year. I've thought of a new entrance for you, Uncle Flea."

"Have you, though? Have you? Have you?"

"From outside. Through the french windows behind the tree."

"Outside!" Mrs. Forrester barked. "Do I understand you, Hilary? Do you plan to put your uncle out on the terrace on a midwinter night—in a snowstorm, I said a snowstorm?"

"It'll only be for a moment, Aunt Bed."

"You have not forgotten, I suppose, that your uncle suffers from a circulatory complaint."

"I'll be all right, B."

"I don't like it, I said—"

"But I assure you! And the undergarment is quilted."

"Pshaw! I said—"

"No, but do listen!"

"Don't fuss, B. My boots are fur-lined. Go on, old boy. You were saying—?"

"I've got a lovely tape recording of sleigh bells and snorting reindeer. Don't interrupt, anybody. I've done my research and I'm convinced that there's an overlap here, between the Teutonic and the druidical and if there's not," Hilary said rapidly, "there ought to be. So. We'll hear you shout 'Whoa,' Uncle Flea, outside, to the reindeer, and then you'll come in."

"I don't shout very loud nowadays, old boy," he

said worriedly. "Not the Pirbright note any more, I'm afraid."

"I thought of that. I've had the 'whoa' added to the bells and snorts. Blore did it. He has a stentorian voice."

"Good. Good."

"There will be thirty-one children and about a dozen parents. And the usual assortment of county and farmers. Outside hands and, of course, the staff."

"Warders?" asked Mrs. Forrester. "From That Place?"

"Yes. From the married quarters. Two. Wives and families."

"Marchbanks?"

"If he can get away. They have their own commitments. The chaplain cooks up something pretty joyless. Christmas," said Hilary acidly, "under maximum security. I imagine one can hardly hear the carols for the alarm bells."

"I suppose," said his aunt after a good suck at her toddy, "you all know what you're about. I'm sure I don't. I smell danger."

"That's a dark saying, Auntie," remarked Hilary.

Blore came in and announced dinner. It was true that he had a very loud voice.

Two – Christmas Eve

Before they went to bed they listened to the regional weather report. It said that snow was expected to fall through the night and into Christmas Eve but that it was unlikely to continue until Christmas Day itself. A warm front was approaching over the Atlantic Ocean.

"I always think," Hilary remarked, "of a warm front as belonging to a décolleté Regency lady thrusting her opulent prow, as it were, into some consequential rout or ball and warming it up no end. The ball, I mean."

"No doubt," his aunt tartly rejoined, "Cressida will fulfil that questionable role at the coming function."

"Well, you know, darling, I rather think she may," said Hilary and kissed his aunt good-night.

When Troy hung her red dress in her wardrobe that night she discovered that the recess in which it had been built must be flanked by a similar recess in the Forresters' room so that the ancient wall that separated them had been, in this section, removed, and a thin partition separated their respective hanging cupboards.

Mrs. Forrester, at this very moment, was evidently disposing of her own garments. Troy could hear the scrape of coat hangers on the rail. She jumped violently when her own name was shouted, almost, as it seemed, into her ear.

"*Troy!* Odd sort of Christian name."

Distantly, Colonel Forrester could be heard to say: ". . . no . . . understand . . . famous . . ." His head, Troy thought was momentarily engulfed in some garment. Mrs. Forrester sounded extremely cross.

"You know what *I* think about it," she shouted and rattled the coat hangers, "I said you know . . ."

Troy, reprehensibly, was riveted in her wardrobe.

". . . don't trust . . ." continued the voice. "Never have. You know that." A pause and a final shout: ". . . sooner it was left straight out to the murderers. Now!" A final angry clash of coat hangers and a bang of wardrobe doors.

Troy went to bed in a daze but whether this condition was engendered by the Lucullan dinner Hilary and Kittiwee had provided or by the juxtaposition of unusual circumstances in which she found herself, she was quite unable to determine.

She had thought she was sleepy when she got into bed, but now she lay awake, listening to small noises made by the fire in her grate as it settled into glowing oblivion and to faint sighs and occasional buffets of the nightwind outside. "Well," Troy thought, "this *is* a rum go and no mistake."

After a period of disjointed but sharp reflections she began to fancy she heard voices somewhere out in the dark. "I must be dozing, after all," Troy thought but knew that it was not so. A gust of wind rumbled in the chimney, followed by a silence into which there intruded the wraith of a voice, belonging nowhere and diminished as if the sound had been turned off in a television dialogue and only the ghost of itself remained.

Now, positively, it was out there below her window: a man's voice—two voices—engaged in indistinguishable talk.

Troy got out of bed and, by the glow from her dying fire, went to her window and parted the curtains.

It was not as dark as she had expected. She looked out at a subject that might have inspired Jane Eyre to add another item to her portfolio. A rift had been blown in the clouds and the moon in its last quarter shone on a morbid-looking prospect of black shadows thrown across cadaverous passages of snow. In the background rose the moors and in the foreground, the shambles of broken glass beneath her window. Beyond this jogged two torchlights, the first of which cast a yellow circle on a white ground. The second bobbed about the side of a large wooden crate with the legend: "Musical instrument. Handle with Extreme Care," stencilled across it. It seemed to be mounted on some kind of vehicle, a sledge, perhaps since it made no noise.

The two men wore hooded oilskins that glinted as they moved. The leader gesticulated and pointed and then turned and leant into the wind. Troy saw that he had some kind of tow-rope over his shoulder. The second man placed his muffled hands against the rear end of the crate and braced himself. He tilted his head sideways and glanced up. For a moment she caught sight of his face. It was Nigel.

Although Troy had only had one look at Vincent, the nonpoisoner-chauffeur-gardener, and that look from the top of a hill, she felt sure that the leader was he.

"Hup!" cried the disembodied voice and the ridiculous outfit moved off round the east wing in the direction of the main courtyard of Halberds. The moon was overrun by clouds.

Before she got back into bed Troy looked at a little

Sèvres clock on her chimney-piece. She was greatly surprised to find that the hour was no later than ten past twelve.

At last she fell asleep and woke to the sound of opening curtains. A general pale glare was admitted.

"Good-morning, Nigel," said Troy.

"Good-morning," Nigel muttered, "madam."

With downcast eyes he placed her morning tea tray at her bedside.

"Has there been a heavy fall of snow?"

"Not to say heavy," he sighed, moving towards the door.

Troy said boldly, "It was coming down quite hard last night, wasn't it? You must have been frozen pulling that sledge."

He stopped. For the first time he lifted his gaze to her face. His almost colourless eyes stared through their white lashes like a doll's.

"I happened to look out," Troy explained, and wondered why on earth she should feel frightened.

He stood motionless for a few seconds and then said "Yes?" and moved to the door. Like an actor timing an exit line he added, "It's a surprise," and left her.

The nature of the surprise became evident when Troy went down to breakfast.

A moderate snowfall had wrought its conventional change in a landscape that glittered in the thin sunshine. The moors had become interfolding arcs of white and blue, the trees wore their epaulettes with an obsequious air of conformity, and the area under treatment by tractors was simplified as if a white dust-sheet had been dropped over it.

The breakfast-room was in the east wing of Halberds. It opened off a passage that terminated in a door into the adjoining library. The library itself, being the foremost room of the east wing, commanded views on three sides.

Troy wanted to have a stare at her work. She went into the library and glowered at the portrait for some minutes, biting her thumb. Then she looked out of the windows that gave on the courtyard. Here, already masked in snow and placed at dead centre, was a large rectangular object that Troy had no difficulty in recognizing since the stencilled legend on its side was not as yet obliterated.

And there, busy as ever, were Vincent and Nigel, shovelling snow from wheelbarrows and packing it round the case in the form of a flanking series of steps based on an understructure of boxes and planks. Troy watched them for a moment or two and then went to the breakfast-room.

Hilary stood in the window supping porridge. He was alone.

"Hullo, hullo!" he cried. "Have you seen the work in progress? Isn't it exciting: the creative urge in full spate. Nigel has been inspired. I *am* so pleased, you can't think."

"What are they making?"

"A reproduction of my many-times-great grand-father's tomb. I've given Nigel photographs and of course he's seen the original. It's a compliment and I couldn't be more gratified. Such a change from wax-works and horses for roundabouts. The crate will represent the catafalque, you see, and the recumbent figure will be life-size. Really it's extraordinarily nice of Nigel."

"I saw them towing the crate round the house at midnight."

"It appears he was suddenly inspired and roused Vincent up to assist him. The top of the crate was already beautifully covered by snow this morning. It's so *good* for Nigel to become creative again. Rejoice with me and have some kedgeree or something. Don't you adore having things to look forward to?"

Colonel and Mrs. Forrester came in wearing that air of spurious domesticity peculiar to guests in a country house. The Colonel was enchanted by Nigel's activities and raved about them while his porridge congealed in its bowl. His wife recalled him to himself.

"I daresay," she said with a baleful glance at Hilary, "it keeps them out of mischief." Troy was unable to determine what Mrs. Forrester really thought about Hilary's experiment with murderers.

"Cressida and Uncle Bert," said Hilary, "are coming by the 3:30 at Downlow. I'm going to meet them unless, of course, I'm required in the library."

"Not if I may have a sitting this morning," said Troy.

"The light will have changed, won't it? Because of the snow?"

"I expect it will. We'll just have to see."

"What *sort* of portraits do you paint?" Mrs. Forrester demanded.

"Extremely good ones," said her nephew pretty tartly. "You're in distinguished company, Aunt Bedelia."

To Troy's intense amusement Mrs. Forrester pulled a long, droll face and immediately afterwards tipped her a wink.

"Hoity-toity," she said.

"Not at all," Hilary huffily rejoined.

Troy said, "It's hopeless asking what sort of things I paint because I'm no good at talking about my work. If you drive me into a corner I'll come out with the most awful jabberwocky."

And in a state of astonishment at herself Troy added like a shamefaced schoolgirl, "One paints as one must."

After a considerable pause Hilary said: "How generous you are."

"Nothing of the sort," Troy contradicted.

"Well!" Mrs. Forrester said. "We shall see what we shall see."

Hilary snorted.

"I did some watercolours," Colonel Forrester remembered, "when I was at Eton. They weren't very good but I did them, at least."

"That was something," his wife conceded, and Troy found herself adding that you couldn't say fairer than that.

They finished their breakfast in comparative silence and were about to leave the table when Blore came in and bent over Hilary in a manner that recalled his own past as a headwaiter.

"Yes, Blore," Hilary asked, "what is it?"

"The mistletoe, sir. It will be on the 3:30 and the person wonders if it could be collected at the station."

"I'll collect it. It's for the kissing bough. Ask Vincent to have everything ready, will you?"

"Certainly, sir."

"Good."

Hilary rubbed his hands with an exhilarated air and proposed to Troy that they resume their sittings. When the session was concluded, they went out into the sparkling morning to see how Nigel was getting on with his effigy.

It had advanced. The recumbent figure of a sixteenth-century Bill-Tasman was taking shape. Nigel's mittened hands worked quickly. He slapped on fistfuls of snow and manipulated them into shape with a wooden spatula: a kitchen implement, Troy supposed. There was something frenetic in his devotion to his task. He didn't so much as glance at his audience. Slap, slap, scoop, scoop, he went.

And now, for the first time, Troy encountered Cooke, the cook, nicknamed Kittiwee.

He had come out-of-doors wearing his professional hat, checked trousers and snowy apron with an over-coat slung rather stylishly over his shoulders. He carried an enormous ladle and looked, Troy thought, as if he had materialized from a Happy Families playing card. Indeed, his round face, large eyes and wide mouth were comically in accord with such a notion.

When he saw Troy and Hilary he beamed upon them and raised a plump hand to his starched hat.

"*Good* morning, sir," said Kittiwee. "*Good* morning, ladies."

" 'Morning, Cooke," Hilary rejoined. "Come out to lend a hand with the icing?"

Kittiwee laughed consumedly at this mildest of joke-lets. "Indeed, *no* sir," he protested. "I wouldn't dare. I just thought a *ladle* might assist the *artist*."

Nigel thus indirectly appealed to merely shook his head without pausing in his task.

"All going well in your department?" Hilary asked.

"Yes, thank you, sir. We're doing nicely. The Boy from Downlow is ever such a bright lad."

"Oh, Good. Good," Hilary said, rather hurriedly, Troy thought. "What about the mince pies?"

"Ready for nibbles and wishes immediately after tea, sir, if you please," cried Kittiwee, gaily.

"If they are on the same level as the other things you've been giving us to eat," Troy said, "they'll be the mince pies of the century."

It was hard to say who was the more delighted by this eulogy, Hilary or his cook.

Vincent came round the east wing wheeling another

barrowful of snow. At close quarters he turned out to be a swarthy, thin man with a haggard expression in his eyes. He looked sidelong at Troy, tipped out his load, and trundled off again. Kittiwee, explaining that he had only popped out for one second, embraced them all in the very widest of dimpled smiles and retired into the house.

A few minutes later Blore came into the courtyard and boomingly proclaimed that luncheon was served.

2.

Cressida Tottenham was blond and extremely elegant. She was so elegant that her beauty seemed to be a second consideration: a kind of bonus, a gloss. She wore a sable hat. Sable framed her face, hung from her sleeves, and topped her boots. When her outer garments were removed she appeared to be gloved rather than clad in the very ultimate of expensive simplicity.

Her eyes and her mouth slanted and she carried her head a little on one side. She was very composed and not loquacious. When she did talk she said "you know" with every second breath. She was not by any means the kind of subject that Troy liked to paint. This might turn out to be awkward: Hilary kept looking inquisitively at her as if to ask what she thought of Cressida.

To Mr. Bert Smith, Troy took an instant fancy. He was a little old man with an impertinent face, a bright eye and a strong out-of-date cockney habit of speech. He was smartly dressed in an aggressive countrified way. Troy judged him to be about seventy years old and in excellent health.

The encounter between the new arrivals and the Forresters was interesting. Colonel Forrester greeted

Miss Tottenham with timid admiration, calling her "Cressy dear."

Troy thought she detected a gently avuncular air, tempered perhaps by anxiety. The Colonel's meeting with Mr. Smith was cordial to a degree. He shook hands with abandon. "How are you? How are you, my dear fellow?" he repeatedly asked and with each inquiry broke into delighted laughter.

"How's the Colonel anyway?" Mr. Smith responded. "You're looking lovely, I'll say that for you. Fair caution, you are, and no error. What's all this they're givin' us abaht you dressing yourself up like Good King Thingummy? Wiv whiskers! *Whiskers!*" Mr. Smith turned upon Mrs. Forrester and suddenly bellowed: "Blimey, 'e must be joking—at 'is age! *Whiskers!*"

"It's my husband who's deaf, Smith," Mrs. Forrester pointed out, "not me. You've made that mistake before, you know."

"What *am* I thinking of," said Mr. Smith, winking at Troy and slapping Colonel Forrester on the back. "Slip of the tongue, as the butcher said when he dropped it accidental in the tripe."

"Uncle Bert," Hilary said to Troy, "is a comedian manqué. He speaks nicely when he chooses. This is his 'aren't I a caution, I'm a cockney' act. He's turning it on for Uncle Flea's benefit. You always bring him out, Uncle Flea, don't you?"

Miss Tottenham caught Troy's eyes and slightly cast up her own.

"Really?" asked the enchanted Colonel. "Do I really, though?"

Mr. Smith quietened down after this exchange and they all went in to tea, which had been set out in the dining-room and had none of the cosiness of Troy's and Hilary's tête-à-têtes by the boudoir fire. Indeed an air of constraint hung over the party which Cressida's refusal to act as chatelaine did nothing to relieve.

"You're not asking me to do the pouring-out bit, darling, for God's sake," Cressida said. "It'd, you know, frankly bore the pants off me. I've got, you know, a kind of thing against it. Not my scene, you know."

Mrs. Forrester stared fixedly at Cressida for some moments and then said, "Perhaps, Hilary, you would like me to perform."

"Darling Auntie, please do. It will be like old times, won't it? When Uncle Bert used to come to Eaton Square after you'd made it up over my upbringing."

"That's the ticket," Mr. Smith agreed. "No hard feelings. Live and let live. That's the story, Missus, isn't it?"

"You're a decent fellow in your own way, Smith," Mrs. Forrester conceded. "We've learnt to understand each other, I daresay. What sort of tea do you like, Mrs. Alleyn?"

Troy thought, "I am among people who say what they think when they think it. Like children. This is a most unusual circumstance and might lead to anything."

She excepted Mr. Smith from her blanket appraisal. "Mr. Smith," she considered, "is a tricky little old man, and what he really thinks about the company he keeps is nobody's business but his."

"How's all the villains, 'Illy?" he asked, putting his head on one side and jauntily quizzing his muffin. "Still keepin' their noses clean?"

"Certainly, Uncle Bert, but do choose your words. I wouldn't for the world Blore or Mervyn heard you talking like that. One of them might walk in at any moment."

"Oh dear," said Mr. Smith, unmoved.

"That yawning void over the fireplace," Cressida

said. "Is that where you meant? You know, about my picture?"

"Yes, my darling," Hilary responded. "As a matter of fact," he looked anxiously at Troy, "I've already ventured a tentative probe."

Troy was saved the awkwardness of a reply by Cressida, who said, "I'd rather it was the drawing-room. Not all mixed in with the soup, and, you know, your far from groovy ancestors." She glanced discontentedly at a Lely, two Raeburns and a Winterhalter. "You know," she said.

Hilary turned rather pink: "We'll have to see," he said.

Mervyn came in with the cook's compliments and the mince pies were ready when they were.

"What is he on about?" Cressida asked fretfully. "On top of tea? And anyway I abhor mincemeat."

"Darling, I *know*. So, privately, do I. But it appears to be an authentic old custom. On taking one's first bite" Hilary explained, "one makes a wish. The ceremony is held by tradition in the kitchen. One need only take a token nibble. It will give him so much pleasure."

"Are there still cats in the kitchen?" Cressida asked. "There's my thing about cats, remember."

"Mervyn," Hilary said, "ask Cooke to put Slyboots and Smartypants out, will you? He'll understand."

"He'd better. I'm allergic," Cressida told Troy. "Cats send me. But totally. I've only got to catch the eye of a cat and I am a psychotic wreck." She enlarged upon her theme. It would be tedious to record how many times she said Troy knew.

"I should be pleased," Mrs. Forrester said loudly, "to renew my acquaintance with Slyboots and Smartypants."

"Rather you than me," Cressida retorted, addressing herself to Mrs. Forrester for the first time but not looking at her.

"I so far agree with you, Hilary," said Mrs. Forrester, "in your views on your staff, as to consider Cooke was well within his rights when he attacked the person who maltreated cats. Well within his rights I consider he was, I said—"

"Yes, Auntie, I know you did. Don't we all! No, darling," Hilary said, anticipating his beloved. "You're the adorable exception. Well, now. Shall we all go and mumble up our mince?"

In the kitchen they were received by Kittiwee with ceremony. He beamed and dimpled but Troy thought there was a look of glazed displeasure in his eyes. This impression became unmistakable when infuriated yowls broke out behind a door into the yard. "Slyboots and Smartypants," thought Troy.

A red-cheeked boy sidled in through the door, shutting it quickly on a crescendo of feline indignation.

"We're sorry," Hilary said, "about the puss-cats, Cooke."

"It takes all sorts, doesn't it, sir?" Kittiwee cryptically rejoined with a sidelong glance at Miss Tottenham. The boy, who was sucking his hand, looked resentfully through the window into the yard.

The mince pies were set out on a lordly dish in the middle of the kitchen table. Troy saw with relief that they were small. Hilary explained that they must take their first bites in turn, making a wish as they did so.

Afterwards Troy was to remember them as they stood sheepishly round the table. She was to think of those few minutes as almost the last spell of general tranquility that she experienced at Halberds.

"You first, Auntie," Hilary invited.

"Aloud?" his aunt demanded. Rather hurriedly he assured her that her wish need not be articulate.

"Just as well," she said. She seized her pie, and took a prodigious bite out of it. As she munched she fixed her eyes upon Cressida Tottenham, and suddenly Troy was alarmed. "I know what she's wishing," Troy thought. "As well as if she were to bawl it out in our faces. She's wishing the engagement will be broken. I'm sure of it."

Cressida herself came next. She made a great to-do over biting off the least possible amount and swallowing it as if it were medicine.

"Did you wish?" Colonel Forrester asked anxiously.

"I forgot," she said and then screamed at the top of her voice. Fragments of mince pie escaped her lovely lips.

Mr. Smith let out a four-letter word and they all exclaimed. Cressida was pointing at the window into the yard. Two cats, a piebald and a tabby, sat on the outer sill, their faces slightly distorted by the glass, their eyes staring and their mouths opening and shutting in concerted meows.

"My dear *girl*," Hilary said and made no attempt to disguise his exasperation.

"My poor pussies," Kittiwee chimed in like a sort of alto to a leading baritone.

"I can't take *cats*," Cressida positively yelled.

"In which case," Mrs. Forrester composedly observed, "you *can* take yourself out of the kitchen."

"No, no," pleaded the Colonel. "No, B. No, no, no! Dear me! Look here!"

The cats now began to make excruciating noises with their claws on the windowpane. Troy, who liked cats and found them amusing, was almost sorry to see them abruptly cease this exercise, reverse themselves on the sill, and disappear, tails up. Cressida, however, clapped her hands to her ears, screamed again, and stamped her feet like an exotic dancer.

Mr. Smith said drily, "No trouble!"

But Colonel Forrester gently comforted Cressida with a wandering account of a brother-officer whose abhorrence of felines in some mysterious way brought about a deterioration in the lustre of his accoutrements. It was an incomprehensiable narrative, but Cressida sat on a kitchen chair and stared at him and became quiet.

"Never mind!" Hilary said on a note of quiet despair. "As we were." He appealed to Troy: "Will you?" he asked.

Troy applied herself to a mince pie, and as she did so there came into her mind a wish so ardent that she could almost have thought she spoke it aloud. "Don't," she found herself dottily wishing, "let anyting beastly happen. Please." She then complimented Kittiwee on his cooking.

Colonel Forrester followed Troy. "You *would* be surprised," he said, beaming at them, "if you knew about *my* wish. *That* you would." He shut his eyes and heartily attacked his pie. "Delicious!" he said.

Mr. Smith said: "How soft can you get!" and ate the whole of his pie with evident and noisy relish.

Hilary brought up the rear, and when they had thanked Kittiwee they left the kitchen. Cressida said angrily that she was going to take two aspirins and go to bed until dinner time. "And I don't," she added, looking at her fiancé, "want to be disturbed."

"You need have no misgivings, my sweet," he rejoined and his aunt gave a laugh that might equally have been called a snort. "Your uncle and I," she said to Hilary, "will take the air, as usual, for ten minutes."

"But—Auntie—it's too late. It's dark and it may be snowing."

"We shall confine ourselves to the main courtyard. The wind is in the east, I believe."

"Very well," he agreed. "Uncle Bert, shall we have our business talk?"

"Suits me," said Mr. Smith, "Any time."

Troy wanted to have a glower at her work and said as much. So they went their several ways.

As she walked through the hall and along the passage that led to the library, Troy was struck by the extreme quietude that obtained indoors at Halberds. The floor was thickly carpeted. Occasional lamps cast a subdued light on the walls but they were far apart. Whatever form of central heating had been installed was almost too effective. She felt as if she moved through a steamed-up tunnel.

Here was the door into the library. It was slightly ajar. She opened it, took two steps, and while the handle was still in her grasp was hit smartly on the head.

It was a light blow and was accompanied by the reek of turpentine. She was neither hurt nor frightened but so much taken by surprise that for a moment she was bereft of reasoning. Then she remembered there was a light switch inside the door and turned it on.

There was the library: warm, silent, smelling of leather, wood fires and paint. There was the portrait on its easel and the workbench with her familiar gear.

And there, on the carpet at her feet, the tin palette-can in which she put her oil and turpentine.

And down her face trickled a pungent little stream.

The first thing Troy did after making this discovery was to find the clean rag on her bench and wipe her face. Hilary, dimly lit on her easel, fixed her with an enigmatic stare. "And a nice party," she muttered, "*you've* let me in for, haven't you?"

She turned back towards the door which she found, to her surprise, was now shut. A trickle of oil and turpentine made its sluggish way down the lacquer-red paint. But *would* the door swing to of its own accord? As if to answer her, it gave a little click and opened a couple of inches. She remembered that this was habitual with it. A faulty catch, she supposed.

But someone had shut it.

She waited for a moment, pulling herself together. Then she walked quickly to the door, opened it, and repressed a scream. She was face-to-face with Mervyn.

This gave her a much greater shock than the knock on her head. She heard herself make a nightmarish little noise in her throat.

"Was there anything madam?" he asked. His face was ashen.

"Did you shut the door? Just now?"

"No, madam."

"Come in, please."

She thought he was going to refuse but he did come in, taking four steps and then stopping where the can still lay on the carpet.

"It's made a mess," Troy said.

"Allow me, madam."

He picked it up, walked over to the bench, and put it down.

"Look at the door," Troy said.

She knew at once that he had already seen it. She knew he had come into the room while she cleaned her face and had crept out again, shutting the door behind him.

"The tin was on the top of the door," Troy said. "It fell on my head. A booby-trap."

"Not a very nice thing," he whispered.

"No. A booby-trap."

"I never!" Mervyn burst out. "My God, I never. My God, I swear I never."

"I can't think—really—why you should."

"That's right," he agreed feverishly. "That's dead right. Christ, why should I! Me!"

Troy began to wipe the trickle from the door. It came away cleanly, leaving hardly a trace.

Mervyn dragged a handkerchief from his pocket, dropped on his knees, and violently attacked the stain on the string-coloured carpet.

"I think plain turpentine might do it," Troy said.

He looked round wildly. She fetched him a bottle of turpentine from the bench.

"Ta," he said and set to work again. The nape of his neck shone with sweat. He mumbled.

"What?" Troy asked. "What did you say?"

"He'll see. He notices everything. They'll say I done it."

"Who?"

"Everybody. That lot. Them."

Troy heard herself saying: "Finish it off with soap and water and put down more mats." The carpet round her easel had, at her request, been protected by upside-down mats from the kitchen quarters.

He gazed up at her. He looked terrified and crafty like a sly child.

"You won't do me?" he asked. "Madam? Honest? You won't grass? Not that I done it, mind. I never. I'd be balmy, woon't I? I never."

"All right, *all right*," Troy almost shouted. "Don't let's have all that again. You say you didn't and I— As a matter of fact, I believe you."

"Gor' bless you, lady."

"Yes, well, never *mind* all that. But if you didn't," Troy said sombrely, "who on earth did?"

"Ah! That's diffrent, ainnit? What say I know?

"You *know*!"

"I got me own idea, ain' I? Trying to put one acrost me. Got it in for all of us, that sod, excuse me for mentioning it."

"I don't know what you're talking about. It seems to me that I'm the one——"

"Do me a favour. You! Lady—you're just the mug, see? It's me it was set up for. Use your loaf, lady."

Mervyn sat back on his heels and stared wildly at Troy. His face, which had reminded her of Kittiwee's pastry, now changed colour: he was blushing.

"I'm sure I don't know what you'll think of me, madam," he said carefully. "I forgot myself, I'm that put out."

"That's all right," she said. "But I wish you'd just explain——"

He got to his feet and backed to the door, screwing the rag round his hand. "Oh madam, madam, madam," he implored. "I do wish you'd just use your loaf."

And with that he left her.

It was not until she reached her room and set about washing the turpentine and oil out of her hair that Troy remembered Mervyn had gone to gaol for murdering someone with a booby-trap.

3.

If Cressida had lost any ground at all with her intended over the affair of the cats, it seemed to Troy that she made it up again and more during the course of the evening. She was the last to arrive in the main drawing-room where tonight, for the first time, they assembled before dinner.

She wore a metallic trousered garment so adhesive that her body might itself have been gilded like the two quattrocento victories that trumpeted above the chimney-piece. When she moved, her dress, recalling Herrick, seemed to melt about her as if she were clad in molten gold. She looked immensely valuable and of course tremendously lovely. Troy heard Hilary catch his breath. Even Mrs. Forrester gave a slight grunt while Mr. Smith, very softly, produced a wolf whistle. The Colonel said, "My dear, you are quite bewildering," which was, Troy thought, as apt a way of putting it as any other. But still, she had no wish to paint Cressida and again she was uneasily aware of Hilary's questioning looks.

They had champagne cocktails that evening. Mervyn was in attendance under Blore's supervision, and Troy was careful not to look at Mervyn. She was visited by a sense of detachment as if she hovered above the scene rather than moved through it. The beautiful room, the sense of ease, the unforced luxury, of a kind of aesthetic liberation, seemed to lose substance and validity and to become—what? Sterile?

"I wonder," said Hilary at her elbow, "what that look means. An impertinent question, by the way, but of course you don't have to give me an answer." And before she could do so he went on. "Cressida is lovely, don't you think?"

"I do indeed but you mustn't ask me to paint her."

"I thought that was coming."

"It would be no good."

"How can you be so sure?"

"It would give you no pleasure."

"Or perhaps too much," Hilary said. "Of a dangerous kind."

Troy thought it better not to reply to this.

"Well," Hilary said, "it shall be as it must be. Already I feel the breath of Signor Annigoni down the nape of my neck. Another champagne cocktail? Of course you will. Blore!"

He stayed beside her, rather quiet for him, watching his fiancée, but Troy felt, in some indefinable way, still communicating with her.

At dinner Hilary put Cressida in the chatelaine's place and Troy thought how wonderfully she shone in it and how when they were married Hilary would like to show her off at much grander parties than this strange little assembly. Like a humanate version of his great possessions, she thought, and was uncomfortable in the notion.

Stimulated perhaps by champagne, Cressida was much more effervescent than usual. She and Hilary had a mock argument with amorous overtones. She began to tease him about the splendour of Halberds and then when he looked huffy added, "Not that I don't devour every last bit of it. It sends the Tottenham blood seething in my veins like . . ." She stopped and looked at Mrs. Forrester, who, over folded arms and with a magisterial frown, steadily returned her gaze.

"Anyway," Cressida said, waving a hand at Hilary, "I adore it all."

Colonel Forrester suddenly passed his elderly, veined fingers across his eyes and mouth.

"Darling!" Hilary said and raised his glass to Cressida.

Mr. Bert Smith also became a little flown with champagne. He talked of his and Hilary's business affairs and Troy thought he must be quite as shrewd as he gave himself out to be. It was not at all surprising that he had got on in such a spectacular manner. She wondered if, in the firm of Bill-Tasman and Smith Associates, which was what their company seemed to be called, Mr. Smith was perhaps the engine and Hilary the exquisite bodywork and upholstery.

Colonel Forrester listened to the high-powered talk with an air of wonderment. He was beside Troy and had asked to "take her in" on his arm, which she had found touching.

"Do you follow all this?" he asked her in a conspiratorial aside. He was wearing his hearing aid.

"Not very well. I'm an ass at business," she muttered and delighted him.

"So am I! I know! So am I! But we have to pretend, don't we?"

"I daren't. I'd give myself away, at once."

"But it's awfully clever. All the brainwork, you know!" he murmured, raising his brow and gazing at Troy. "Terrific! Phew! Don't you agree?"

She nodded and he slyly bit his lip and hunched his shoulders.

"We mustn't let on we're so muddly," said the Colonel.

Troy thought: this is how he used to talk to thoroughly nice girls when he was an ensign fifty years ago. All gay and playful with the "Destiny Waltz" swooning away on the bandstand and an occasional flutter in the conservatory. The chaperones thought he was just the job, no doubt. And she wondered if he proposed to Aunt Bed on a balcony at a regimental ball. But what the devil was Aunt Bed like in her springtide, Troy wondered, and was at a loss. A dasher, perhaps? A fine girl? A spanker?

". . . so I said, 'Do me a favour, chum. You call it what you like: for my book you're at the fiddle! Distinguished and important collection! Yeah? So's your old man!' Nothing but a bunch of job-burgers, that lot."

"I'm sure you're right, Uncle Bert," said Hilary definitively and bent towards his aunt.

"That's a very nice grenade you're wearing, Auntie darling," he said. "I don't remember it, do I?"

"Silver wedding," she said. "Your uncle. I don't often get it out."

It was a large diamond brooch pinned in a haphazard fashion to the black cardigan Mrs. Forrester wore over her brown satin dress. Her pearls were slung about her neck and an increased complement of rings had been shoved down her fingers.

Mr. Smith, his attention diverted from high finance, turned and contemplated her.

"Got 'em all on, eh?" he said. "Very nice, too. Here! Do you still cart all your stuff round with you? Is that right? In a tin box? Is that a fact?"

"Pas," Mrs. Forrester said, *"devant les domestiques."*

"How does the chorus go?"

Hilary intervened. "No, *honestly,* Aunt B," he protested throwing an agitated glance at Blore, who was at the sideboard with his back turned.

"Hilary," said Cressida, "that reminds me."

"Of what, my sweet?" Hilary asked apprehensively.

"It doesn't really matter. I was just wondering about tomorrow. The party. The tree. It's in the drawing-room isn't it? I've been wondering, what's the scene? You know? The stage-management and all that."

It was the first time Troy had heard Cressida assume an air of authority about Halberds, and she saw that Hilary was delighted. He embarked on a long explanation. The sleigh bells, the tape-recorded sounds, the arrival of Colonel Forrester as a Druid through the french windows. The kissing bough. The tree. The order of events. Colonel Forrester listened with the liveliest satisfaction.

This discussion took them through the rest of dinner. Cressida continued to fill out the role of hostess with considerable aplomb, and before Mrs. Forrester, who was gathering herself together, could do anything more about it, leant towards her and said, "Shall we, Aunt B?" with a ravishing smile. It was the first time, Troy suspected, that she had ever addressed her future aunt-by-marriage in those terms. Mrs. Forrester looked put out. She said, "I was going to, anyway," rose with alacrity, and made for the door. Her husband got there first and opened it.

"We shan't stay long over our port," he confided, looking from his wife to Troy. "Hilary says there are any number of things to be done. The tree and the kissing bough and all. Don't you like, awfully," he said to Troy, "having things to look forward to?"

When the ladies reached the drawing-room it was to find Vincent, Nigel and the apple-cheeked boy in the very act of wheeling in through the french windows a fine Christmas tree lightly powdered with snow. It was housed in a green tub and mounted on the kind of trolly garage hands lie upon when working underneath a car. At the far end of the room a green canvas sheet had been spread over Hilary's superb carpet, and to the centre of this the tree was propelled.

Winter had entered the room with the tree and laid its hands on their faces. Cressida cried out against it. The men shut the french windows and went away. A stepladder and an enormous box of decorations had been left beside the tree.

From the central chandelier in the drawing-room someone—Nigel, perhaps—had hung the traditional kissing bough, a bell-shaped structure made from mistletoe and holly with scarlet apples depending from it by golden tinsel. It was stuck about with scarlet candles. The room was filled with the heady smell of resinous greenery.

Troy was almost as keen on Christmas trees as Colonel Forrester himself and thought the evening might well be saved by their joint activities. Mrs. Forrester eyed the tree with judicious approval and said there was nothing the matter with it.

"There's a Crib," she said. "I attend to that. I bought it in Oberammergau when Hilary was a Pagan child of seven. He's still a Pagan of course, but he brings it out to oblige me. Though how he reconciles it with Fred in his heathen beard and that brazen affair on the chandelier is best known to himself. Still, there is the service. Half-past ten in the chapel. Did he tell you?"

"No," Troy said. "I didn't even know there was a chapel."

"In the east wing. The parson from the prison takes it High Church, which Hilary likes. Do you consider him handsome?"

"No," Troy said. "But he's paintable."

"Ho," said Mrs. Forrester.

Mervyn came in with the coffee and liqueurs. When he reached Troy he gave her a look of animal subservience that she found extremely disagreeable.

Cressida's onset of hostesslike responsibility seemed to have been left behind in the dining-room. She stood in front of the fire jiggling her golden slipper on her toe and leaning a superb arm along the chimney-piece. She waited restively until Mervyn had gone and then said, "That man gives me the horrors."

"Indeed," said Mrs. Forrester.

"He's such a *creep*. They all are, if it comes to that. Oh yes, I know all about Hilly's ideas and I grant you it's one way out of the servant problem. I mean *if* we're to keep Halberds up and all that, this lot is one way of doing it. Personally, I'd rather have Greeks or something. You know."

"You don't see it, as Hilary says he does, from the murderer's point of view?" Mrs. Forrester observed.

"Oh, I know he's on about all that," Cressida said, jiggling her slipper, "but, let's face it, gracious living is what really turns him on. Me, too. You know?"

Mrs. Forrester stared at her for several seconds and then, with an emphatic movement of her torso, directed herself at Troy. "How do *you* manage?" she asked.

"As best we can. My husband's a policeman and his hours are enough to turn any self-respecting domestic into a psychotic wreck."

"A *policeman*?" Cressida exclaimed and added, "Oh, yes, I forgot. Hilly told me. But he's madly high-powered and famous, isn't he?"

As there seemed to be no answer to this, Troy did not attempt to make one.

"Shouldn't we be doing something about the tree?" she asked Mrs Forrester.

"Hilary likes to supervise. You should know that by now."

"Not exactly a jet-set scene, is it?" Cressida said. "You know. Gaol-boss. Gaol-doctor. Warders. Chaplain. To say nothing of the gaol-kids. Oh, I forgot. A groovy shower of neighbours, all very county and not one under the age of seventy. Hilarious. Let the bells chime."

"I am seventy years of age and my husband is seventy-three."

"There I go," Cressida said. "You know? The bottom." She burst out laughing and suddenly knelt at Mrs. Forrester's feet. She swung back the glossy burden of her hair and put her hands together. "I'm not as lethally awful as I make out," she said. "You've both

been fantastic to me. Always. I'm grateful. Hilly will
have to beat me like a gong. You know? Bang-bang.
Then I'll behave beautifully. Sweetie-pie, Aunt B, forgive me."

Troy thought, "Aunt Bed would have to be a Medusa
to freeze her," and sure enough a smile twitched at
the corners of Mrs. Forrester's mouth. "I suppose you're
no worse than the rest of your generation," she conceded. "You're clean and neat: I'll say that for you."

"As clean as a whistle and as neat as a new pin,
aren't I? Do you think I'll adorn Hilly's house, Aunt
B?"

"Oh, you'll *look* nice," said Mrs. Forrester. "You
may depend upon that. See you behave yourself."

"*Behave* myself," Cressida repeated. There was a
pause. The fire crackled. A draught from somewhere
up near the ceiling caused the kissing bough to turn
a little on its cord. In the dining-room, made distant
by heavy walls and doors, Hilary's laugh sounded.
With a change of manner so marked as to be startling
Cressida said, "Would you call me a sinful lady, Aunt
Bedelia?"

"What on earth are you talking about, child? What's
the matter with you?"

"Quite a lot, it appears. Look."

She opened her golden bag and took out a folded
piece of paper. "I found it under my door when I
went up to dress. I was saving it for Hilary," she
said, "but you two may as well see it. Go on, please.
Open it up. Read it. Both of you."

Mrs. Forrester stared at her for a moment, frowned,
and unfolded the paper. She held it away from her so
that Troy could see what was printed on it in enormous capitals.

SINFUL LADY BEWARE
AN UNCHASTE WOMAN IS AN ABOMINATION.
HE SHALL NOT SUFFER THEE TO DWELL IN HIS HOUSE.

"What balderdash is this! Where did you get in?"

"I told you. Under my door."

Mrs. Forrester made an abrupt movement as if to crush the paper, but Cressida's hand was laid over hers. "No, don't," Cressida said, "I'm going to show it to Hilary. And I must say I hope it'll change his mind about his ghastly Nigel."

4.

When Hilary was shown the paper, which was as soon as the men came into the drawing-room, he turned very quiet. For what seemed a long time he stood with it in his hands, frowning at it and saying nothing. Mr. Smith walked over to him, glanced at the paper, and gave out a soft, protracted whistle. Colonel Forrester looked inquiringly from Hilary to his wife, who shook her head at him. He then turned away to admire the tree and the kissing bough.

"Well, boy," said Mrs. Forrester. "What do you make of *that?*"

"I don't know. Not, I think, what I am expected to make of it, Aunt Bed."

"Whatever anybody makes of it," Cressida pointed out, "it's not the nicest kind of thing to find in one's bedroom."

Hilary broke into a strange apologia: tender, oblique, guarded. It was a horrid, silly thing to have happened, he told Cressida, and she mustn't let it trouble her. It wasn't worth a second thought. "Look," he said, "up the chimney with it, vulgar little beast," and threw it on the fire. It blackened, its preposterous legend turned white and started out in momentary prominence, it was reduced to a wraith of itself and flew out of sight. "Gone! Gone! Gone!" chanted Hilary rather wildly and spread his arms.

"I don't think you ought to have done that," Cressida said, "I think we ought to have kept it."

"That's right," Mr. Smith chimed in. "For dabs," he added.

This familiar departmental word startled Troy. Mr. Smith grinned at her. "That's correct," he said. "Innit? What your good man calls routine, that is. Dabs. You oughter kep' it, 'Illy."

"I think, Uncle Bert, I must be allowed to manage this ridiculous little incident in my own way."

"Hullo-ullo-ullo!"

"I'm quite sure, Cressida darling, it's merely an idiot-joke on somebody's part. *How* I detest practical jokes!" Hilary hurried on with an unconvincing return to his usual manner. He turned to Troy, "Don't you?"

"When they're as unfunny as this. If this is one."

"Which I don't for a moment believe," Cressida said. "Joke! It's a deliberate insult. Or worse." She appealed to Mrs. Forrester. "Isn't it?" she demanded.

"I haven't the remotest idea what it may be. What do you say to all this, Fred, I said what—"

She broke off. Her husband had gone to the far end of the room and was pacing out the distance from the french windows to the tree.

"Thirteen, fourteen, fifteen—fifteen feet exactly," he was saying. "I shall have to walk fifteen feet. Who's going to shut the french window after me? These things need to be worked out."

"Honestly, Hilly darling, I do *not* think it can be all shrugged off, you know, like a fun thing. When you yourself have said Nigel always refers to his victim as a sinful lady. It seems to me to be perfectly obvious he's set his sights at me and I find it terrifying. You know, terrifying."

"But," Hilary said, "it isn't. I promise you, my lovely child, it's not at all terrifying. The circumstances are entirely different—"

"I should hope so considering she was a tart."

"—and of course I shall get to the bottom of it. It's too preposterous. I shall put it before—"

"You can't put it before anybody. You've burnt it."

"Nigel is completely recovered."

" 'Ere," Mr. Smith said. "What say one of that lot's got it in for 'im? What say it's been done to discredit 'im? Planted? Spiteful, like?"

"But they get on very well together."

"Not with the Colonel's chap. Not with Moult they don't. No love lost there, I'll take a fiver on it. I seen the way they look at 'im. And 'im at them."

"Nonsense, Smith," said Mrs. Forrester. "You don't know what you're talking about. Moult's been with us for twenty years."

"What's that got to do with it?"

"Oh *Lord!*" Cressida said loudly and dropped into an armchair.

"—and who's going to read out the names?" the Colonel speculated. "I can't wear my specs. They'd look silly."

"Fred!"

"What, B?"

"Come over here, I said come over here."

"Why? I'm working things out."

"You're overexciting yourself. Come here. It's about Moult, I said it's . . ."

The Colonel, for him almost crossly, said, "You've interrupted my train of thought, B. What about Moult?"

As if in response to a heavily contrived cue and a shove from offstage, the door opened and in came Moult himself, carrying a salver.

"Beg pardon, sir," Moult said to Hilary, "but I thought perhaps this might be urgent, sir. For the Colonel, sir."

"What *is* it, Moult?" the Colonel asked quite testily.

Moult advanced the salver in his employer's direction. Upon it lay an envelope addressed in capitals: "COL. FORRESTER."

"It was on the floor of your room, sir. By the door, sir. I thought it might be urgent," said Moult.

Three – Happy Christmas

When Colonel Forrester read the message on the paper he behaved in much the same way as his nephew before him. That is to say for some seconds he made no move and gave no sign of any particular emotion. Then he turned rather pink and said to Hilary, "Can I have a word with you, old boy?" He folded the paper and his hands were unsteady.

"Yes, of course—" Hilary began when his aunt loudly interjected, "No!"

"B, you must let me . . ."

"No. If you've been made an Object," she said, "I want to know how, I said . . ."

"I heard you. No, B. No, my dear. It's not suitable."

"Nonsense. Fred, I insist . . ." She broke off and in a completely changed voice said, "Sit down, Fred. Hilary!"

Hilary went quickly to his uncle. They helped him to the nearest chair. Mrs. Forrester put her hand in his breast pocket and took out a small phial. "Brandy," she said and Hilary fetched it from the tray Mervyn had left in the room.

Mr. Smith said to Troy, "It's 'is ticker. He takes turns."

He went to the far end of the room and opened a

window. The North itself returned, stirring the tree
and turning the kissing bough.

Colonel Forrester sat with his eyes closed, his hair
ruffled and his breath coming short. "I'm perfectly all
right," he whispered. "No need to fuss."

"Nobody's fussing," his wife said. "You can shut that
window, if you please, Smith."

Cressida gave an elaborate and prolonged shiver.
"Thank God for that, at least," she muttered to Troy,
who ignored her.

"Better," said the Colonel without opening his eyes.
The others stood back.

The group printed an indelible image across Troy's
field of observation: an old man with closed eyes,
fetching his breath short; Hilary, elegant in plum-
coloured velvet and looking perturbed; Cressida, loung-
ing discontentedly and beautifully in a golden chair;
Mrs. Forrester, with folded arms, a step or two removed from her husband and watchful of him. And
coming round the Christmas tree, a little old cockney
in a grand smoking jacket.

In its affluent setting and its air of dated formality
the group might have served as subject matter for
some Edwardian problem-painter: Orchardson or, better still, the Hon. John Collier. And the title? "The
Letter." For there it lay where the Colonel had dropped
it, in exactly the right position on the carpet, the
focal point of the composition.

To complete the organization of this hopelessly
obsolete canvas, Mr. Smith stopped short in his tracks
while Mrs. Forrester, Hilary and Cressida turned
their heads and looked, as he did, at the white paper
on the carpet.

And then the still picture animated. The Colonel
opened his eyes. Mrs. Forrester took five steps across
the carpet and picked up the paper.

"Aunt Bed—!" Hilary protested but she shut him up with one of her looks.

The paper had fallen on its face. She reversed it and read and—a phenomenon that is distressing in the elderly—blushed to the roots of her hair.

"Aunt Bed—?"

Her mouth shut like a trap. An extraordinary expression came into her face. Fury? Troy wondered. Fury certainly but something else? Could it possibly be some faint hint of gratification? Without a word she handed the paper to her nephew.

As Hilary read it his eyebrows rose. He opened his mouth, shut it, reread the message, and then, to Troy's utter amazement, made a stifled sound and covered his mouth. He stared wildly at her, seemed to pull himself together, and in a trembling voice said, "This is—no—I mean—this is preposterous. My dear Aunt Bed!"

"Don't call me *that*," shouted his aunt.

"I'm most dreadfully sorry. I always do—oh! Oh! I see."

"Fred. Are you better?"

"I'm all right now, thank you, B. It was just one of my little go's. It wasn't—that thing that brought it on, I do assure you. Hilly's quite right, my dear. It *is* preposterous. I'm very angry, of course, on your account, but it *is* rather ridiculous, you know."

"I *don't* know. Outrageous, yes. Ridiculous, no. This person should be horsewhipped."

"Yes, indeed. But I'm not quite up to horsewhipping, B, and in any case one doesn't know who to whip."

"One can find out, I hope."

"Yes, well, that's another story. Hilly and I must have a good talk."

"What you must do is go to bed," she said.

"Well—perhaps. I do want to be all right for

tomorrow, don't I? And yet—we were going to do the tree and I love that."

"Don't be a fool, Fred. We'll ring for Moult. Hilary and he can—"

"I don't want Hilary and Moult. There's no need. I'll go upstairs backwards if you like. Don't *fuss,* B." Colonel Forrester stood up. He made Troy a little bow. "I am so awfully sorry," he said, "for being such a bore."

"You're nothing of the sort."

"Sweet of you. Good-night. Good-night, Cressida, my dear, Good-night, Bert. Ready, B?"

"He's the boss, after all," Troy thought as he left on his wife's arm. Hilary followed them out.

"What a turn-up for the books," Mr. Smith remarked. "Oh dear!"

Cressida dragged herself out of her chair. "Everybody's on about the Forrester bit," she complained. "Nobody seems to remember *I've* been insulted. We're not even allowed to know what this one said. You know. What was written. They could hardly call Aunt B a sinful lady, could they? Or could they?"

"Not," said Mr. Smith, "with any marketing potential they couldn't."

"I'm going to bed," Cressida said, trailing about the room. "I want a word with Hilary. I'll find him upstairs, I suppose. Good-night, Mrs. Alleyn."

"Do we just abandon all this—the tree and so on?"

"I daresay he'll do it when he comes down. It's not late, after all, is it? Good-night, Mr. Smith."

" 'Nighty-night, Beautiful," said Mr. Smith. "Not to worry. It's a funny old world but we don't care, do we?"

"I must say I do, rather. You know?" said Cressida and left them.

"Marvellous!" Mr. Smith observed and poured himself a drink. "Can I offer you anything, Mrs. A?"

"Not at the moment, thank you. Do *you* think this is all a rather objectionable practical joke?"

"Ah! That's talking. Do I? Not to say practical joke, exactly, I don't. But in a manner of speaking . . ."

He broke off and looked pretty sharply at Troy. "Upset your apple-cart a bit, has it?"

"Well—"

"Here! *You* haven't been favoured, yourself? Have you?"

"Not with a message."

"With something, though?"

"Nothing that matters," said Troy, remembering her promise to Mervyn and wishing Mr. Smith was not quite so sharp.

"Keeping it to yourself?" he said. "Your privilege of course, but whatever it is if I was you I'd tell 'Illy. Oh, well. It's been a long day and all. I wouldn't say no to a bit of kip, myself." He sipped his drink. "Very nice," he said, "but the best's to come."

"The best?"

"My nightcap. Know what it is? Barley water. Fact. Barley water with a squeeze of lemon. Take it every night of my life. Keeps me regular and suits my fancy. 'Illy tells that permanent spectre of his to set it up for me in my room."

"Nigel?"

"That's right. The bloodless wonder."

"What's your opinion of the entourage, Mr. Smith?"

"Come again?"

"The setup? At Halberds?"

"Ah. I get you. Well, now: it's peculiar. Look at it any way you like, it's eccentric. But then in a manner of speaking, so's 'Illy. It suits him. Mind, if he'd set 'imself up with a bunch of smashers and grabbers or job-buyers or magsmen or any of that lot, I'd of spoke

up very strong against. But murderers—when they're
oncers, that is—they're different."

"My husband agrees with you."

"And *he* ought to know, didn't 'e? Now, you won't
find Alf Moult agreeing with that verdict. Far from it."

"You think he mistrusts the staff?"

"Hates their guts, if you'll pardon me. He comes of
a class that likes things to be done very, very regular
and respectable does Alf Moult. Soldier-servant. Super-
snob. I know. I come from the one below myself:
not up to his mark, he'd think, but near enough to
know how he ticks. Scum of the earth, he calls them.
If it wasn't that he can't seem to detect any difference
between the Colonel and Almighty God, he'd refuse
to demean hisself by coming here and consorting
with them."

Mr. Smith put down his empty glass, wiped his
fingers across his mouth and twinkled. "Very nice,"
he said. "You better come and see my place one of
these days. Get 'Illy to bring you. I got one or two
works might interest you. We do quite a lot in the old
master lurk ourselves. Every now and then I see something I fancy and I buy it in. What's your opinion of
Blake?"

"Blake?"

"William. Tiger, tiger."

"Superb."

"I got one of 'is drawings."

"Have you, now!"

"Come and take a butcher's."

"Love to," said Troy. "Thank you."

Hilary came in overflowing with apologies. "What
you must think of us!" he exclaimed. "One nuisance
treads upon another's heels. Judge of my mortification."

"What's the story up to date, then?" asked Mr.
Smith.

"Nothing more, really, except that Cressida has been very much disturbed."

"What a shame. But she's on the road to recovery, I see."

"What do you see?"

"It was worse when they favoured the blood red touch. Still and all, you better wipe it off."

"What a really dreadful old man you are, Uncle Bert, said Hilary, without rancour but blushing and using his handkerchief.

"I'm on me way to me virtuous couch. If I find a dirty message under the door I'll scream. Good-night, all."

They heard him whistling as he went upstairs.

"You're not going just yet, are you?" Hilary said to Troy. "Please don't or I'll be quite sure you've taken umbrage."

"In that case I'll stay."

"How heavenly cool you are. It's awfully soothing. Will you have a drink? No? I shall. I need one." As he helped himself Hilary said, "Do you madly long to know what was in Uncle Flea's note?"

"I'm afraid I do."

"It's not really so frightful."

"It can't be since you seemed inclined to laugh."

"You *are* a sharp one, aren't you? As a matter of fact, it said quite shortly that Uncle Flea's a cuckold spelt with three *k*'s. It was the thought of Aunt Bed living up to her pet name that almost did for me. Who with, one asks oneself? Moult?"

"No wonder she was enraged."

"My dear, she wasn't. Not really. Basically she was as pleased as Punch. Didn't you notice how snappy she got when Uncle Flea said it was ridiculous?"

"I don't believe you."

"You may as well, I promise you."

Troy giggled.

"Of course she'd love it if Uncle Flea did go into action with a horsewhip. I can never understand how it's managed, can you? It would be so easy to run away and leave the horsewhipper laying about him like a ringmaster without a circus."

"I don't think it's that kind of horsewhip. It's one of the short jobs like a jockey's. You have to break it in two when you've finished and contemptuously throw the pieces at the victim."

"You're wonderfully well informed, aren't you?"

"It's only guesswork."

"All the same, you know, it's no joke, this business. It's upset my lovely Cressida. *She* really *is* cross. You see, she's never taken to the staff. She was prepared to put up with them because they do function quite well, don't you think? But unfortunately she's heard of the entire entourage of a Greek millionaire who died the other day, all wanting to come to England because of the Colonels. And now she's convinced it was Nigel who did her message and she's dead set on making a change."

"You don't think it was Nigel?"

"No. I don't think he'd be such an ass."

"But if—I'm sorry but you did say he was transferred to Broadmoor."

"He's as sane as sane can be. A complete cure. Oh, I know the message to Cressida is rather in his style but I consider that's merely a blind."

"*Do* you!" Troy said thoughtfully.

"Yes, I do. Just as—well—Uncle Flea's message is rather in Blore's vein. You remember Blore slashed out at the handsome busboy who had overpersuaded Mrs. Blore. Well, it came out in evidence that Blore made a great to-do about being a cuckold. The word cropped up all over his statements."

"How does he spell it?"

"I've no idea."

"What is your explanation?"

"To begin with I don't countenance any notion that both Nigel and Blore were inspired, independently, to write poison pen notes on the same sort of paper (it's out of the library), in the same sort of capital letters."

(Or, thought Troy, that Mervyn was moved at the same time to set a booby-trap.)

"—Or, equally," Hilary went on, "that one of the staff wrote the messages to implicate the other two. They get on extremely well together, all of them."

"Well, then?"

"What is one left with? Somebody's doing it. It's not me and I don't suppose it's you."

"No."

"No. So we run into a reductio ad absurdum, don't we? We're left with a most improbable field. Flea. Bed. Cressida. Uncle Bert."

"And Moult?"

"Good Heavens," said Hilary. "Uncle Bert's fancy! I forgot about Moult. Moult, now. *Moult*."

"Mr. Smith seems to think—"

"Yes, I daresay." Hilary glanced uneasily at Troy and began to walk about the room as if he were uncertain what to say next. "Uncle Bert," he began at last, "is an oddity. He's not a simple character. Not at all."

"No?"

"No. For instance there's his sardonic-East-End-character act. 'I'm so artful, you know, I'm a cockney.' He *is* a cockney, of course. Vintage barrow-boy. But he's put himself in inverted commas and comes out of them whenever it suits him. You should hear him at the conference table. He's as articulate as the next man and, in his way, more civilized than most."

"Interesting."

"Yes. He's got a very individual sense of humour, has Uncle Bert."

"Tending towards black comedy?"

"He might have invented the term. All the same," Hilary said, "he's an astute judge of character and I—I can't pretend he isn't, although—"

He left this observation unfinished. "I think I'll do the tree," he said. "It settles one's nerves."

He opened the lid of the packing-case that had been placed near the tree.

Mr. Smith had left ajar the double doors into the great hall from whence there now came sounds of commotion. Somebody was stumbling rapidly downstairs and making ambiguous noises as he came. A slither was followed by an oath and an irregular progress across the hall. The doors burst wide open and in plunged Mr. Smith: an appalling sight.

He was dressed in pyjamas and a florid dressing gown. One foot was bare, the other slippered. His sparse hair was disordered. His eyes protruded. And from his open mouth issued dollops of foam.

He retched, gesticulated, and contrived to speak.

"Poisoned!" he mouthed. "I been poisoned."

An iridescent bubble was released from his lips. It floated towards the tree, seemed to hang for a moment like an ornament from one of the boughs, and then burst.

2.

"Soap," Hilary said. "It's soap, Uncle Bert. Calm yourself for Heaven's sake and wash your mouth out. Go to a downstairs cloakroom, I implore you."

Mr. Smith incontinently bolted.

"Hadn't you better see to him?" Troy asked.

"What next, what next! How inexpressibly distasteful. However."

Hilary went. There followed a considerable interval, after which Troy heard them pass through the hall on their way upstairs. Soon afterwards Hilary returned looking deeply put out.

"In his barley water," he said. "The strongest possible solution of soap. Carnation. He's been hideously sick. This settles it."

"Settles—?"

"It's some revolting practical joker. No, but it's too bad! And in the pocket of his pyjama jacket another of these filthy notes. 'What price Arsnic.' He might have died of fright."

"How is he, in fact?"

"Wan but recovering. In an mounting rage."

"Small blame to him."

"Somebody shall smart for this," Hilary threatened.

"I suppose it couldn't be the new boy in the kitchen?"

"I don't see it. He doesn't know their backgrounds. This is somebody who knows about Nigel's sinful lady and Blore's being a cuckold and Vincent's slip over the arsenical weed-killer."

"And Mervyn's booby-trap," Troy said before she could stop herself. Hilary stared at her.

"You're not going to tell me—? *You are!*"

"I promised I wouldn't. I suppose these other jobs sort of let me out but—all right, there was an incident. I'm sure he had nothing to do with it. Don't corner me."

Hilary was silent for some time after this. Then he began taking boxes of Christmas tree baubles out of the packing case.

"I'm going to ignore the whole thing," he said. "I'm going to maintain a masterly inactivity. Somebody wants me to make a big scene and I won't. I won't upset my staff. I won't have my Christmas ruined. Sucks-boo to whoever it may be. It's only ten to eleven, believe it or not. Come on, let's do the tree."

They did the tree. Hilary had planned a golden colour scheme. They hung golden glass baubles, big in the lower branches and tapering to miniscule ones at the top, where they mounted a golden angel. There were festoons of glittering gold tinsel and masses of gilded candles. Golden stars shone in and out of the foliage. It was a most fabulous tree.

"And I've even gilded the people in the crib," he said. "I hope Aunt Bed won't object. And just you wait till the candles are lit."

"What about the presents? I suppose there are presents?"

"The children's will be in golden boxes brought in by Uncle Flea, one for each family. And ours, suitably wrapped, on a side table. Everybody finds their own because Uncle Flea can't read the labels without his specs. He merely tows in the boxes in a little golden car on runners."

"From outside? Suppose it's a rough night?"

"If it's too bad we'll have to bring the presents in from the hall."

"But the Colonel will still come out of the storm?"

"He wouldn't dream of doing anything else."

With some hesitation Troy suggested that Colonel Forrester didn't seem very robust and was ill-suited to a passage, however brief, through the rigours of a midwinter storm, clad, she understood, in gold lamé. Hilary said he could wear gloves. Noticing, perhaps, that she was not persuaded, he said Vincent would hold an umbrella over the Colonel and that in any case it wouldn't do for his wig and crown of mistletoe to get wet although, he added, a sprinkling of snow would be pretty. "But of course it would melt," he added. "And that could be disastrous."

Hilary was perched on the top of the stepladder. He looked down through green foliage and golden baubles at Troy.

"You don't approve," he said. "You think I'm effete and heartless and have lost my sense of spiritual values."

This came uncomfortably near to what in fact Troy had been thinking.

"You may be right," he went on before she could produce an answer. "But at least I don't pretend. For instance, I'm a snob. I set a lot of importance on my being of ancient lineage. I wouldn't have proposed to my lovely, lovely Cressida if she'd had a tatty origin. I value family trees even more than Christmas trees. And I love being rich and able to have a truly golden tree."

"Oh," Troy said, "I've nothing but praise for the golden tree."

"I understand you perfectly. You must pray for me in the chapel tomorrow."

"I'm not qualified."

Hilary said, "Never mind about all that. I've been keeping the chapel as a surprise. It really is quite lovely."

"Are you a Christian?"

"In the context," said Hilary, "it doesn't arise. Be an angel and hand up a bauble."

It was midnight when they had completed their work. They stood at the other end of the long room before the dying fire and admired it.

"There will be no light but the candles," Hilary said. "It will be perfectly magical. A dream-tree. I hope the children will be enchanted, don't you?"

"They can't fail. I shall go to bed, now, I think."

"How nice it's been, doing it with you," he said, linking his arm in hers and leading her down the room. "It has quite taken away all that other beastly nonsense. Thank you so much. Have you admired Nigel's kissing bough?"

They were under it. Troy looked up and was kissed.

"Happy Christmas," said Hilary.

She left him there and went up to her room.

When she opened her wardrobe she was surprised to hear a murmur of voices in the Forresters' room. It was distant and quite indistinguishable but as she hung up her dress she heard footsteps tread towards her and the Colonel's voice, close at hand, said very loudly and most decisively: "No, my dear, that is absolutely final. And if you don't, I will."

A door slammed. Troy had a picture of Mrs. Forrester banging her way into their bathroom but a moment later had to reverse this impression into one of her banging her way back into the bedroom. Her voice rose briefly and indistinctly. The Colonel's footfall receded. Troy hastily shut the wardrobe door and went to bed.

3.

Christmas day came in with a wan glint of sunshine. The view from Troy's bedroom might have been framed by robins, tinsel and holly. Snow took the sting out of a landscape that could have been set up during the night for Hilary's satisfaction.

As she dressed, Troy could hear the Forresters shouting to each other next door and concluded that the Colonel was back on his usual form. When she opened her wardrobe she heard the now familiar jangle of coat hangers on the other side.

"Good-morning!" Troy shouted. She tapped on the common wall. "Happy Christmas!" she cried.

A man's voice said, "Thank you, madam. I'll tell the Colonel and Mrs. Forrester."

Moult.

She heard him go away. There was a distant conjunction of voices and then he returned, discreetly tapping on the wall.

"The Colonel and Mrs. Forrester's compliments, madam, and they would be very happy if you would look in."

"In five minutes," Troy shouted. "Thank you."

When she made her call she found Colonel and Mrs. Forrester in bed and bolt upright under a green-lined umbrella of the sort associated with Victorian missionaries and Empire builders. The wintry sun lay across their counterpane. Each wore a scarlet dressing gown the skirts of which were deployed round the wearer like some monstrous calyx. They resembled gods of a sort.

In unison they wished Troy a Happy Christmas and invited her to sit down.

"Being an artist," Mrs Forrester said, "you will not find it out-of-the-way to be informally received."

At the far end of the room a door into their bathroom stood open and beyond that a second door into a dressingroom where Moult could be seen brushing a suit.

"I had heard," said Troy, "about the umbrella."

"We don't care for the sun in our eyes. I wonder," said Mrs. Forrester, "if I might ask you to shut the bathroom door. Thank you very much. Moult has certain prejudices which we prefer not to arouse. Fred, put in your aid. I said put in your aid."

Colonel Forrester, who had smiled and nodded a great deal without seeming to hear anything much, found his hearing aid on his bedside table and fitted it into his ear.

"It's a wonderful invention," he said. "I'm a little worried about wearing it tonight, though. But, after all, the wig's awfully long. A Druid with a visible hearing aid would be *too* absurd, don't you think?"

"First of all," Mrs. Forrester began, "were there any developments after we went to bed?"

"We're dying to know," said the Colonel.

Troy told them about Mr. Smith and the soap. Mrs. Forrester rubbed her nose vexedly. "That's very tiresome," she said. "It upsets my theory. Fred, it upsets my theory."

"Sickening for you, B."

"And yet, does it? I'm not so sure. It might be a ruse, you know, I said . . ."

"I'm wearing my aid, B."

"What," Troy asked, "is your theory?"

"I was persuaded that Smith wrote the letters."

"But surely . . ."

"He's a good creature in many ways but his sense of humour is coarse and he dislikes Cressida Tottenham."

"B, my dear, I'm sure you're mistaken."

"No you're not. You're afraid I'm right. He doesn't think she's good enough for Hilary. Nor do I."

"Be that as it may, B——"

"Be that as it is, you mean. Don't confuse me, Fred."

"——Bert Smith would certainly not write that disgraceful message to me. About you."

"I don't agree. He'd think it funny."

The Colonel looked miserable. "But it's not," he said.

"Hilary thought it funny," Mrs. Forrester said indignantly and turned to Troy. "Did *you*? I suppose Hilary told you what it said."

"In general terms."

"Well? Funny?"

Troy said, "At the risk of making myself equally objectionable I'm afraid I've got to confess that—"

"Very well. You need go no further." Mrs. Forrester looked at her husband and remarked, astoundingly. "Impertinent, yes. Unfounded, of course. Preposterous, not so farfetched as you may suppose."

A reminiscent gleam, Troy could have sworn, came into Mrs. Forrester's eye.

"I don't believe Bert would make himself sick," the Colonel urged.

"I wouldn't put it past him," Mrs. Forrester said darkly. "However," she continued with a wave of her hand, "that is unimportant. What I wished to talk to you about, Mrs. Alleyn, is the line I hope we shall all take in this matter. Fred and I have decided to ignore it. To dismiss it—" she swept her arm across the Colonel, who blinked and drew back "—entirely. As if it had never been. We refuse to give the perpetrator of these insults, the satisfaction of paying them the slightest attention. We hope you will join us in this stand."

"Because," her husband added, "it would only spoil everything—the tree and so on. We're having a rehearsal after church and one must give one's full attention."

"And you're quite recovered, Colonel?"

"Yes, yes, quite, thank you. It's my old ticker, you know. A leaky valve or some nonsense of that sort, the quacks tell me. Nothing to fuss about."

"Well," Troy said, getting up, "I'll agree—mum's the word."

"Good. That settles that. I don't know how this gel of yours is going to behave herself, Fred."

"She's *not mine,* B."

"She was your responsibility."

"Not now, though." The Colonel turned towards Troy but did not look at her. His face was pink. He spoke rapidly as if he had memorized his observations and wished to get rid of them. "Cressida," he explained, "is the daughter of a young fellow in my regiment. Germany. 1950. We were on an exercise and my jeep overturned." Here the Colonel's eyes filled with tears. "And do you know this dear fellow got me out? I was pinned face down in the mud and he got me out and then the most dreadful things happened. Collapse. Petrol. And I promised him I'd keep an eye on the child."

"Luckily," said Mrs. Forrester, "she was well provided for. School in Switzerland and all that. I say nothing of the result."

"Her mother died, poor thing. In childbirth."

"And now," said Mrs. Forrester, suddenly shutting up their umbrella with a definite snap, "now she's in some sort of actressy business."

"She's an awfully pretty girl, don't you think?"

"Lovely," said Troy warmly and went down to breakfast.

Hilary was busy during the morning, but Troy did a certain amount of work on the portrait before making herself ready for church.

When she looked through the library windows that gave on the great courtyard, she got quite a shock. Nigel had completed his effigy. The packing case was mantled in frozen snow and on top of it, sharply carved and really quite impressive in his glittering iciness, lay Hilary's Bill-Tasman ancestor, his hands crossed, rather like flatfish, on his breast.

At half-past ten, the monk's rang fast and exuberantly in its tower as if its operator was a bit above himself. Troy made her way downstairs and across the hall and, following instructions, turned right into the corridor which served the library, the breakfast-room, the boudoir, Hilary's study and, as it now transpired, the chapel.

It was a superb chapel. It was full, but by no means too full, of treasures. Its furniture, including monstrance and candlesticks, quattrocento confessional—the lot—was in impeccable taste and, no doubt, awfully valuable.

Troy experienced a frightful desire to hang crinkly paper garlands on some insipid plaster saint.

Blore, Mervyn, Nigel, Vincent, Kittiwee and the Boy were already seated. They were supplemented by a cluster of odd bodies whom she supposed to be outside workers at Halberds and their wives and children. Hilary and Cressida were in the front pew. The rest of the houseparty soon assembled and the service went through with High Church decorum. The prison chaplain gave a short, civilized sermon. Colonel Forrester, to Troy's surprise and pleasure, played the lovely little organ for the seasonable hymns. Hilary read the gospel, and Mr. Smith, with surprising aplomb and the full complement of aitches, the epistle.

At three o'clock that afternoon the ceremony of the tree was rehearsed.

It was all very thoroughly planned. The guests would assemble in the library, Troy's portrait and impedimenta having been removed for the occasion to Hilary's study. Vincent, with umbrella and a charming little baroque car on runners, loaded with Christmas boxes, would be stationed outside the drawing-room windows. At eight o'clock recorded joybells would be usher in the proceedings. The children would march in procession two-by-two from the library across the hall to the drawing-room, where they would find the golden tree blazing in the dark. The adults would follow.

These manoeuvres executed, Colonel Forrester, fully accoutred as a Druid, would emerge from the little cloak-room next the drawing-room, where Cressida had helped to make him up. He would slip through a door into the entrance porch and from there into the wintry courtyard. Here he would effect a liaison with Vincent. The recorded music, sleigh bells, snorts and cries of "Whoa!" would be released. The french windows, flung open from within by Blore and Mervyn, would admit the Colonel towing his guilded car. To a fanfare ("Of trumpets also and shawms," Hilary said) he would encircle the tree and then, abandoning his load, would bow to his audience, make one or two esoteric gestures, and retire to the limbo from whence he had come. He would then pick up his skirts and bolt back through the hall and into the cloakroom, where with Cressida's help he would remove his beard, moustache and eyebrows, his wig, his boots and his golden gown. In due course he would appear in his native guise among the guests.

The rehearsals did not go through without incidents, most of which were caused by the extreme excitability of the Colonel himself. Troy became very anxious about him, and Mrs. Forrester, whose presence he had feebly tried to prevent, finally put her foot down and told Hilary that if he wanted his uncle to perform that evening he must stop making him run about like a madman. She would not be answerable for the consequences, she said, if he did not. She then removed her husband to rest in his room, obliging him, to his mild annoyance, to ascend the stairs backwards and stop for ten seconds at every fifth step.

Cressida, who seemed to be extremely unsettled, drifted up to Troy and watched this protracted exit.

The Colonel begged them not to wait, and at Cressida's suggestion they went together to the boudoir.

"There are moments," Cressida said, "when I catch myself wondering if this house is not a loony-bin. Well, I mean, look at it. It's like one of those really trendy jobs. You know, the Happening thing. We did them in Organic-Expressivists."

"What *are* Organic-Expressivists?" Troy asked.

"You can't really *explain* O-E. You know. You can't say it's 'about' that or the other thing. An O-E Exposure is one thing for each of *us* and another for each of the *audience*. One simply hopes there will be a spontaneous emotional release," Cressida rapidly explained. "Zell—our director—well *not* a director in the establishment sense—he's our *source*—he puts enormous stress on spontaneity."

"Are you rejoining the group?"

"No. Well, Hilary and I are probably getting married in May, so if we do there wouldn't really be much point, would there? And anyway the O-E's in recess at the moment. No lolly."

"What did you yourself do in the performances?"

"At first I just moved about getting myself released and then Zell felt I ought to develop the yin-yang bit, if that's what it's called. You know, the male-female bit. So I did. I wore a kind of net trouser-token on my leg and I had long green crepe-hair pieces stuck to my left jaw. I must say I hated the spirit-gum. You know, on your skin? But it had an erotic-seaweed connotation that seemed to communicate rather successfully."

"What else did you wear?"

"Nothing else. The audiences met me. You know? Terribly well. It's because of my experience with crepe hair that I'm doing Uncle Fred's beard. It's all ready-made and only has to be stuck on."

"I do hope he'll be all right."

"So do I. He's all uptight about it, though. He's fantastic, isn't he? Not true. I'm way up there over him and Auntie B. I think he's the mostest. You know? Only I don't exactly send Auntie B, I'm afraid."

She moved gracefully and irritably about the beautiful little room. She picked up an ornament and put it down again with the half-attention of an idle shopper.

"There's been a row in the kitchen," she said. "Did you know? This morning?"

"Not I."

"About me, in a sort of way. Kittiwee was on about me and his ghastly cats and the others laughed at him and—I don't exactly—but it all got a bit out of hand. Moult was mixed up in it. They all hate Moult like poison."

"How do you know about it?"

"I heard. Hilly asked me to look at the flowers that have been sent. The flower-room's next the servants' hall only we're meant to call it the staff common-room. They were at it hammer-and-tongs. You know. Yelling. I was just wondering whether I ought to tell Hilly when I heard Moult come into the passage. He was shouting back at the others. He said, 'You lot! You're no more than a bloody squad of bloody thugs,' and a good deal more. And Blore roared like a bull for Moult to get out before one of them did him over. And I've told Hilly. I thought he might have told you, he likes you so much."

"No."

"Well, anyway, let's face it; I'm not prepared to marry into a permanent punch-up. I mean it's just crazy. It's not my scene. If you'd heard! Do you know what Blore said? He said: 'One more crack out of you and I'll bloody block your light.' "

"What do you suppose that means?"

"I know what it sounded like," Cressida said. "It sounded like murder. And I mean that. Murder."

4.

It was at this point that Troy began to feel really disturbed. She began to see herself, as if she was another person, alone among strangers in an isolated and falsely luxurious house and attended by murderers. That, she thought, like it or lump it, is the situation. And she wished with all her heart she was out of it and spending her Christmas alone in London or with any one of the unexceptionable friends who had so warmly invited her.

The portrait was almost finished. Perhaps quite finished. She was not sure it hadn't reached the state when somebody with wisdom should forcibly remove her from it and put it out of her reach. Her husband had been known to perform this service, but he was twelve thousand miles away and unless, as sometimes happened, his job in the Antipodes came to a quick end, would not be home for a week. The portrait was not dry enough to pack. She could arrange for it to be sent to the framers and she could tell Hilary she would leave—when? Tomorrow? He would think that very odd. He would smell a rat. He would conclude that she was afraid and he would be dead right. She was.

Mr. Smith had said that he intended returning to London the day after tomorrow. Perhaps she could leave with him. At this point Troy saw that she would have to take a sharp look at herself. It was an occasion for what Cressida would probably call maintaining her cool.

In the first place she must remember that she was often overcome, in other people's houses, by an overpowering desire to escape, a tyrannical restlessness as inexplicable as it was embarrassing. Every nerve in her body would suddenly telegraph "I must get out of this." It could happen, even in a restaurant, where, if the waiter was slow with the bill, Troy suffered agonies of frustration. Was her present most ardent desire to be gone no more than the familiar attack exacerbated by the not inconsiderable alarms and eccentricities of life at Halberds? Perhaps Hilary's domestics were, after all, as harmless as he insisted. Had Cressida blown up a servants' squabble into a display of homicidal fury?

She reminded herself of the relatively quick recovery of the Forresters from the incidents and, until the soap episode, of Mr. Smith. She took herself to task, tied her head in a scarf, put on her overcoat, and went for a short walk.

The late afternoon was icily cold and still, the darkening sky was clear and the landscape glittered. She looked more closely at Nigel's catafalque, which was now frozen as hard as its marble progenitor in the chapel. Really Nigel had been very clever with his kitchen instruments. He had achieved a sharpness and precision far removed from the blurred clumsiness of the usual snow effigy. Only the northern aspect, Troy thought, had been partly defaced by the wind and occasional drifts of rain and even there it was the snow-covered box steps that had suffered rather than the effigy itself. Somebody should photograph it, she thought, before the thaw comes.

She walked as far as the scarecrow. It was tilted sideways, stupid and motionless, at the impossible angle in which the wind had left it. A disconsolate thrush sat on its billycock hat.

By the time she had returned, tingling, to the warm house, Troy had so far got over her impulsive itch as to postpone any decision until the next day. She even began to feel a reasonable interest in the party.

And indeed Halberds simmered with expectation. In the enormous hall with its two flights of stairs, giant swags of fir, mistletoe and holly caught up with scarlet tassels hung in classic loops from the gallery and picture rails. Heroic logs blazed and crackled in two enormous fireplaces. The smell was superb.

Hilary was there, with a written timetable in his hand, issuing final instructions to his staff. He waved gaily to Troy and invited her to stay and listen.

"Now! Blore! To go over it once more," Hilary was saying. "You will make sure the drawing-room door is locked. Otherwise we shall have children screaming in before they should. When everybody is here (you've got your guest list) check to make sure Vincent is ready with the sledge. You wait until half-past seven when the first recorded bells will be played and Colonel Forrester will come downstairs and go into the cloakroom near the drawing-room, where Miss Tottenham will put on his beard."

"Choose your words, sweetie," Cressida remarked. "I'd look a proper Charlie, wouldn't I?"

Kittiwee sniggered.

"Miss Tottenham," Hilary said, raising his voice, "will help the Colonel with his beard. You now check that Nigel is at hand to play his part and at a quarter to eight you tap on the door of the cloakroom near the drawing-room to let Colonel Forrester and Miss Tottenham know we are ready. Yes?"

"Yes, sir. Very good, sir."

"You and Nigel then light the candles on the tree

and the kissing bough. That's going to take a little
time. Be sure you get rid of the stepladder and turn
off the lights. *Most* important. Very well. That done,
you tell Nigel to return to the record player in the hall
here. Nigel: at five to eight precisely, you increase the
indoor recording of the bells. Plenty of volume, remember. We want the house to be *full* of bells. Now!
Mervyn! When you hear the bells, unlock the drawing-
room doors and, I implore you, be sure you have the
key to hand."

"I've got it on me, sir."

"Good. Very well. You, Blore, come to the library
and announce the tree. Full voice, you know, Blore.
Give it everything, won't you?"

"Sir."

"You and Mervyn, having thrown open the drawing-room doors, go right through the room to the
french windows. Check that the Colonel is ready outside. Vincent will by this time be with him and will
flash his torch. Wait by the windows. Now, then. The
crucial moment," Hilary excitedly continued, "has
arrived. *When* everybody has come in and settled in
their places—I shall see to that and I daresay Mrs.
Alleyn will be very kind and help me—you, Blore,
stand in the window where Vincent can see you and
give him his signal. Vincent, be ready for this. You
must keep out of sight with the sleigh, until the last
moment. When the inside bells stop, bring the sleigh
into the courtyard, where you will join the Colonel.
And when you get your signal, the sound effects for
the entrance will be turned on. The loudspeakers,"
Hilary explained to Troy, "are outside for greater verisi-
militude. And now, *now* Blore! Keep your heads, you
and Mervyn, I implore you. Coolness is all. Coolness
and coordination. *Wait* for your own voice shouting
'Whoa' on the loudspeakers, *wait* for the final cascade

of sleigh bells and then—and *only* then—fling wide the french windows and admit the Colonel with his sledge. Vincent, you must watch the Colonel like a lynx for fear that in his zeal he tries to effect an entrance before we are ready for him. Make certain he removes his gloves. Take them off him at the last moment. He has to wear them because of chilblains. See he's well *en train* beforehand with the tow-ropes of the sledge over his shoulders. He may show a hideous tendency to tie himself up in them like a parcel. Calm him."

"Do my best, sir," said Vincent, "but he does show the whites of his eyes, like, when he gets up to the starting cage."

"I know. I depend on your tact, Vincent. Miss Tottenham will see him out of the cloakroom and you take over in the courtyard. After that he's all yours."

"Thank you, sir," said Vincent dubiously.

"Those," said Hilary, surveying his troops, "are my final words to you. That is all. Thank you." He turned to Troy. "Come and have tea," he said. "It's in the boudoir. We help ourselves. Rather like the Passover with all our loins, such as they are, girded up. I do hope you're excited. Are you?"

"Why—yes," she agreed, surprised to find that it was so, "I am. I'm very excited."

"You won't be disappointed, I promise. Who knows," said Hilary, "but what you won't look back on tonight as a unique experience. There, now!"

"I daresay I shall," Troy said, humouring him.

Four – The Tree and the Druid

Bells everywhere. The house sang with their arbitrary clamour: it might have been the interior of some preposterous belfry. Nigel was giving zealous attention to his employer's desire for volume.

"Whang-whang-whang-*whang*," yelled an overstimulated little boy making extravagant gestures and grimaces. Sycophantic little girls screamed their admiration in his face. All the children leapt to their feet and were pounced upon by their parents, assisted by Hilary and Troy. Three of the parents who were also warders at the Vale began to walk purposefully about the room, and with slightly menacing authority soon reformed the childish rabble into a mercurial crocodile.

"Bells, bells, bells, *bells!*" shouted the children, like infant prodigies at grips with Edgar Allan Poe.

Blore entered, contemplated his audience, fetched a deep breath, and bellowed: "The Tree, Sir."

An instant quiet was secured. The bells having given a definitive concerted crash hummed into silence. All the clocks in the house and the clock in the stable tower struck eight and then, after a second or two, the bells began again, very sweetly, with the tune of St. Clement Dane.

"Come along," said Hilary.

With the chanciness of their species the children suddenly became angelic. Their eyes grew as round as saucers, their lips parted like rosebuds, they held hands and looked enchanting. Even the overstimulated little boy calmed down.

Hilary, astonishingly, began to sing. He had a vibrant alto voice and everybody listened to him.

> " 'Oranges and lemons,' say the Bells of St. Clement's
> 'You owe me five farthings,' say the Bells of St. Martin's."

Two and two they walked, out of the library, into the passage, through the great hall now illuminated only by firelight, and since the double doors of the drawing-room stood wide open, into the enchantment that Hilary had prepared for them.

And really, Troy thought, it *was* an enchantment. It was breathtaking. At the far end of this long room, suspended in darkness, blazed the golden Christmas tree alive with flames, stars and a company of angels. It quivered with its own brilliance and was the most beautiful tree in all the world.

> " 'When will you pay me," say the bells of Old Bailey
> 'When I am rich,' say the bells of Shoreditch."

The children sat on the floor in the light of the tree. Their elders—guests and the household staff—moved to the far end of the room and were lost in shadow.

Troy thought, "This is Uncle Flea's big thing and here, in a moment, will come Uncle Flea."

Hilary, standing before the children, raised his hands for quiet and got it. From outside in the night came sounds that might have been made by insubstantial flutes piping in the north wind. Electronic music, Troy thought, and really almost *too* effective: it raised goose-pimples, it turned one a little cold. But through the music came the jingle of approaching sleigh bells. Closer and closer to an insistent rhythm until they were outside the french windows. Nothing could be seen beyond the tree, but Hilary in his cunning had created an arrival. Now came the stamp of hooves, the snorts, the splendid cries of "Whoa." Troy didn't so much as think of Blore.

The windows were opened.

The tree danced in the cold air, everything stirred and glittered: the candle flames wavered, the baubles tinkled.

The windows were shut.

And round the tree, tugging his golden car on its runners, came the Druid.

Well, Troy thought, it may be a shameless concoction of anachronisms and Hilary's cockeyed sense of fantasy, but it works.

The Druid's robe, stiff, wide-sleeved and enveloping, was of gold lamé. His golden hair hung about his face in formal strands and his golden beard spread like a fan across his chest. A great crown of mistletoe shaded his eyes, which were spangled and glinted in the dark. He was not a comic figure. He was strange. It was as if King Lear had been turned into Ole-Luk-Oie the Dream God. He circled the tree three times to the sound of trumpets and pipes.

Then he dropped the golden cords of his car. He raised his arms, made beckoning gestures, and bowed with extended hands.

Unfortunately he had forgotten to remove his gloves, which were of the sensible knitted kind.

"Fred. Your gloves, I said—"

But he was gone. He had returned from whence he

came. A further incursion of cold air, the windows
were shut, the bells receded.

He was gone.

2.

The joyful pandemonium that now broke out among
the children was kept within reasonable bounds by
Hilary and Troy, who had become a sort of A.D.C.
to the action. The names of the families were em-
blazoned in glitter on the boxes and the children
broke into groups, found, delved, and exclaimed.

Mervyn stood by the tree with an extinguisher,
watching the candles. Hilary signalled to Nigel, who
switched on the lights by a wall table where the grown-
up presents were assembled. Troy found herself alongside Mrs. Forrester.

"He was splendid," Troy cried. "He was really
splendid."

"Forgot his gloves. I knew he would."

"It didn't matter. It didn't matter in the least."

"It will to Fred," said Mrs. Forrester. And after a
moment: "I'm going to see him." Or Troy thought
that was what she said. The din was such that even
Mrs. Forrester's well-projected observations were hard
to hear. Hilary's adult visitors and the household staff
were now opening their presents. Nigel had begun to
circulate with champagne cocktails. To Troy they
seemed to be unusually potent.

Cressida was edging her way towards them. At
Hilary's request she wore her dress of the previous
night, the glittering trouser suit that went so admirably
with his colour scheme. She raised her arm and signalled to Mrs. Forrester over the heads of the intervening guests. Something slightly less lackadaisical
than usual in her manner held Troy's attention. She

watched the two women meet in the crowd. Cressida stooped her head. The heavy swag of her pale hair swung across her face and hid it but Mrs. Forrester was caught by the wall light. Troy saw her frown and set her mouth. She hurried to the door, unceremoniously shoving through groups of visitors.

Cressida made for Troy.

"I say," she said, "was he all right? I tried to see but I couldn't get a good look."

"He was splendid."

"Good. You spotted him, of course?"

"What?"

"Spotted him, I said—Great Grief!" Cressida ejaculated, "I'm beginning to talk like Aunt Bed. You *saw,* didn't you?"

"Saw? What?"

"Him."

"Who?"

"Moult."

"Moult?"

"You don't tell me," Cressida bawled, "that you didn't realize? Sharp as you are and all."

"I don't know what you mean."

"It wasn't—" An upsurge of laughter among the guests drowned Cressida's next phrase but she advanced her lovely face towards Troy's and screamed, *"It was Moult.* The Druid was Moult."

"Moult!"

"Uncle Flea's had a turn. Moult went on for the part."

"Good Lord! Is he all right?"

"Who?"

"Uncle—Colonel Forrester?"

"I haven't seen him. Aunt B's gone up. I expect so. It seems he got overexcited again."

"Oh!" Troy cried out. "I *am* so sorry."

"I know. Still," Cressida shouted, "just one of those things. You know."

Nigel appeared before them with his champagne cocktails.

"Drink up," Cressida said, "and have another with me. I need it. Do."

"All right. But I think there's rather a lot of brandy in them, don't you?"

"There'd better be."

Hilary broke through the crowd to thank Troy for her present, a wash drawing she had made of the scarecrow field from her bedroom window. He was, she could see, as pleased as Punch: indistinguishable thanks poured out of him. Troy watched his odd hitched-up mouth (like a camel's, she thought) gabbling away ecstatically.

At last he said, "It all went off nicely, don't you think, except for Uncle Flea's gloves? How he could!"

Troy and Cressida, one on each side of him, screamed their intelligence. Hilary seemed greatly put out and bewildered. "Oh *no!*" he said. "You *don't* tell me! *Moult!*" And then after further ejaculations, "I must say he managed very creditably. Dear me, I must thank him. Where is he?"

The overstimulated little boy appeared before them. He struck an attitude and blew a self-elongating paper squeaker into Hilary's face. Toy trumpets, drums and whistles were now extremely prevalent.

"Come here," Hilary said. He took Cressida and Troy by their arms and piloted them into the hall, shutting the doors behind them. The children's supper was laid out in great splendour on a long trestle table. Kittiwee, the Boy and some extra female helps were putting final touches.

"That's better," Hilary said. "I must go and see

Uncle Flea. He'll be cut to the quick over this. But first tell me, Cressida darling, what exactly happened?"

"Well, I went to the cloakroom as arranged, to do his makeup. Moult was there already, all dressed up for the part. It seems he went to their rooms to help Uncle Fred and found him having a turn. Moult gave him whatever he has, but it was as clear as clear he couldn't go on for the show. He was in a great taking on. You know? So they cooked it up that Moult would do it. He'd heard all about it over and over again, of course, he'd seen the rehearsals and knew the business. So when Uncle Fred had simmered down and had put his boots up and all that (he wouldn't let Moult get Aunt B), Moult put on the robe and wig and came down. And I slapped on his whiskers and crown and out he went into the courtyard to liaise with Vincent."

"Splendid fellow."

"He really did manage all right, didn't he? I came in for his entrance. I couldn't see him awfully well because of being at the back but he seemed to do all the things. And then when he eggzitted I returned to the cloakroom and helped him clean up. He was in a fuss to get back to Uncle Fred and I said I'd tell Aunt B. Which I did."

"Darling, too wonderful of you. Everybody has clearly behaved with the greatest expedition and aplomb. Now I must fly to poorest Flea and comfort him."

He turned to Troy. "*What* a thing!" he exclaimed. "Look! Both you darlings, continue in your angelic ways like loves and herd the children in here to their supper. Get Blore to bellow at them. As soon as they're settled under the eyes of these splendid ladies, Blore and the staff will be ready for us in the dining-room. He'll sound the gong. If I'm late don't wait for me.

Get the grown-ups into the dining-room. There are place cards but it's all very informal, really. And ask Blore to start the champagne at once. *Au revoir, au 'voir, 'voir,*" cried Hilary, running upstairs and wagging his hand above his head as he went.

"All jolly fine," Cressida grumbled. "I'm worn to a frazzle. But still. Come on."

She and Troy carried out Hilary's instructions and presently the adult party was seated round the dinner table. Troy found herself next to her acquaintance of the moors, Major Marchbanks, who said politely that this was a piece of luck for him.

"I was too shy to say so when we met the other afternoon," he said, "but I'm a great admirer of your work. I've actually got one of your pictures, and who do you suppose gave it to me?"

"I can't imagine."

"Can't you? Your husband."

"Rory!"

"We are old friends. And associates. He gave it to me on the occasion of my marriage. And long before yours, I expect. He may not have even met you then."

"I don't paint in the same way now."

"But it's been a development, I venture? Not an abandonment?"

"Well," said Troy, liking him, "I choose to think so."

Mr. Smith was on her other side. He had heard about Moult's gallant effort and was greatly intrigued. Troy could feel him there at her left elbow, waiting to pounce. Several times he made a rather sly ejaculation of "Oi," but as Major Marchbanks was talking she disregarded it. When she was free she turned and found Mr. Smith with his thumbs in his armholes and his head on one side, contemplating her. He gave her a sideways chuck of his head and a click of his tongue. "Oi," he repeated. Troy had taken a certain amount of champagne. "Oi, yourself," she replied.

"Turn up for the books, Alf Moult making like he was Nebuchadnezzar in a bathrobe."

Troy stared at him. "You know, you're right," she said. "There was something distinctly Blakean. Disallowing the bathrobe."

"Where's he got to?"

"He's up with the Colonel, I think."

" 'E's meant to be doling out mince pies to the little angels."

"That's as it may be," Troy said darkly and drank some more champagne.

Hilary had arrived and had sat down beside a lady on Major Marchbanks' left. He looked slightly put out. Mr. Smith called up the table to him. " 'Ow's the Colonel?" and he said, "Better, thank you," rather shortly.

"The old lady's keeping him company, then?"

"Yes." Hilary added some appropriate general remarks about his uncle's disappointment and signalled to Blore, who bent over him with a majordomo's air. None of the servants, Troy thought, seemed to be at all put out by the presence of so many of Her Majesty's penal servants. Perhaps they enjoyed displaying for them in their new roles.

Hilary spoke quietly to Blore but Blore, who seemed incapable of quiet utterance, boomingly replied, "He's not there, sir," and after a further question: "I couldn't say, sir. Shall I enquire?"

"Do," said Hilary.

Blore made a slight, majestic signal to Mervyn, who left the room.

"That's peculiar," said Mr. Smith. "Where's Alf gone to hide 'is blushes?"

"How do you know it's Moult they're talking about?"

"They said so, di'n they?"

"I didn't hear them."

"It's peculiar," Mr. Smith repeated. He leant back in his chair and fixed his beady regard upon Hilary. He did not pick his teeth. Troy felt that this was due to some accidental neglect in his interpretation of the role for which he so inscrutably cast himself.

She drank some more champagne. "Tell me," she began recklessly, "Mr. Smith. Why do you—or do you—"

But Mr. Smith was paying no attention to Troy. His attention was fixed upon Mervyn, who had returned and was speaking to Blore. Blore again bent over his employer.

"Moult, sir," he intoned, "is not on duty in the hall."

"Why the devil not!" Hilary snapped quite loudly.

"I'm sure I can't say, sir. He received instructions, sir. Very clear."

"All right, well *find* him, Blore. He's wanted with the Colonel. Mrs. Forrester won't leave the Colonel by himself. Go *on,* Blore. Find him, Go yourself."

Blore's eyebrows mounted his forehead. He inclined, returned to Mervyn, and raised a finger at Nigel, with whom he finally left the dining-room. Mervyn remained in sole command.

Hilary looked round his table and said, laughingly, and in French, something about the tyranny of one's dependents which, Troy imagined, was incomprehensible to all but a fraction of his guests.

She turned to Major Marchbanks. She was now fairly certain within herself that she would be showing great strength of character if she were to refuse any more champagne. She looked severely at her glass and found it was full. This struck her as being ex-

quisitely funny but she decided not to interfere with
it.

"Who," asked Major Marchbanks, "is Moult?"

Troy was glad to find that she was able to give him
a coherent answer. "Do you," she asked, "find this
party very extraordinary?"

"Oh, but completely fantastic," he said, "when one
looks at it objectively. I mean four hours ago I was
doing the honours at the Vale Christmas feast and
here I am with three of my warders, drinking Bill-
Tasman's champagne and waited upon by a company
of you know what."

"One of them—Blore, I think—was actually at the
Vale, wasn't he?"

"Oh yes. He's an Old Boy. I recommended him.
With appropriate warnings, you know. I really think
he rather likes displaying his waiter's expertise for
us Vale persons. He was at the top of his profession,
was Blore."

"He's given me a morsel too much to drink," Troy
said carefully.

Major Marchbanks looked at her and burst out
laughing. "You don't tell me you're tiddly?"

"That would be going too far, which is what I hope
I haven't. Gone," Troy added with dignity.

"You seem all right to me."

"Good."

"I say," Hilary said, leaning towards Troy and speaking across the intervening guests, "isn't it too boring
about Moult? Aunt Bed won't budge until he relieves
her."

"What can he be doing?"

"Flown with success, I daresay, and celebrating it.
Here's to your bright eyes," Hilary added and raised his
glass to her.

Troy said. "Look. I'll nip up and relieve Mrs. Forrester. Do let me."

"I can't possibly—"

"Yes, you can. I've finished my lovely dinner. Don't stir, please, anybody," said Troy and was up and away with a celerity that greatly pleased her. "At least," she thought, "I'm all right on my pins."

In the hall the children's supper party was breaking up and they were being drafted back into the drawing-room. Here they would collect their presents, move to the library, and gradually be put in order for departure. On their account the party would be an early one.

At the foot of the stairs Troy encountered Blore.

"Have you found Moult?" she asked.

"No, madam," Blore said, making a sour face. "I don't understand it at all, madam. It's very peculiar behaviour."

("So," Troy irrelevantly thought, "is killing a busboy while you're carving a wing-rib.")

She said, "I'm going up to relieve Mrs. Forrester."

"Very kind, I'm sure, madam. And too bad, if I may say so, that you should be put upon."

"Not a bit of it," said Troy lightly.

"Moult!" Blore said. He actually spoke softly but with such a wealth of venom that Troy was quite taken aback. She continued upstairs and finding herself a bit swimmy in the head, went first to her own room. There she took two aspirins, put a cold sponge on the back of her neck, opened her window, stuck her head out, and gasped.

Two snowflakes touched her face: like the Ice Maiden's fingers in Hans Andersen. The moon was up. She paused for one moment to look at the deadened landscape it offered, and then shut her window, drew her curtains, and went to call on the Forresters.

Colonel Forrester was in bed and awake. He was propped up by pillows and had the look of a well-washed patient in a children's ward. Mrs. Forrester sat before the fire, knitting ferociously.

"Thought you might be Moult," she said.

Troy explained her errand. At first it looked as if Mrs. Forrester was going to turn her down flat. She didn't want any dinner, she announced, and in the same breath said they could send up a tray.

"Do go, B," her husband said. "I'm perfectly well. You only fuss me, my dear. Sitting angrily about."

"I don't believe for a moment they've really looked for him, I said——"

"All right, then. *You* look. Go and stir everybody up. I bet if you go, they'll find him."

If this was cunning on the part of 'the Colonel, it was effective. Mrs. Forrester rammed her knitting into a magenta bag and rose.

"It's very kind of you," she snarled at Troy. "More than that yellow doll of Hilary's thought of offering. Thank you. I shall not be long."

When she had gone the Colonel bit his underlip, hunched his shoulders, and made big eyes at Troy. She made the same sort of face back at him and he gave a little giggle.

"I do so hate fusses," he said, "don't you?"

"Yes, I do rather. Are you really feeling better?"

"Truly. And I'm *beginning* to get over my disappointment though you must admit it *was* provoking for me, wasn't it?"

"Absolutely maddening."

"I hoped you'd understand. But I'm glad Moult did it nicely."

"When did you decide to let him?"

"Oh—at the last moment. I was actually in the dressing room, putting on my robe. I got a bit stuck inside it as one can, you know, with one's arms above one's head and one's mouth full of material, and I rather panicked and had a Turn. Bad show. It was a crisis. There had to be a quick decision. So I told him to carry on," said the Colonel as if he described a tight corner in a military engagement, "and he did. He put me in here and made me lie down and then he went back to the dressing-room to put on the robe. And carried on. Efficiently, you thought?"

"Very. But it's odd of him not to come back, isn't it?"

"Of course it is. He should have reported at once. Very poor show indeed," said the Colonel, drawing himself up in bed and frowning.

"You don't think he could have gone straight to your dressing-room to take off the robe? There's a door from the passage into the dressing-room, isn't there?"

"Yes. But he should have made his report. There's no excuse.

"Would you mind if I just looked in the dressing-room? To see if the robe is there?"

"Do, do, do, do," said the Colonel.

But there was no golden robe in the dressing-room which, as far as Troy could judge, was in perfect order. A little crimson room, it was, with a flock wallpaper and early Victorian furniture. Heavy red curtains on brass rings were drawn across the windows. It might have been a room in Bleak House, and no doubt that was exactly the impression Hilary had intended it to make. She looked in the cupboards and drawers and even under the bed, where she found a rather battered tin box with "Col. F. F. Forrester" painted in white letters on it. Remembering Hilary's remarks upon their normal luggage she supposed this must contain the Forresters' valuables.

Somewhere, a long way off, a car door slammed. She thought she could hear voices.

She half opened the curtains and heard more doors slam and engines start up. The guests were leaving. Rays from invisible headlamps played across the snowy prospect, horns sounded, voices called.

Troy rattled the curtains shut and returned to the Colonel.

"Not there," she said. "I suppose he left it in the cloakroom downstairs. I must ask Cressida—she'll know. She took his whiskers off."

"Well, I'm jolly furious with Moult," said the Colonel, rather drowsily. "I shall have to discipline him, I can see that."

"Did he show himself to you? In the robe? Before he went downstairs?"

"Eh? Did he, now? Well, yes, but—Well, in point of fact I dozed off after my Turn. I do that, you know," said the Colonel, his voice trailing away into a drone. "After my Turns. I do doze off."

He did so now, gently puffing his cheeks in and out and making little noises that reminded Troy of a baby.

It was very quiet in the bedroom. The last car had left and Troy imagined the houseparty standing round the drawingroom fire talking over the evening. Or perhaps, she thought, they are having a sort of hunt-for-Moult game. Or perhaps he's been found sleeping it off some forgotten corner.

The Colonel himself now slept very soundly and peacefully and Troy thought there was really no need for her to stay any longer. She turned off all the lights except the bedside lamp and went downstairs.

She found a sort of public meeting going on in the hall. The entire staff was assembled in a tight, apprehensive group being addressed by Hilary. Mrs. Forrester balefully sat beside him as if she was in the chair. Mr. Smith, smoking a cigar, stood on the outskirts like a heckler. Cressida, looking exhausted, was stretched in a porter's chair and her arms dangling and her feet half out of her golden sandals.

"—and all I have to tell you," Hilary was saying, "is that he must be *found*. He must be somewhere and he must be *found*. I know you've got a lot to do and I'm sorry and really it's too ridiculous but there it is. I don't know if any of you have suggestions to make. If you have I'd be glad to hear them."

From her place on the stairs Troy looked at Hilary's audience. Blore. Mervyn. Nigel. Vincent. Kittiwee. The Boy. Standing further back, a clutch of extra helpers, male and female, brought in for the occasion. Of these last, one could only say that they looked tired and puzzled.

But the impression was very different when she considered the regular staff. Troy was sure she hadn't concocted this impression and she didn't think it stemmed from preknowledge. If she hadn't known anything about their past, she believed, she would still have thought that in some indefinable way the staff had closed their ranks and that fear had inspired them to do so. If they had picked up death masks of their faces and clapped them over their own, they could scarcely have been less communicative. This entravagant notion was given a kind of validity by the fact that—surely—they were all most uncommonly pale? They stared straight in front of themselves as if they were on parade.

"Well," Hilary said, "Blore? You're the chief of staff. Any ideas?"

"I'm afraid not, sir. We have made, I think I may

say, sir, a thorough search of the premises. Very thorough, sir."

"Who," Mrs. Forrester snapped out, "saw him last?"

"Yes. All right. Certainly, Aunt Bed. Good question," said Hilary, who was clearly flustered.

There was a considerable pause before Cressida said: "Well, I've *said,* sweeties, haven't I? When he eggzitted after his thing I went back as arranged to the cloakroom and he came in from the outside porch and I took off his robe, wig and makeup and he said he'd go and report to Uncle Fred and I went back to the party."

"Leaving him there?" Hilary and Mrs. Forrester asked in unison.

"Like I said, for Heaven's sake. Leaving him there."

Nobody had paid any attention to Troy. She sat down on the stairs and wondered what her husband would make of the proceedings.

"All right. Yes. Good. All right," said poor Hilary. "So far so good. Now then. Darling, you therefore came into the hall, here, didn't you, on your way to the drawing-room?"

"I didn't do an Uncle Tom's Cabin, darling, and take to the snow."

"Of course not. Ha-ha. And—let me see—the people in charge of the children's supper were here, weren't they?" Hilary looked appealingly in their direction. "Kitti—Cooke—and all his helpers?" he wheedled.

"That's right," said Cressida. "Busy as bees." She closed her eyes.

"And I expect," Hilary said, "some of you can remember Miss Tottenham coming into the hall, don't you?"

Kittiwee said huffily, "Well, sir, I'm sure we *were* very busy round the supper table at the far end of the hall and, personally speaking, I didn't take notice to anythink but my work. However, sir, I do call the incident to mind because of a remark that was passed."

"Oh?" Hilary glanced at Cressida who didn't open her eyes.

"I asked him," she said, "if his bloody cats were shut up."

"Yes, I see."

Mrs. Forrester adjusted her thick-lensed spectacles to look at Cressida.

"The thing is," Hilary hurried on, "did any of you happen to notice Moult when he came out of the cloakroom there? After Miss Tottenham? Because he must have come out and he ought to have gone up the right-hand flight of the stairs to the Colonel's room and then returned to help with the children."

Hilary's reference to the stairs caused his audience to shift their attention to them and discover Troy. Mrs. Forrester ejaculated: "Has he—?" and Troy said quickly, "No. Not a sign. The Colonel's quite all right and fast asleep."

Nobody, it transpired, had seen Moult come out of the cloakroom or go anywhere. Kittiwee again pointed out that the hall was large and dark and they were all very busy. When asked if they hadn't wondered why Moult didn't turn up to do his job, Blore replied with unmistakable spitefulness that this didn't surprise them in the least.

"Why?" Mrs. Forrester barked.

Kittiwee simpered and Blore was silent. One of the women tittered.

Mr. Smith removed his cigar from his mouth. "Was 'e sozzled?" he asked of nobody in particular, and as there was no response added, "What I mean, did 'e take a couple to celebrate 'is triumph?"

"That's a point," Cressida conceded. She opened her eyes. "He was in a tizzy about going on for the part. It was pretty silly, really, because after all—no dialogue. Round the tree, business with arms, and off. Still, he was nervous. And when I fixed his whiskers I must say it was through a pretty thick Scotch mist."

"There y'are," said Mr. Smith.

"Aunt Bed—does Moult sometimes—?"

"Occasionally," said Mrs. Forrester.

"I think he had it on him," Cressida said. "That's only my idea, mind. But he sort of patted himself—you know?"

Hilary said, "He was already wearing the robe when you went in to make him up, wasn't he?"

"That's right. He put it on upstairs, he said, for Uncle Fred to see."

"Which he didn't," Troy said. "He'd gone to sleep."

"Moult didn't say anything about that. Though, mind you," Cressida added, "I was only with him for a matter of a minute. There was nothing to fixing his beard: a couple of spots of spirit gum and Bob was your uncle. But I did notice he was all uptight. He was in no end of a taking-on. Shaking like a leaf, he was."

"Vincent!" Hilary suddenly exclaimed, and Vincent gave a perceptible start. "Why didn't I think of you! You saw Moult, outside, when he left the drawing-room, didn't you? After his performance?"

Vincent, almost indistinguishably, acknowledged that he did.

"Well—what about it? Did he say anything or—or—look anything—or do anything? Come *on,* Vincent?"

But no. It appeared that Vincent had not even noticed it was Moult. His manner suggested that he and Moult were not on such terms that the latter would have divulged his secret. He had emerged from his triumph into the icy cold, hunched his shoulders against the wind, and bolted from the courtyard into the porch. Vincent saw him enter the little cloakroom.

"Which gets us nowhere," Mrs. Forrester said with a kind of stony triumph.

"I don't know why there's all the carry-on, 'Illy," said Mr. Smith. "Alf Moult's sleeping it orf."

"Where?" Mrs. Forrester demanded.

"Where, where, where! Anywhere. You don't tell me there's not plenty of lay-bys for a spot of kip where nobody's thought of looking! 'Ow about the chapel?"

"My dear Uncle Bert—surely—"

"Or all them old stables and what-'ave-you at the back. Come orf it!"

"Have you—?" Hilary asked his staff.

"I looked in the chapel," Mrs. Forrester announced.

"Has anybody looked—well—outside. The laundries and so on?"

It appeared not. Vincent was dispatched to do this. "If 'e's there," Troy heard him mutter " 'e'll 'ave froze."

"What about the top story? The attics?" Mr. Smith asked.

"No, sir. We've looked," said Blore, addressing himself exclusively to Hilary. It struck Troy that the staff despised Mr. Smith for the same reason that they detested Moult.

A silence followed: mulish on the part of the staff, baffled on the part of the houseparty, exhausted on all counts. Hilary finally dismissed the staff. He kept up his grand seignorial role by thanking his five murderers, congratulating them upon their management of the party and hoping, he said, that their association would continue as happily throughout the coming year.

Those of the temporary helpers who live in the district he excused from further duties.

The houseparty then retired to the boudoir, it being, Hilary said, the only habitable room in the house.

Here, after a considerable amount of desultory speculation and argument, everybody but Troy, who found she detested the very sight of alcohol, had a nightcap. Hilary mixed two rum toddies and Mrs. Forrester said she would take them up to her room. "If your uncle's awake," she said. "He'll want one. If he isn't—"

"You'll polish them both off yourself, Auntie?"

"And why not?" she said. "Good-night, Mrs. Alleyn. I am very much obliged to you. Good-night, Hilary. Good-night, Smith." She looked fixedly at Cressida. "Good-night," she said.

"What have *I* done?" Cressida demanded when Mrs. Forrester had gone. "Honestly, darling, your relations!"

"Darling, you *know* Auntie Bed, none better. One can only laugh."

"Heh, heh, heh. Anyone'd think I'd made Moult tight and then hidden him in the boot cupboard." Cressida stopped short and raised a finger. *"A propos,"* she said. "Has anybody looked in the cupboards?"

"Now, my darling child, why on earth should he be in a cupboard? You talk," said Hilary, "as if he were a Body," and then looked extremely perturbed.

"If you ask my opinion which you haven't," said Mr. Smith, "I think you're all getting yourselves in a muck sweat about nothing. Don't you lose any sleep over Alf Moult. He knows how to look after 'imself, none better. And since it's my practice to act as I speak I'll wish you good-night. Very nice show, 'Illy, and none the worse for being a bit of a mockup. Wouldn't of done for the pipe-and-tabor lot, would it? Bells, Druids, Holy Families and angels! What a combination! Oh dear! Still, the kids appreciated it so we don't care, do we? Well. Bye, bye, all."

When he had gone Hilary said to Troy, "You see what I mean about Uncle Bert? In his way he's a purist."

"Yes, I do see."

"I think he's fantastic," said Cressida. "You know? There's something basic. The grass-roots thing. You *believe* in him. Like he might be out of Genêt."

"My darling girl, what dreadful nonsense you do talk! Have you so much as *read* Genêt?"

"Hilly! For Heaven's sake—he's where O-E *begins*."

Hilary said with unusual acerbity, "And I'm afraid he's where I leave off."

"Of course I've known all along you'll never get the message."

Troy thought, "This is uncomfortable. They're going to have a row," and was about to leave them to it when Cressida suddenly laughed and wound her arms round Hilary's neck. He became very still. She drew his head down and whispered. They both laughed. Their embrace became so explicit that Troy thought on the whole she had better evaporate and proceeded to do so.

As the door she half turned, wondering if she should throw out a jolly good-night. Hilary, without releasing Cressida, lifted his face and gave Troy not so much a smile as the feral grimace of an antique Hylaeus. When she had shut the door behind her she thought: that was the sort of thing one should never see.

On her way through the hall she found a great clearance had been made and could hear voices in the drawing-room. Well, she thought, Hilary certainly has it both ways. He gets all the fun of setting up his party and none of the tedious aftermath. That's done for him by his murderers.

She reached her room, with its well-tended fire, turned-down bed and impeccably laid-out dressing gown, pyjamas and slippers. She supposed Nigel had found time to perform these duties, and found this a disagreeable reflection.

She hung her dress in the wardrobe and could just catch the drone of the Forresters' voices joined, it seemed, in no very urgent conversation. Troy was wide awake and restless. Too much had happened and happened inconclusively over the last few days. The anonymous messages, which, with astonishment, she realized she had almost forgotten. The booby-trap, Cressida's report of the row in the staff common-room. Uncle Flea's turns. Moult as Druid. The disappearance of Moult. Should these elements, wondered Troy, who had been rereading her Forster, connect? What would Rory think? He was fond of quoting Forster. "Only connect. Only connect." What would he make of all this? And now, in a flash, Troy was perfectly certain that he would think these were serious matters.

As sometimes happens in happy marriages, Troy and her husband, when parted, often found that before one of them wrote or cabled or telephoned, the other was visited by an intensified awareness, a kind of expectation. She had this feeling very vividly now and was glad of it. Perhaps in the morning there would be news.

She heard midnight strike and a moment later Cressida, humming the "Bells of St. Clement's," passed the door on her way to her room at the south end of the corridor.

Troy yawned. The bedroom was overheated and

at last she was sleepy. She went to her window, slipped
through the curtains without drawing them, and opened
it at the top. The north wind had risen and the rumour
of its progress was abroad in the night. Flights of
cloud were blown across the heavens. The moon was
high now, casting a jetty shadow from the house across
the snow. It was not a deserted landscape, for round
the corner of the east wing came Vincent and his
wheelbarrow and in the barrow the dead body of the
Christmas tree denuded of its glory. He plodded on
until he was beneath the Forresters' windows and then
turned into the shadow and was swallowed. She heard
a swish and tinkle as he tipped his load into the debris
of the ruined conservatory.

Shivering and immoderately tired, she went to bed
and to sleep.

Five — Alleyn

Troy woke next morning at the sound of Nigel's discreet attentions to her fire. He had placed her early tea tray by her bed.

She couldn't make up her mind, at once, to speak to him, but when he opened her window curtains and let in the reflected pallor of snow she wished him good morning.

He paused, blinking his white eyelashes, and returned the greeting.

"Is it still snowing?" she asked.

"Off and on, madam. There was sleet in the night but it changed to snow, later."

"Has Moult appeared?"

"I believe not, madam."

"How very odd, isn't it?"

"Yes, madam. Will that be all, madam?"

"Yes, thank you."

"Thank you, madam."

But it's all phony, Troy thought. He turns it on. He didn't talk like that when he made rocking-horses and wax effigies. Before he reached the door she said, "I think you made a wonderful job of that catafalque."

He stopped. "Ta," he said.

"I don't know how you managed to get such precision and detail with a medium like snow."

"It was froze."

"Even so. Have you ever sculpted? In stone?"

"It was all working from moulds like. But I always had a fancy to carve."

"I'm not surprised."

He said, "Ta," again. He looked directly at her and went out.

Troy bathed and dressed and took her usual look at the landscape. Everywhere except in areas close to the house, a coverlet of snow. Not a footprint to be seen. Over on the far left the canvas-covered bulldozers and their works were mantled. Every tree was a Christmas tree. Somebody had reerected the scarecrow, or perhaps with a change in the wind it had righted itself. It looked, if anything, more human than before. Quite a number of birds had settled on it.

Troy found Hilary and Mr. Smith at breakfast. Hilary lost no time in introducing the Moult theme.

"No Moult! It really is beyond a joke, now," he said. "Even Uncle Bert agrees, don't you, Uncle Bert?"

"I give you in, it's a rum go," he conceded. "Under existing circs, it's rather more than that. It's upsetting.

"What do you mean by 'existing circs'?"

"Ask yourself."

"I asked you."

Mervyn came in with a fresh supply of toast.

"Pas devant les domestiques," quoted Mr. Smith.

Mervyn withdrew. "Why not before them?" Hilary asked crossly.

"Use your loaf, boy."

"I don't know what you're talking about, Uncle Bert."

"No? Ah: Fancy."

"Oh, *blast* everything!" said Hilary. He turned to

Troy. "He really *isn't* on the premises," he said. "Not in the house or the outbuildings. If he wandered into the grounds somewhere, he didn't go off the drive or swept paths because there aren't any unaccountable footprints in the snow."

"Could he have got into the back of one of the cars and gone to sleep and been driven away unnoticed?"

"He'd have woken up and declared himself by now, surely?"

"It's an idea, though," said Mr. Smith. "What say he got into the boot of the station wagon from the Vale and come to behind bars? That'd be a turn-up for the books, wouldn't it?"

"Excessively droll," said Hilary sourly. "Well!" he said, throwing up his hands, "what's the next step? I don't know! The Fleas are becoming difficult, I can tell you that much. I looked in on them and found Aung Bed trying to valet Uncle Flea and getting it all wrong. Aunt Bed's in a rage because she can't put her jewelry away."

"Why can't she?"

"It seems she keeps it in their locked tin box with all their securities under the bed in the dressing-room."

"I know," said Troy. "I saw it."

"Well, Moult's got the key."

"They're potty," said Mr. Smith definitively. "What I mean, potty. What I mean, look at it! Carts her stuff round, and it's good stuff, mind, some of it's very nice stuff. Carts it round in a flipping tin box and gives the key to a bloody disappearing act. No, what I mean, I arst you!"

"All right, Uncle Bert. All right. We all know the Fleas go their own way. That's beside the point. What we have to decide——"

The door was flung open and Mrs. Forrester entered in a temper. She presented a strange front to the breakfast table. She was attired in her usual morning apparel: a Harris tweed skirt, a blouse and three cardigans, the uppermost being puce in colour. Stuck about this ensemble at eccentric angles were any number of brooches. Round her neck hung the elaborate Victorian necklace which had been the *pièce de résistance* of her last night's toilet. She wore many rings and several bracelets. A watch, suspended from a diamond and emerald bow, was pinned to her breast. She twinkled and glittered like—the comparison was inevitable—a Christmas tree.

"Look at me," she unnecessarily demanded.

"Aunt B," Hilary said, "we do. With astonishment."

"As well you might. Under the circumstances, Hilary, I feel obliged to keep my Lares and Penates about me."

"I would hardly describe—"

"Very well. They are not kitchen utensils. That I grant you. The distinction, however, is immaterial."

"You didn't sport all that hardware last night, Mrs. F." Mr. Smith suggested.

"I did not. I had it brought out and I made my choice. The rejected pieces should have been returned to their place. By Moult. They were not and I prefer under the circumstances to keep them about me. That, however is not the matter at issue. Hilary!"

"Aunt Bed?"

"An attempt has been made upon our strongbox."

"Oh my God! What do you mean?"

"There is evidence. An instrument—possibly a poker— has been introduced in an unsuccessful attempt upon the padlock."

"It needed only this," said Hilary and took his head between his hands.

"I am keeping it from your uncle: it would fuss him. What do you propose to do?"

"I? What can I do? Why," asked Hilary wildly, "do you keep it under the dressing-room bed?"

"Because it won't go under our bed, which is ridiculously low."

"What's the story, then?" Mr. Smith asked. "Did Alf Moult try to rob the till and run away in a fright when he foozled the job?"

"With the key in his pocket?" Mrs. Forrester snapped. "You're not very bright this morning, Smith."

"It was a joke."

"Indeed."

Blore came in. "A telephone call, sir, for Mrs. Alleyn," he said.

"*Me?* Is it from London?"

"Yes, madam. Mr. Alleyn, madam."

"Oh how lovely!" Troy shouted before she could stop herself. She apologized and made a bolt for the telephone.

2.

"—so we wound the whole thing up at ninety in the shade and here I am. A Happy Christmas, darling. When shall I see you?"

"Soon. Soon. The portrait's finished. I think. I'm not sure."

"When in doubt, stop. Shouldn't you?"

"I daresay. I want to. But there's just one thing—"

"Troy: is anything the matter?"

"In a way. No—not with me. Here."

"You've turned cagey. Don't you want to talk?"

"Might be better not."

"I see. Well—when?"

"I—Rory, hold on will you? Hold on."

"I'm holding."

It was Hilary. He had come in unnoticed and now made deprecatory gestures and rather silly little faces at Troy. "Please!" he said. "May I? Do forgive me, but may I?"

"Of course." ·

"It's just occurred to me. So dismal for Alleyn to be in an empty house in London at Christmas. So *please*, suggest he comes to us. I know you want to fly on wings of song, but you did say you might need one more sitting, and anyway I should be so delighted to meet him. He might even advise about Moult or would that be anti-protocol? But—please—?"

"I think perhaps—"

"No, you don't. You can't. You mustn't 'think perhaps.' Ask him. Go on, do."

Troy gave her husband the message.

"Do you," he said, speaking close to the receiver, "want this? Or would you rather come home? There's something up, isn't there? Put on a carefree voice, love, and tell me. Would you like me to come? I can. I'm free at the moment."

"Can you? Are you?"

"Then, shall I?"

"I really don't know," Troy said and laughed, as she trusted, gaily. "Yes. I think so."

"When would you leave if I didn't come?"

"Well—don't quite know," she said and hoped she sounded playful and cooperative.

"What the hell," her husband asked, "is all this? Well, never mind. You can't say, obviously."

Hilary was making modest little gestures. He pointed to himself and mouthed, "May I?"

"Hilary," said Troy, "would like to have a word."

"Turn him on," said Alleyn. "Or have you, by any chance, already done so?"

"Here he is," Troy said severely. "Rory: this is Hilary Bill-Tasman."

She handed over the receiver and listened to Hilary. His manner was masterly: not too overtly insistent, not too effusive, but of such a nature that it made a refusal extremely difficult. I suppose, Troy thought, these are the techniques he brings to bear on his rich, complicated business. She imagined her husband's lifted eyebrow. Presently Hilary said: "And you *are* free, aren't you? So why not? The portrait, if nothing else, will be your reward: it's quite superb. You will? I couldn't be more delighted. Now: about trains— there's just time—"

When that was settled he turned, beamingly, to Troy and held out the receiver. "Congratulate me!" cried Hilary and, with that characteristic gesture of his, left the room, gaily wagging his hand above his head.

Troy said, "It's me again."

"Good."

"I'll come to the station."

"Too kind."

"So nice to see you again!"

"Always pleasant to pick up the threads."

"Good-morning."

"Good-morning."

When Hilary announced that Vincent would put on his chauffeur's uniform and take the small car to the main line station, Troy suggested that she herself could so so. This clearly suited him very well. She gathered that some sort of exploratory work was to be carried out in the grounds. ("Though really," Hilary said, "one holds out little hope of it") and that Vincent's presence would be helpful.

Soon after luncheon Troy got ready for the road.

She heard a commotion under her window and looked out.

Vincent and three other men were floundering about in a halfhearted way among broken glass and the dense thicket that invested the site of the old conservatory. They poked and thrust with forks and spades. "But that's ridiculous," thought Troy.

She found Hilary downstairs waiting to see her off.

He stared at her. "You look," he said, "as if somebody had given you a wonderful present. Or made love to you. Or something."

"And that's exactly how I feel," she said.

He was silent for so long and stared so hard that she was obliged to say: "Is anything more the matter?"

"I suppose not," he said slowly. "I hope not. I was just wondering, However! Watch out for icy patches, won't you? You can't miss the turnings. *Bon voyage.*"

He watched her start up her engine, turned on his heel, and went quickly into the house.

In her walks Troy had always taken paths that led up to the moors: "The Land Beyond the Scarecrow," she had called it to herself as if it belonged to a children's story. Now she drove down the long drive that was to become a grand avenue. The bulldozer men were not at work over Christmas. Their halfformed hillock, and the bed for the lake that would reflect it, were covered with snow—the tractors looked ominous and dark under their tarpaulins. Further away stood a copse of bare trees that was evidently a feature of the original estate and beyond this, fields stretching downhill, away from the moors and towards a milder and more humanized landscape. At the end of the drive she crossed a bridge over a rapid brook that Hilary had told her would be developed, further upstream, into water gardens.

A drive of some twelve miles brought her to her destination. The late afternoon sun shone bravely, there was an air of normality and self-containment about the small country town of Downlow. Troy drove along the main street to the station, parked her car, and went through the office to the platform. Here, in the familiar atmosphere of paste, disinfectant and travel posters, Halberds seemed absurd and faintly distasteful.

She was early and walked up and down the platform, partly to keep warm and partly to work off her overstimulated sense of anticipation. Strange notions came into her head. As, for instance, would Cressida in—say—ten years' time, feel more or less like this if she had been absent from Hilary for three weeks? Was Cressida much in love with Hilary? Did she passionately want to be mistress of Halberds? Judging by those representatives of county families who had rather uneasily attended the party, Cressida was unlikely to find a kindred spirit among them. Perhaps she and Hilary would spend most of their time in their S.W.1 flat, which Troy supposed to be on a pretty lavish scale. Would they take some of their murderers to look after them when they came up to London? Troy found that she felt uneasy about Cressida and obscurely sorry for her.

With a loud clank the signal arm jerked up. A porter and one or two other persons strolled onto the platform, and from down the line came the banshee whistle of the London train.

3.

"Mind? Of course I don't mind," Alleyn said. "I thought I should be hanging about the flat waiting for you to come home! Instead of which, here we are, bold as brass, driving somebody else's car through a Christmas tree landscape and suiting each other down to the ground. What's wrong with that?"

"I've no complaints."

"In that case you must now tell me what's up in the Bill-Tasman outfit. You sounded greatly put out this morning."

"Yes, well . . . all right. Hold on to your hat and fetch up all your willing suspension of unbelief. You'll need it."

"I've heard of Bill-Tasman's experiment with villains for flunkies. Your letter seemed to suggest that it works."

"That was early days. That was a week ago. I didn't write again because there wasn't time. Now, listen."

" *'List, list, O list.'* "

"Yes, well, it's an earful."

" *'Speak, I am bound to hear.'* "

"Roy! Don't be a detective."

"Oops! Sorry."

"Here I go, then."

Troy had got about a third of the way through her narrative when her husband stopped her.

"I suppose," he said, "I have to take it that you are *not* making this up as you go along."

"I'm not even making the most of my raw material. Which part do you find difficult to absorb?"

"My trouble is quantitative rather than particular, but I find I jib at Aunt Bed. I don't know why. I suppose she's not somebody in disguise and camping it up?"

"That really would be a more appropriate theory for Mr. Smith."

"Oh," said Alleyn. "I know about your Mr. Smith. The firm of Bill-Tasman and Smith is at the top of the

British if not the European antiquarian trade, and Albert Smith, from the police angle, is as pure as the driven snow. We've sought their opinions before now in cases of fraud, robbery from collections, and art forgeries. He started as a barrow-boy, he had a flair, and with the aid of Bill-Tasman, Senior, he got to the top. It's not an unusual story, darling. It's merely an extreme example. Press on."

Troy pressed on with mileage and narrative. They reached the signpost for the Vale turn-off and began to climb the lower-reaches of the moors. Patches of snow appeared. In the far distance, Troy thought she recognized the high tor above the Vale.

Alleyn became quieter and quieter. Every now and then he questioned her and once or twice asked her to go over the ground again. She had got as far as the anonymous messages and the booby-trap when she interrupted herself. "Look," she said. "See those plumes of smoke beyond the trees? We're nearly there. That's Halberds."

"Could you pull up? I'd like to hear the lot while we're at it."

"O.K."

She turned the car on to the verge of the road and stopped the engine. The sky had begun to darken, mist rose from hollows and blurred their windscreen. Rime glittered on a roadside briar.

"You must be starved with cold after Sydney in midsummer."

"I'm treble-sweatered and quilted. Carry on, my love."

Ten minutes later Troy said, "And that's it. When I left, Vincent and some chaps were tramping about with forks and spades in the ruins of the conservatory."

"Has Bill-Tasman reported to his local police?"

"I don't think so."

"He damn' well ought to."

"I think he's holding back for you."

"Like hell he is!"

"For your advice."

"Which will be to call up the local station. What else, for pity's sake? What's he *like*, Bill-Tasman? He sounded precious on the telephone."

"He's a bit like a good-looking camel. Very paintable."

"If you say so, darling."

"He's intelligent, affected and extremely companionable."

"I see. And what about this chap Moult? Does he drink, did you say?"

"According to Aunt Bed, occasionally."

"Jim Marchbanks is at the Vale."

"I forgot to tell you—we've chummed up."

"Have you now? Nice creature, isn't he?"

They were silent for a minute or so. Presently Alleyn said his wife's nose was as cold as an iced cherry but not as red. After a further interval she said she thought they should move on.

When they reached the turn in the drive where Halberds was fully revealed, Alleyn said that everything had become as clear as mud: Troy had obviously got herself into a film production, on location, of *The Castle of Otranto* and had been written into the script as the best way of keeping her quiet.

Blore and Mervyn came out to meet them. They both seemed to Troy to be excessively glum faced but their behavior was impeccable. Mervyn, carrying Alleyn's suitcase, led the way upstairs to a dressing-room on the far side of Troy's bathroom and connecting with it.

"Mr. Bill-Tasman is in the boudoir, madam," said

Mervyn with his back to Alleyn. He cast a rather wild glance at Troy and withdrew.

"Is that chap's name Cox?" Alleyn asked.

"I've no idea."

"Mervyn Cox. Booby-trap. Flat iron. Killed Warty Thompson the cat-burglar. That's the boy."

"Did you—?"

"No. One of Fox's cases. I just remembered."

"I'm certain he didn't rig that thing up for me."

"You may well be right. Suspect anyone else?"

"No. Unless—"

"Unless?"

"It's so farfetched. It's just that there does appear to have been some sort of feud between Moult and the staff."

"And Moult fixed the things up to look like Mervyn's job? And wrote the messages in the same spirit? Out of spite?"

"He doesn't seem to be particularly spiteful."

"No?"

"He obviously adores the Colonel. You know—one of those unquestioning, dogged sort of attachments."

"I know."

"So what?"

"Well may you ask. What's he like to look at?"

"Oh—rather upsetting, poor chap. He's got a scarred face. Burns, I should imagine."

"Come here to me."

"I think you'd better meet Hilary."

"Blast Hilary," said Alleyn. "All right. I suppose so."

It was abundantly clear to Troy, when they found Hilary alone in the boudoir, that something had been added to the tale of inexplicable events. He greeted Alleyn with almost feverish enthusiasm. He gushed about the portrait (presently they would look at it), and he also gushed about Troy, who refused to catch her husband's eye. He talked more than a little wildly about Alleyn's welcome return from the Antipodes. He finally asked, with a strange and most unsuccessful attempt at off-handedness, if Troy had told Alleyn of their "little mystery." On hearing that she had he exclaimed, "No, but *isn't* it a bore? I do so *hate* mysteries, don't you? No, I suppose you don't, as you perpetually solve them."

"Have there been any developments?" Troy asked.

"Yes, as a matter of fact. Yes. I was leading up to them. I—I haven't made it generally known as yet. I thought I would prefer—"

Cressida came in and Hilary madly welcomed her as if they had been parted for a week. She stared at him in amazement. On being introduced to Alleyn she gave herself a second or two to run over his points and from then until the end of the affair at Halberds made a dead set at him.

Cressida was not, Troy had to admit, a gross practitioner. She kept fractionally to the right of a frontal attack. Her method embraced the attentive ear, the slight smile of understanding, the very occasional glance. She made avoidance about ninety per cent more equivocal than an accidental brush of the hands, though that was not lacking either, Troy noticed, when Cressida had her cigarette lit.

Troy wondered if she always went into action when confronted with a personable man or if Alleyn had made a smash hit. Was Hilary at all affected by the manifestations? But Hilary, clearly, was fussed by other matters and his agitation increased when Mrs. Forrester came in.

She, in her way, also made a dead set at Alleyn, but her technique was widely different. She barely waited for the introduction.

"Just as well you've come," she said. "High time. Now we shall be told what to do."

"Aunt Bed—we mustn't—"

"Nonsense, Hilary. Why else have you dragged him all this way? Not," she added as an afterthought, "that he's not pleased to see his wife, of course."

"I'm delighted to see her," said Alleyn.

"Who wouldn't be!" Hilary exclaimed. Really, Troy thought, he was showing himself in a most peculiar light.

"Well?" Mrs. Forrester began on a rising inflexion.

Hilary intervened. He said, with a show of firmness, that perhaps a little consultation in the study might be an idea. When his aunt tried to cut in he talked her down, and as he talked he seemed to gain authority. In the upshot he took Alleyn by the elbow and, coruscating with feverish jokelets, piloted him out of the boudoir.

"Darling!" said Cressida to Troy before the door had shut. "Your husband! You know? And I mean this. The mostest."

The study was in the east wing, next door to the boudoir. Hilary fussed about, turning on lamps and offering Alleyn tea (which he and Troy had missed), or a drink. "Such a mongrel time of day, I always think," he said. "Are you sure you won't?"

Alleyn said he was sure. "You want to talk about this business, don't you?" he asked. "Troy's told me the whole story. I think you should call your local police."

"She said you'd say that. I did hope you wouldn't mind if I just consulted you first."

"Of course I don't. But it's getting on for twenty-four hours, isn't it? I really don't think you should wait any longer. It might be best to call up your provincial Detective-Superintendent. Do you know him?"

"Yes. *Most* uncongenial. Beastly about the staff. I really couldn't."

"All right. Where's the nearest station? Downlow?"

"Yes. I believe so. Yes."

"Isn't the super there a chap called Wrayburn?"

"I—I did think of consulting Marchbanks. At the Vale, you know."

"I'm sure he'd give you the same advice."

"Oh!" Hilary cried out. "And I'm sure you're right but I do dislike this sort of thing. I can't expect you to understand, of course, but the staff here—they won't like it either. They'll hate it. Policemen all over the house. Asking questions. Upsetting them like anything."

"I'm afraid they'll have to lump it, you know."

"Oh *damn!*" Hilary said pettishly. "All right. I'm sorry, Alleyn. I'm being disagreeable."

"Ring Wrayburn up and get it over. After all, isn't it just possible that Moult, for some reason that hasn't appeared, simply walked down the drive and hitched a lift to the nearest station? Has anyone looked to see if his overcoat and hat and money are in his room?"

"Yes. Your wife thought of that. Nothing missing, as far as we could make out."

"Well—ring up."

Hilary stared at him, fetched a deep sigh, sat down at his desk, and opened his telephone directory.

Alleyn walked over to the window and looked out. Beyond the reflected image of the study he could distinguish a mass of wreckage—shattered glass, rubbish, trampled weeds and, rising out of them close at hand, a young fir with some of its boughs broken. Troy had shown him the view from her bedroom and he realized that this must be the sapling that grew beneath Colonel Forrester's dressing-room window. It was somewhere about here, then, that she had seen Vincent dispose of the Christmas tree at midnight. Here, too, Vincent and his helpers had been trampling about with garden forks and spades when Troy left for Downlow. Alleyn shaded the pane and moved about until he could eliminate the ghostly study and look further into the dark ruin outside. Now he could make out the Christmas tree, lying in a confusion of glass, soil and weeds.

A fragment of tinsel still clung to one of its branches and was caught in the lamplight.

Hilary had got his connection. With his back to Alleyn he embarked on a statement to Superintendent Wrayburn of the Downlow Constabulary and, all things considered, made a pretty coherent job of it. Alleyn, in his day, had been many, many times rung up by persons in Hilary's position who had given a much less explicit account of themselves. As Troy had indicated: Hilary was full of surprises.

Now he carefully enunciated details. Names. Times. A description. Mr. Wrayburn was taking notes.

"I'm much obliged to you," Hilary said. "There is one other point, Superintendent. I have staying with me—"

"Here we go," Alleyn thought.

Hilary screwed round in his chair and made a deprecatory face at him. "Yes," he said. "Yes. At his suggestion, actually. He's with me now. Would you like to speak to him? Yes, by all means." He held out the receiver.

"Hullo," Alleyn said, "Mr. Wrayburn?"

"Would this be Chief-Superintendent Alleyn?"

"That's right."

"Well, well, well. Long time," said Mr. Wrayburn brightly, "no see. When was that case? Back in '65."

"That's it. How are you, Jack?"

"Can't complain. I understand there's some bother up your way?"

"Looks like it."

"What are you doing there, Chief?"

"I'm an accident. It's none of my business."

"But you reckon we ought to take a wee look-see?"

"Your D.C.C. would probably say so. Somebody ought to, I fancy."

"It's a cold, cold world. I was counting on a nice quiet Christmas. So what happens? A church robbery, a suspected arson, and three fatal smashes in my district and half my chaps down with flu. And now this. And look at you! You're living it up, aren't you? Seats of the Mighty?"

"You'll come up, then, Jack?"

"That's correct."

"Good. And Jack—for your information, it's going to be a search-party job."

"Well, ta for the tip anyway. Over and out."

Alleyn hung up. He turned to find Hilary staring at him over his clasped hands.

"Well," Hilary said. "I've done it. Haven't I?"

"It really was advisable, you know."

"You don't—You don't ask me anything. Any questions about that wretched little man. Nothing."

"It's not my case."

"You talk," Hilary said crossly, "like a doctor."

"Do I?"

"Etiquette. Protocol."

"We have our little observances."

"It would have been so much pleasanter—I'd made up my mind I'd—I'd—"

"Look here," Alleyn said. "If you've got any kind of information that might have even a remote bearing on this business, do for Heaven's sake let Wrayburn have it. You said, when we were in the other room, that there's been a development."

"I know I did. Cressida came in."

"Yes—well, do let Wrayburn have it. It won't go any further if it has no significance."

"Hold on," said Hilary. "Wait. Wait."

He motioned Alleyn to sit down and, when he had done so, locked the door. He drew the window curtains close shut, returned to his desk, and knelt down before it.

"That's a beautiful desk," Alleyn said. "Hepplewhite?"

"Yes." Hilary fished a key out of his pocket. "It's intact. No restoration nonsense." He reached into the back of the kneehole. Alleyn heard the key turn. Hilary seemed to recollect himself. With a curious half-sheepish glance at Alleyn, he wrapped his handkerchief about his hand. He groped. There was an interval of a few seconds and then he sat back on his heels.

"Look," he said.

On the carpet, near Alleyn's feet, he laid down a crumpled newspaper package.

Alleyn leant forward. Hilary pulled back the newspaper.

He disclosed a short steel poker with an ornate handle.

Alleyn looked at it for a moment. "Yes?" he said. "Where did you find it?"

"That's what's so—upsetting." Hilary gave a sideways motion of his head towards the window. "Out there," he said. "Where you were looking—I saw you—just now when I was on the telephone. In the tree."

"The Christmas tree?"

"No, no, no. The growing tree. Inside it. Lying

across the branches. Caught up, sort of, by the handle."

"When did you find it?"

"This afternoon. I was in here wondering whether, after all, I should ring up Marchbanks or the police and hating the idea of ringing up anybody because of—you understand—the staff. And I walked over to the window and looked out. *Without* looking. You know? And then I saw something catching the light in the tree. I didn't realize at once what it was. The tree's quite close to the window—almost touching it. So I opened the window and looked more carefully and finally I stepped out the ledge and got it. I'm afraid I didn't think of fingerprints at that juncture."

Alleyn, sitting on the edge of his chair, still looked at the poker. "You recognize it?" he said. "Where it comes from?"

"Of course. I bought it. It's part of a set. Late eighteenth century. Probably Welsh. There's a Welsh press to go with it."

"Where?"

"Uncle Flea's dressing-room."

"I see."

"Yes, but do you? Did Troy tell you? About the Fleas' tin box?"

"Mrs. Forrester says somebody had tried to force the lock?"

"Exactly! Precisely! With a poker. She actually said with a poker. Well: *as if* with a poker. And it wasn't Moult because Moult, believe it or not, keeps the key. So why a poker for Moult?"

"Quite."

"And—there are dark marks on it. At the end. If you look. Mightn't they be stains of black japanning? It's a japanned tin box. Actually, Uncle Flea's old uniform case."

"Have you by any chance got a lens?"

"Of course I've got a lens," Hilary said querulously. "One constantly uses lenses in our business. Here. Wait a moment."

He found one in his desk and gave it to Alleyn.

It was not very high-powered but it was good enough to show, at the business end of the poker, a dark smear hatched across by scratches: a slight glutinous deposit to which the needle from a conifer adhered. Alleyn stooped lower.

Hilary said, "Well? Anything?"

"Did you look closely at this?"

"No, I didn't, I was expecting my aunt to come in. Aunt Bed is perpetually making entrances. She wanted to harry me and I didn't want to add to her fury by letting her see this. So I wrapped it up and locked it away. Just in time, as it turned out. In she come with all her hackles up. If ladies have hackles."

"But you did notice the marks then?"

"Yes. Just."

"They're not made by lacquer."

"Oh?"

"I'm afraid not."

"Afraid? What do you mean—afraid?"

"See for yourself."

Alleyn gave Hilary the glass. Hilary stared at him and then knelt by the crumpled paper with its trophy. Alleyn moved the desk lamp to throw a stronger light on the area. Hilary bent his body as if he performed some oriental obeisance before the poker.

"Do you see?" Alleyn said. "It's not what you supposed, is it? Look carefully. The deposit is sticky, isn't it? There's a fir needle stuck to it. And underneath—I think Mr. Wrayburn would rather you didn't touch it—underneath, but just showing one end, there's a gold-coloured thread. Do you see it?"

"I—yes. Yes, I think—yes—"

"Tell me," Alleyn asked. "What colour was the Druid's wig?"

4.

"Now, I tell you what," Alleyn said to his wife. "This thing has all the signs of becoming a top-ranking nuisance, and I'm damned if I'll have you involved in it. You know what happened that other time you got stuck into a nuisance."

"If you're thinking of bundling me off to a pub in Downlow, I'll jib."

"What I'm thinking of is a quick return by both of us to London."

"Before the local force gets any ideas about you?"

"Exactly."

"You're a bit late for that, darling, aren't you? Where's Mr. Wrayburn?"

"In the study, I imagine. I left Bill-Tasman contemplating his poker and I told him it'd be better if he saw the Super alone. He didn't much like the idea, but there it is."

"Poor Hilary!"

"I daresay. It's a bit of an earthquake under his ivory tower, isn't it?"

"Do you like him, Rory?"

Alleyn said, "I don't know. I'm cross with him because he's being silly but—yes, I suppose if we'd met under normal conditions I'd have quite liked him. Why?"

'He's a strange one. When I was painting him I kept thinking of such incongruous things."

"Such as?"

"Oh—fauns and camels and things."

"Which does his portrait favour?"

"At first, the camel. But the faun has sort of in-tervened—I mean the Pan job, you know, not the sweet little deer."

"So I supposed. If he's a Pan-job I'll bet he's met his match in his intended nymph."

"She went in, boots and all, after you, didn't she?"

"If only," Alleyn said, "I could detect one pinch, one soupçon, of the green-eyed monster in you, my dish, I'd crow like a bloody rooster."

"We'd better finish changing. Hilary will be expect-ing us. Drinks at seven. You're to meet Mr. Smith and the Fleas."

"I can wait."

There was a tap at the door.

"You won't have to," said Troy. "Come in."

It was Nigel, all downcast eyes, to present Mr. Bill-Tasman's compliments to Mr. Alleyn and he would be very glad if Mr. Alleyn would join him in the study.

"In five minutes," Alleyn said, and when Nigel had gone: "Which was that?"

"The one that killed a sinful lady. Nigel."

"I thought as much. Here I go."

He performed one of the lightning changes to which Troy was pretty well accustomed, gave her a kiss, and went downstairs.

Superintendent Wrayburn was a sandy man; big, of course, but on the bonier side. He was princi-pally remarkable for his eyebrows, which resembled those of a Scotch terrier, and his complexion which, in midwinter, was still freckled like a plover's egg.

Alleyn found him closeted with Hilary in the study. The poker, rewrapped, lay on the desk. Before Hilary was a glass of sherry and before Mr. Wrayburn, a pretty generous whisky and water, from which Alleyn deduced that he hadn't definitely made up his mind what sort of job he seemed to be on. He was obviously glad to see Alleyn and said it was quite a coincidence, wasn't it?

Hilary made some elaborate explanations about drinks being served for the houseparty in the drawing-room at seven but perhaps they could join the others a little later and in the meantime—surely now Alleyn would—?

"Yes, indeed. Thank you," Alleyn said. "Since I'm not on duty," he added lightly and Mr. Wrayburn blushed beyond his freckles.

"Well—nor am I," he said quickly. "Yet. I hope. Not exactly."

Superintendent Wrayburn, Hilary explained, had only just arrived, having been held up at the station. He'd had a cold drive. It was snowing again. He was more than pleased to have Alleyn with them. He, Hilary, was about to give Mr. Wrayburn a—Hilary boggled a little at the word—a statement about the "unfortunate mishap."

Alleyn said "of course" and no more than that. Mr. Wrayburn produced his regulation notebook, and away Hilary went, not overcoherently and yet, Alleyn fancied, with a certain degree of artfulness. He began with Moult's last-minute substitution at the Christmas tree, and continued with Vincent's assurance that he had seen Moult (whom he thought to be the Colonel) after the performance, run from the courtyard into the entrance porch and thence to the dressing room. "Actually," Hilary explained, "it's a cloakroom on one's right as one comes into the house. It's in the angle of the hall and the drawing-room which was so convenient. There's a door from it into the hall itself and another one into the entrance porch. To save muddy boots, you know, from coming into the house."

"Quite," said Mr. Wrayburn. He gazed at his notes. "So the last that's known of him, then, is—?"

"Is when, having taken off his robe and makeup with Miss Tottenham's help, he presumably left the cloakroom with the avowed intention of going up to Colonel Forrester."

"Did he leave the cloakroom by the door into the hall, sir?"

"Again—presumably. He would hardly go out into the porch and double back into the hall, would he?"

"You wouldn't think so, sir, would you? And nobody saw him go upstairs?"

"No. But there's nothing remarkable in that. The servants were getting the children's supper ready. The only light, by my express orders, was from the candles on their table. As you've seen, there are two flights of stairs leading to a gallery. The flight opposite this cloakroom door is farthest away from the children's supper table. The staff would be unlikely to notice Moult unless he drew attention to himself. Actually Moult was—" Hilary boggled slightly and then hurried on. "Actually," he said, "Moult was supposed to help them but, of course, that was arranged before there was any thought of his substituting for Colonel Forrester."

"Yes, sir. I appreciate the position. Are there," Wrayburn asked, "coats and so forth in this cloakroom, sir? Mackintoshes and umbrellas and gum boots and so on?"

"Good for you, Jack," thought Alleyn.

"Yes. Yes, there are. Are you wondering," Hilary said quickly, "if, for some reason—?"

"We've got to consider everything, haven't we, Mr. Bill-Tasman?"

"Of course. Of course. Of course."

"You can't think of any reason, sir, however farfetched, like, that would lead Mr. Moult to quit the premises and, if you'll excuse the expression, do a bunk?"

"No. No. I can't. And—" Hilary looked nervously at Alleyn. "Well—there's a sequel. You're yet to hear—"

And now followed the story of the japanned uniform box, at which Mr. Wrayburn failed entirely to conceal his astonishment and, a stunning climax, the exhibition of the poker.

Alleyn had been waiting for this. He felt a certain amusement in Mr. Wrayburn's change of manner, which was instant and sharp. He became formal. He looked quickly from Hilary to the object on the desk and upon that his regard became fixed. The lens lay near at hand. Mr. Wrayburn said, "May I?" and used it with great deliberation. He then stared at Alleyn.

"I take it," he said, "You've seen this?"

Alleyn nodded.

Hilary now repeated his account of the finding of the poker, and Mr. Wrayburn peered out of the window and asked his questions and made his notes. All through this procedure he seemed in some indefinable way to invite Alleyn to enter into the discussion and to be disappointed that he remained silent.

Hilary avoided looking at the object on his desk. He turned his back, bent over the fire, made as if to stir it and, apparently disliking the feel of the study poker, dropped it with a clatter in the hearth.

Wrayburn said, "Yes," several times in a non-committal voice and added that things had taken quite a little turn, hadn't they, and he must see what they could do about it. He told Hilary he'd like to take care of the poker and was there perhaps a cardboard box? Hilary offered to ring for one, but Wrayburn said he wouldn't bother the staff at this stage. After some rummaging in his bureau, Hilary found a long tabular carton with a number of maps in it. He took them out and Wrayburn slid the wrapped poker tenderly into it. He suggested that it might be as well not to publicize the poker and Hilary was in feverish agreement. Wrayburn thought he would like to have a wee chat with the Detective Chief-Superintendent about the turn this seemed to be taking. Hilary winced. Wrayburn then asked Alleyn if he would be kind enough to show him the cloakroom. Hilary began to say that he himself would do so, but stopped short and raised his shoulders.

"I see," he said. "Very well." Alleyn went to the door, followed by Wrayburn carrying the carton. "Mr. Wrayburn!" Hilary said loudly.

"Sir?"

"I am sure you are going to talk about my staff."

"I was only," Wrayburn said in a hurry, "going to ask, as a matter of routine, for the names of your guests and the staff. We—er—we have to make these inquiries, sir."

"Possibly. Very well, you shall have them. But I must tell you, at once, that whatever theory you may form as to the disappearance of this man, there is no question, there can never be any question, no matter what emerges, that any one of my staff, in even the remotest fashion, is concerned in it. On that point," said Hilary, "I am and I shall remain perfectly adamant."

"Strong," said Mr. Wrayburn.

"And meant to be," said Hilary.

Six – Storm Rising

"It's a very impressive residence, this," Superintendent Wrayburn observed.

He and Alleyn paused in the hall, which was otherwise deserted. Great swags of evergreen still hung from the gallery. Fires blazed on the enormous hearths.

"What I mean," Superintendent Wrayburn said, "it's impressive," and after a moment: "Take a look at this."

A framed plan of Halberds hung near the entrance.

"Useful," said Wrayburn. They studied it and then stood with their backs to the front doors getting, as Wrayburn put it, the hang of the place. Beyond that, the open courtyard, flanked east and west by the projecting wings. On their left was the east wing with a corridor opening off the hall serving library, breakfast-room, boudoir, study and, at the rear angle of the house, the chapel. On their right were the drawing-room, dining-room serveries and, at the northwest rear corner, the kitchen. Doors under the gallery, one of them the traditional green baize swinger, led from the back of the hall, between the twin flights of stairs;

into a passage which gave on the servants' quarters and various offices, including the flower-room.

Alleyn looked up at the gallery. It was dimly lit, but out of the shadows there glimmered a pale greenish shape of extreme elegance. One's meant to look at that, he thought. It's a treasure.

"So what about this cloakroom, then?" Wrayburn suggested. "Before I take any further action?"

"Why not? Here you are."

It was in the angle between the entrance porch and the drawing-room and, as Hilary said, had a door to the hall and another to the porch. "The plan," Alleyn pointed out, "shows a corresponding room on the east side. It's a symmetrical house, isn't it?"

"So when he came out," Wrayburn mused, "he should have walked straight ahead to the right-hand flight of stairs and up them to the gallery?"

"And along the gallery to the east corridor in the visitors' wing. Where he disappeared into thin air?"

"Alternatively—Here! Let's look."

They went into the cloakroom, shutting the door behind them and standing close together, just inside the threshold.

Alleyn was transported backstage. Here was that smell of face cream and spirit-gum. Here was the shelf with a towel laid over it and the looking-glass. Neatly spread out, fanwise, on one side of this bench, was the Druid's golden beard and moustache and, hooked over a table lamp in lieu of a wigblock, the golden wig itself, topped by a tall crown of mistletoe.

A pair of knitted woollen gloves lay nearby.

A collection of mackintoshes, gum boots, and shooting-sticks had been shoved aside to make room for the Druid's golden robe. There was the door opening on the porch and beside it a small lavatorial compartment. The room was icy cold.

Under the makeup bench, neatly aligned, stood a pair of fur-lined boots. Their traces from the outside door to where they had been removed were still quite damp and so were they.

"We'd better keep clear of them," Alleyn said, "hadn't we?" From where he stood he reached over to the bench, moved the table lamp and, without touching the wig, turned its back towards them. It had been powdered, like the beard, with gold dust. But at the place where the long hair would have overhung the nape of the neck there was a darker patch.

"Wet?" Wrayburn said, pointing to it. "Snow, would that have been? He was out in the snow, wasn't he? But the rest of the thing's only—" he touched the mistletoe crown "—damp."

Alleyn flicked a long finger at the cardboard carton which Wrayburn still carried. "Did you get a good look at it?" he asked.

"That's right," Wrayburn said, answering a question that Alleyn had not asked. "You're dead right. This is getting altogether different. It looks to me," he said, "as if we'd got a bit of case on our hands."

"I believe you have."

"Well," Wrayburn said, making small movements of his shoulders and lifting his chin. "There'll have to be an adjustment, I mean to say in the approach, won't there?" He laid the carton on the bench as if it was made of porcelain. "There'll need to be an analysis, of course, and a comparison. I'd better—I'd better report it to our C.I.D. But—just let's—

He shot a glance at Alleyn, fished in his pockets, and produced a small steel rule. He introduced the end under the hair and raised it.

"Take a look," he said. "It's wet, of course, but d'you reckon there's a stain?"

"Might be."

"I'm going to damn' well—" Without completing his sentence, Wrayburn lifted a strand and with a fingernail and thumb separated a single hair and gave it a tweak. The wig tipped sideways and the crown of mistletoe fell off. Wrayburn swore.

"They make these things pretty solidly, don't they?" Alleyn said. He righted the wig and held it steady. Wrayburn wound the single hair round the rule and this time jerked it free. Alleyn produced an envelope and the hair was dropped into it. Wrayburn stowed it in his tunic pocket.

"Let's have a look at the robe," Alleyn said. He lifted it off on its coat hanger and turned it round. A slide fastener ran right down the back, separating the high-standing collar, which showed a wet patch and was frayed.

"Cripes," said Wrayburn, and then: "We'll have to get this room locked up."

"Yes."

"Look. What seems to come out of this? I mean it's pretty obvious the hair on the poker matches this, and there's not much doubt, is there, that the deposit on the poker is blood. And what about the wet patch on the wig? And the collar? That's not blood. So what? They've been cleaned. What with? Water? Wiped clear or washed. Which? Where? When?

"You're going like a train, Jack."

"Must have been here, after the young lady left him. Unless—well, unless she did it and left him cold, in which case who got rid of him? *She* didn't. Well— did she?"

"Have you met the young lady?"

"No."

"She's not the body-carrying type. Except her own, which she carries like Cleopatra, Queen of Egypt."

"Is that right?" Wrayburn mused. "Is that a fact?

Now, about this wig and beard and all that carry-on. To begin with, this gear's upstairs in a dressing-room. Moult supposedly puts it on, all except the whiskers, and comes down here, where the young lady meets him and fixes the whiskers. She goes to the drawing-room and he goes out by that door into the porch and then into the courtyard, where this Vincent liaises with him, then into the drawing-room, where he does a Daddy Christmas, or what passes for it, round the tree. Then he returns the same way as he came and Vincent sees him come in here by the same door and the young lady takes off his whiskers and leaves him here. And that's the last anybody sees of him. Now. What say, somebody who knows he's here comes in from outside *with* the poker from the upstairs dressing-room and lets him have it. Say he's sitting there, nice and handy, still wearing his wig. Right. Then this character hauls him outside and dumps him, God knows where, but—Here!" Wrayburn ejaculated. "Wait a bit! What's out there? There's a sledge out there. And there's this chap Vincent out there. Isn't there?"

"There is, indeed."

"Well!" Wrayburn said. "It's a start, isn't it? It may not do in the finish. And I've read your book. I know what you think about drawing quick conclusions."

"It's a start."

"Following it up, then. This character, before he goes, sees the condition of the wig and cleans the stains off at the handbasin there and hitches it over the lamp like we found it with that blasted tiara on it. And he goes out and chucks the poker into the fir tree and disposes—God knows where—of the—if it's homicide—of the body. How about it? Come on. Prove me a fool. Come on."

"My dear chap, I think it's a well-reasoned proposition."

"You do?"

"There are difficulties, though."

"There are?"

"The floor, for instance. The carpet. Clear traces of the returning wet boots but nothing else. No other boots. And nothing to suggest a body having been dragged to the door. O.K., suppose it was carried out? You'd still expect some interference with the original prints and a set of new ones pointing both ways, wouldn't you?"

Wrayburn stared moodily at the string-coloured carpet with its clear damp incoming impressions. He picked up a boot and fitted it to the nearest print. "Tallies," he said. "That's something. And the boot's still wet. No drying in here and it was only last night, after all. Well—what next? What's left? Alternative— he did go upstairs and get clobbered."

"Wearing his wig?"

"All right. Fair enough. Wearing his wig. God knows why, but wearing his wig. And goes up to the dressing-room. And gets clobbered with the dressing-room poker. And—here! Hold on! Hold on! And the clobberer throws the poker out of the window and it gets stuck in the tree?"

"It seems possible."

"It does?"

"And the body? If he's dead?" Alleyn asked.

"Through the window too? Hang on. Don't rush me."

"Not for the world. Is the body wearing the wig when it takes the high jump?"

Wrayburn swallowed. "The bloody wig," he said. "Leave the wig for the time being. Now. I know this bunch of domestic villains are supposed to have searched the area. I know that. But what say some-one—all right, one of that lot for the sake of argument—had already removed the body? In the night? Will you buy that?"

"I'll take it on approval. Removed the body and to confuse the issue returned the unmentionable wig to the cloakroom?"

"I quite like it," said Wrayburn with a slight attempt at modesty. "Well, anyway, it does sort of fit. It snowed up here, last night. We won't get anything from the ground, worse luck."

"Until it thaws."

"That's right. That's dead right." Wrayburn cleared his throat. "It's going to be a big one," he said and after a considerable pause: "Like I said, It's for our C.I.D. I'll have to ring the Detective Chief Super about this one and I reckon I know what he'll say. He'll say we set up a search. Look, I'll get onto this right away. You wait here. Will you?"

"Well—"

"I'd be obliged."

"All right."

So Wrayburn went off to telephone his Detective Chief Superintendent and Alleyn, a prey to forebodings, was left to contemplate the cloakroom.

Wrayburn came back, full of business. "There you are!" he said. "Just as I thought: He's going to talk to his senior 'tecs and in the meantime I'm to carry on here. As from now. I'm to lay on a search party and ask Major Marchbanks for dogs. You'll hang on, won't you?" Alleyn promised and did so. When Wrayburn had gone he reexamined the wig, plucked a hair for himself, touched the still-damp robe, and fell into an abstraction from which Mr. Wrayburn's return aroused him.

"No joy," grumbled Wrayburn. "Breaking and entering *with* violence and Lord knows what else at the D.C.S.'s. He is calling up as many chaps as he can and the Major's sending us what *he* can spare. They should be here within the hour. In the meantime—" he broke off, glanced at Alleyn, and made a fresh start. "There'll have to be confirmation of all this stuff—statements from the party. The lot."

"Big thing for you."

"Are you joking? While it lasts, which will be until the C.I.D. comes waltzing in. Then back down the road smartly for me, to the drunks-in-charge. Look!" he burst out. "I don't reckon our lot can handle it. Not on their own. Like the man said: we're understaffed and we're busy. We're fully extended. I don't mind betting the D.C.S.'ll talk to the C.C. before the hour's out."

"He'll be able to call on the county for extra men."

"He'd do better to go straight to the Yard. Now!"

Alleyn was silent.

"You know what I'm getting at, don't you?"

"I do, but I wish you wouldn't. The situation's altogether too freakish. My wife's a guest here and so am I. I'm the last person to meddle. I've told Bill-Tasman as much. Let them call in the Yard if they like, but not me. Leave me out. Get a statement from my wife, of course. You'll want to do that. And then, unless there's any good reason against it, I'll take her away and damn' glad to do so. And that's final. I'll leave you to it. You'll want to lock up this place and then you can get cracking. Are there keys? Yes. There you are."

"But—"

"My dear man, no. Not another word. Please."

Alleyn went out, quickly, into the hall.

He encountered Hilary standing about six feet away with an air strangely compounded of diffidence flavoured with defiance.

"I don't know what you'll think of me," said Hilary.

"I daresay you may be very cross. You see, I've been talking to our local pundit. The Detective Chief Superintendent. And to your boss-person at the C.I.D."

2.

"—It's just," Hilary blandly explained, "that I do happen to know him. Soon after I was first settled with the staff here, he paid a visit to the Vale, and March-banks brought him over for tea. He was interested in my experiment. But we mustn't keep him waiting, must we?"

"He's still on the line?"

"Yes. He'd like to have a word with you. There's a telephone over there. I *know* you're going to forgive me," Hilary said to Alleyn's back.

"Then you know a damn' sight more than's good for you," Alleyn thought. He gave himself a second or two to regain his temper and lifted the receiver. Hilary left him with ostentatious tact. Alleyn wondered if he was going to have a sly listen in from wherever he had established the call.

The Assistant Commissioner was plaintive and slightly facetious. "My dear Rory," he said, "what very odd company you keep: no holiday like a busman's, I see."

"I assure you, sir, it's none of my seeking."

"So I supposed. Are you alone?"

"Ostensibly."

"Quite. Well, now your local D.C. Super rang me before Bill-Tasman did. It seems there's no joy down your way: big multiple stores robbery, with violence, and a near riot following some bloody sit-in. They're sending a few chaps out but they're fully extended and can't really spare them. As far as I can gather this show of yours—"

"It's not mine."

"Wait a minute. This show of yours looks as if it might develop into something, doesn't it?" This was the Assistant Commissioner's stock phrase for suspected homicide.

"It might, yes."

"Yes. Your host would like you to take over."

"But the D.C.S. is in charge, sir. In the meantime Wrayburn, the Div. Super from Downlow's holding the fort."

"Has the D.C.S. expressed his intention of going it alone?"

"I understand he's bellyaching—"

"He is indeed. He wants the Yard."

"But he'll have to talk to his Chief Constable, sir, before—"

"His Chief Constable is in the Bermudas."

"Damnation!"

"This is a very bad line. What was that you said?" Alleyn repressed an impulse to say "you 'eard."

"I swore," he said.

"That won't get you anywhere, Rory."

"Look, sir—my wife—Troy—she's a guest in the house. So am I. It's a preposterous setup. Isn't it?"

"I've thought of that. Troy had better come back to London, don't you agree? Give her my best respects and tell her I'm sorry to visit the policeman's lot upon her."

"But, sir, if I held the other guests I'd have to— you see what a farcical situation it is."

"Take statements and let 'em go if you think it's O.K. You've got a promising field without them, haven't you?"

"I'm not so sure. It's a rum go. It's worse than that, it's lunatic."

"You're thinking of the homicidal domestics? An

excellent if extreme example of rehabilitation. But of course you may find that somewhere among them there's a twicer. Rory," said the A.C., changing his tone, "I'm sorry but we're uncommonly busy in the department. This job ought to be tackled at once, and it needs a man with your peculiar talents."

"And that's an order?"

"Well, yes. I'm afraid it is."

"Very good, sir."

"We'll send you down Mr. Fox for a treat. Would you like to speak to him?"

"I won't trouble him." Alleyn said sourly. "But— wait a moment."

"Yes?"

"I believe Wrayburn has a list of the domestic staff here. I'd like to get a C.R.O report."

"Of course. I'd better have a word with this Super. What's his name? Wrayburn? Turn him on, will you?"

"Certainly, sir."

"Thank you. Sorry. Good luck to you."

Alleyn went in search of his wife. She was not in their rooms, which gave evidence of her having bathed and changed. He spent a minute or two with his head through the open window, peering into the wreckage below, and then went downstairs. As he crossed the hall he encountered Blore with a tray of drinks and a face of stone.

"The party is in the library, sir," Blore said. "Mr. Bill-Tasman wished me to inform you. This way, if you please, sir."

They were all there including Troy, who made a quick face at him.

Hilary was in full spate. "My dears," he was saying, "*what* a relief it is." He advanced upon Alleyn with outstretched hands, took him by the biceps and gently shook him. "My dear fellow!" Hilary gushed. "I was just saying—I can't tell you how relieved we all are. Now do, do, do, do." This seemed to be an invitation to drink, sit down, come to the fire, or be introduced to the Colonel and Mr. Smith.

The Colonel had already advanced. He shook hands and said there was almost no need for an introduction because Troy had been "such a dear and so kind," and added that he was "most awfully worried" about Moult. "You know how it is," he said. "The feller's been with one, well, more years than one cares to say. One feels quite lost. And he's a nice feller. I—we—" he hesitated, glanced at his wife, and then said in a rush, "We're very attached to him. Very. And, I do assure you, there's no harm in him. No harm at all in Moult."

"Upsetting for you," Alleyn said.

"It's so awful," said the Colonel, "to think he may have got that thing, whatever it is. Be wandering about? Somewhere out there? The cold! I tell my nephew we ought to ring Marchbanks up and ask him to lay on his dogs. They must have dogs at that place. What do you say?"

Alleyn said, and meant it, that it was a good idea. He found Mr. Smith bearing down upon him.

"Met before," said Mr. Smith, giving him a knuckle-breaking handshake. "I never caught on you was you, if you get me. When was it? Ten years ago? I gave evidence for your lot in the Blake forgery case. Remember me?"

Alleyn said he remembered Mr. Smith very well.

Cressida, in a green velvet trousered garment, split down the middle and strategically caught together by an impressive brooch, waggled her fingers at Alleyn and said, "Hi, there."

Hilary began offering Alleyn a drink and when he

said he wouldn't have one was almost comically non-plussed. "You won't?" he exclaimed.

"Not on duty, alas," said Alleyn.

"But—no, *really!* Surely under these conditions. I mean, it's not as if you were—well, my dear man, you know what I mean."

"Yes, I do," Alleyn said. "But I think we must as far as possible reduce the rather bizarre circumstances to something resembling routine police procedure."

Hilary said, "I know, I know but—" and boggled. He appealed dumbly to Troy.

"It would have been lovely to have come as a visitor," Alleyn said politely, "but I turn out to be no such thing. I turn out to be a policeman on a job and I must try to behave accordingly."

A complete silence followed. Hilary broke it with a slight giggle.

Mrs. Forrester said, "Very sensible," and to her nephew: "You can't have it both ways, Hilary, and you'd best make your mind up to it."

"Yes. All right," Hilary said and gulped. "Well," he asked Alleyn, "what's the form then? What would you like us to do?"

"For the moment—nothing. The first thing of course, is to set up an organized search for the missing man. Wrayburn is bringing in people to that end as soon as they can be assembled. They'll be here within the hour. Later on I shall ask each of you for as detailed an account of the events leading up to the disappearance as you can give me. In the meantime I shall have a word with Mr. Wrayburn and then, if you please, I would like to look at Moult's bedroom and at Colonel Forrester's dressing-room. After that we'll have a word with the staff. Perhaps you'd be very kind and tell them, would you?"

"Oh, God," said Hilary. "Yes. I suppose so. Yes, of

course. But you will remember, won't you, they are in a rather special position?"

"You can say that again," Mr. Smith remarked.

"I think that's all for the moment," Alleyn said. "So if you'll excuse me—?"

"But you'll join us for dinner, at least?" Hilary expostulated. "Of course you will!"

"You're very kind but I think we should press on."

"But that's fantastic," Cressida cried. "You can't starve. Hilly, he can't starve." She appealed to Troy. "Well, can he? You know? Can he?"

Before Troy could answer Hilary began to talk rather wildly about Alleyn joining them when he could and then about game pie or at the very least, sandwiches. He rang and on the arrival of Blore seemed to collect himself.

Blore stood inside the door with his gaze fixed on a distant point above all their heads.

"Oh, Blore," Hilary said. "Mr. Alleyn has very kindly agreed to help us. He's going to take complete charge and we must all assist him as much as we possibly can. I know you and the staff will cooperate. Mr. Alleyn may not be dining. Please arrange a cold supper, will you? Something he can take when he's free. In the dining-room."

"Very good, sir."

"And Blore. Mr. Alleyn would like, later on, to have your account, and the others', of what you've all told me. In case I've forgotten anything or got it wrong. You might just let them know, will you?"

"Certainly, sir."

"Thank you."

"Thank you, sir."

When Blore had gone Cressida said: "Hilly, is it my imagination or does that man seem all uptight to you?"

"I hope not, darling. I do hope not. Of course, naturally they're a bit on edge," Hilary pleaded. "But nobody's going to draw any false conclusions, are they? Of course they're not. Which is why," he added, reaching for a graceful turn of phrase, "one is so thankful that you," he turned to Alleyn, "have taken us under your wing. If you see what I mean."

"I don't know," Alleyn said pleasantly, "that you've quite defined the function of an investigating officer, but it's nice of you to put it that way."

Hilary laughed extravagantly and then, with an air of elaborate and anxious solicitation, asked Alleyn if there was *anything, anything at all,* that *anybody* could do to help.

"Not at the moment, I think," he said. "Troy's given me a pretty comprehensive idea of the situation. But there is one point, as you're all here—"

"Yes? Yes?" urged Hilary, all concern.

"Nobody recognized Moult as the Druid, it seems. You did all see him, didn't you? In action?"

A general chorus of assent was followed by elaborations from which it emerged that the houseparty, with the exception of Colonel Forrester, had "mixed" with the other guests and the children in the library and had followed the children in procession to the drawing-room. They had stood together during the tree. When the grown-ups, joined by Cressida, opened their parcels, the houseparty again congealed, thanking each other and exclaiming over the gifts.

Alleyn asked if anyone, apart from his employers, had seen or spoken to Moult during the day. They all looked blank and said they might have but didn't really remember. If they had spoken it would only be to say "Merry Christmas."

"Right," Alleyn said. "Thank you. And now, if I may be excused, I'll talk to Wrayburn. By the way, may I borrow that lens of yours? It'll make me feel less of a phony."

"Of course—I'll—"

"Don't move. I'll get it. It's on your desk. One other thing—may I take a look at your quarters, Colonel?"

"Certainly. Certainly. If there's anything you'd like me to show you," said Colonel Forrester with obvious keenness, "I'll be glad—"

"No, Fred," said his wife. "You don't start that sort of nonsense. Rushing up and down stairs and looking for clues. I said rushing—"

"I know you did, B. It doesn't apply."

"If I need help," Alleyn said, "I'll come and ask for it. May I?"

"You do that," said the Colonel warmly and threw a bold look at his wife. "I'll be delighted. By all means. You do that."

So Alleyn collected the lens, found Wrayburn and took him upstairs, and Troy, in an extraordinary state of semidetachment, went in with the houseparty to dinner.

3.

Moult's bedroom in the top story at Halberds gave evidence, in its appointments, of Hilary's consideration for his staff. It exhibited, however, the pathological orderliness of an army barracks and had the same smell: a compound of boot-polish, leather, fag-ends, heavy cloth and an indefinable stale masculinity.

Moult's topcoat, outdoor suit and shoes, hat and gloves were all properly disposed. His empty suitcase was stowed at the back of his wardrobe. His blameless underwear lay impeccably folded in his clothespress. Even his borderline-pornographic reading was neatly stacked on his bedside table. On the dressing table was a pigskin case with his initials on it. Opened, it revealed two old-fashioned silverbacked brushes, a comb and a card. Alleyn showed the card to Wrayburn. "Lt. Col. F. Fleaton Forrester" on one side and on the other, in a sharply pointed hand, "A. Moult. On the twenty-fifth anniversary of a very happy association. F. F."

When they found Moult's wallet in a drawer of his dressing table it too proved to be initialled and of pigskin. The card inside, Mrs. Fleaton Forrester's, said abruptly, "Moult. 1946–1971. B. F." It contained no money but a list of telephone numbers and three snapshots. The first showed the Colonel in uniform, mounted on a charger, and Sergeant Moult in uniform and on foot saluting him. A round-faced man with monkeylike cheeks heavily scarred. The second showed the Colonel and Mrs. Forrester gazing disconsolately at a tract of moorland and Moult gazing respectfully at them. The third was faded and altogether had the appearance of being much older. It was a snapshot of a younger Moult with one stripe up, holding by the hand an overdressed little girl of about four.

"That'll be the man himself in all three, will it?" Wrayburn speculated.

"Yes. You notice the scarred face?"

"Married? With a kid?"

"Doesn't follow as the night the day. It may be anybody's infant-phenomenon."

"I suppose so."

"When my chaps get here," Alleyn said, "we'll take dabs. And when we lay the dogs on, we'll show them one of his shoes. Did I tell you the Colonel also suggested dogs from the Vale? Hullo! Listen to this!"

A hullabaloo of sorts had broken out in the chimney: a confusion of sound, thrown about and distorted, blown down and sucked back as if by some gigantic and inefficient flautist.

"That's the Nor'east Buster getting up," Wrayburn said. "That's bad. That's a nuisance."

"Why?"

"It means rain in these parts. Very heavy as a rule."

"Snow?"

"More likely floods. Here she comes."

The window rattled violently and was suddenly hit by a great buffet of rain.

"Lovely hunting weather," Alleyn grunted. "Still— you never know. It may do us more good than harm. We'll lock up here and penetrate the Forrester suite. Come on."

They went down to the next floor and walked along the heavily carpeted corridor serving the guest rooms. It was lit by only a third of its shaded wall lamps and very quiet. No rumour of the storm outside or of life within the house. Alleyn supposed the guests and Hilary were all in the dining-room and suddenly felt ravenous. He was about to say so but instead laid his hand on Wrayburn's arm and motioned him to be quiet. He pointed ahead. From under one of the doors a sliver of light showed on the red carpet.

Alleyn counted doors. Troy had told him which room belonged to which guest. They now approached his dressing-room, linked by a bathroom with Troy's bedroom. Next came the Forresters' bedroom, bathroom and dressing-room. Beyond these were Mr. Smith and, on the front corner of the east wing in a large room with its own bathroom, Cressida. Where Hilary himself slept—no doubt in some master apartment of great stateliness—Troy had had no idea.

It was from under the Forresters' bedroom door that the light showed.

Alleyn listened for a moment and could hear nothing. He made a quick decision. He motioned Wrayburn to stay where he was and himself opened the door and walked straight in.

He did so to the accompaniment of a loud crash.

A man at the window turned to face him: a blond, pale man whom he had seen before, wearing dark trousers and an alpaca jacket.

"Good evening again," Alleyn said. "I've made a mistake. I thought this was my wife's room."

"Next door," the man barely articulated.

"Stupid of me. You must be Nigel, I think."

"That's right, sir."

"I've been admiring your work in the courtyard. It really is quite something."

Nigel's lips moved. He was saying, inaudibly, "Thank you very much."

The windowpane behind him streamed with driven rain. His head, face and the front of his jacket were wet.

"You've been caught," Alleyn said lightly.

Nigel said: "It's come down very sudden. I was—I was closing the window, sir. It's very awkward, this window."

"It'll ruin your snow sculpture, I'm afraid."

Nigel suddenly said, "It may be a judgment."

"A judgment? On whom? For what?"

"There's a lot of sin about," Nigel said loudly. "One way and another. You never know."

"Such as?"

"Heathen practices. Disguised as Christian. There's hints of blasphemy there. Touches of it. If rightly looked at."

"You mean the Christmas tree?"

"Heathen practices round graven images. Caperings. And see what's happened to him."

"What *has* happened to him?" asked Alleyn and wondered if he'd struck some sort of lunatic bonanza.

"He's *gone*."

"Where?"

"Ah! Where! That's what sin does for you. I know. Nobody better. Seeing what I been myself."

Nigel's face underwent an extraordinary change. His mouth hung open, his nostrils distended, his white eyelashes fluttered and then, like a microcosm of the deluge outside, he wept most copiously.

"Now, look here——" Alleyn began but Nigel with an unconsicionable roar fled from the room and went thudding down the corridor.

Wrayburn appeared in the doorway. "What the hell's all that in aid of?" he asked. "Which of them was it?"

"That was Nigel, the second houseman, who once made effigies but became a religious maniac and killed a sinful lady. He is said to be cured."

"Cured!"

"Although I believe Mr. Bill-Tasman has conceded that when Nigel remembers his crime he is inclined to weep. He remembered it just now."

"I overheard some of his remarks. The chap's certifiable. Religious maniac."

"I wonder why he leaned out of the window."

"He did?"

"I fancy so. He was too wet to match his story about just shutting it. And there's a very little rain on the carpet. I don't believe it was open until he opened it."

"Funny!"

"It is, rather. Let's have a look about, shall we?"

They found nothing in the bedroom more remarkable than the Forresters' green-lined tropical umbrella. Niegel had turned down their bed, laid out their Viyella nightclothes, and banked up their fire. The windows were shut.

"Wouldn't you think," Mr. Wrayburn observed, "that they'd have heaters in these rooms? Look at the work involved! It must be dynamite."

"He's trying to re-create the past."

"He's lucky to have a lunatic to help him, then."

They went through the bathroom with its soap, mackintosh and hair lotion smells. Mr. Wrayburn continued to exclaim upon the appointments at Halberds: "Bathrooms! All over the shop like an eight-star-plus hotel. You wouldn't credit it." He was somewhat mollified to discover that in the Colonel's dressing-room a radiator had been built into the grate. It had been switched on, presumably by Nigel. "Look at that!" said Mr. Wrayburn. "What about his electrical bill! No trouble!"

"And here," Alleyn pointed out, "are the Welsh fire irons. Minus the poker. Highly polished and, of course, never used. I think the relative positions of the fireplace, the bed, the window and the doors are worth noticing, Jack. If you come in from the bathroom, the window's on your right, the door into the corridor on your left and the bed, projecting from the outside wall facing you, with the fireplace beyond it in the far wall. If I were to sit on the floor on the far side of the bed and you came through the bathroom door, you wouldn't see me, would you?"

"No?" said Mr. Wrayburn, expecting an elaboration but getting none. Alleyn had moved to the far side of the bed: a single high-standing Victorian four-poster unadorned with curtains. Its authentic patchwork quilt reached to the floor and showed a sharp bulge at one side. He turned it back and exposed Colonel Forrester's uniform box black-japanned, white-lettered, and quite noticeably dented and scarred about the padlock area.

"I do hate," Alleyn said, sitting on his heels, "this going on a job minus my kit. It makes one feel such a damned, piddling amateur. However, Fox will bring it and in the meantime I've the Bill-Tasman lens. Look here, Jack. Talk of amateurism! This isn't the handiwork of any master cracksman, is it?"

Mr. Wrayburn squatted down beside him. "Very clumsy attempt," he agreed. "What's he think he'd achieve? Silly."

"Yes," Allen said, using the lens, "a bit of hanky-panky with the padlock. Something twisted in the hoop."

"Like a poker?"

"At first glance perhaps. We'll have to take charge of this. I'll talk to the Colonel."

"What about the contents?"

"It's big enough, in all conscience, to house the crown jewels but I imagine Mrs. Forrester's got the lion's share dotted about her frontage. Troy thinks they carry scrip and documents in it. And you did hear, didn't you, that Moult has charge of the key?"

Wrayburn, with a hint of desperation in his voice, said, "I don't know! Like the man said: you wouldn't credit it if you read it in a book. I suppose we pick the lock for them, do we?"

"Or pick it for ourselves if not for them? I'll inquire of the Colonel. In the meantime they mustn't get their hands on it."

Wrayburn pointed to the scarred area. "By Gum! I reckon it's the poker," he said.

"Oh for my Bailey and his dab-kit."

"The idea being," Wrayburn continued, following out his thought, "that some villain unknown was surprised trying to break open the box with the poker."

"And killed? With the poker? After a struggle? That seems to be going rather far, don't you think? And when you say 'somebody'—"

"I suppose I mean Moult."

"Who preferred taking a very inefficient whang at the box to using the key?"

"That's right—we dismiss that theory, then. It's ridiculous. How about Moult coming in after he'd done his Christmas tree act and catching the villain at it and getting knocked on the head?"

"And then—?"

"Pushed through the window? With the poker after him?"

"In which case," Alleyn said, "he was transplanted before they searched. Let's have a look at the window."

It was the same as all the others: a sash window with a snib locking the upper to the lower frame.

"We'd better not handle anything. The damn' bore of it is that with this high standard of house management the whole place will have been dusted off. But if you look out of this window, Jack, it's at the top of the sapling fir where Bill-Tasman picked up the poker. His study is directly beneath us. And if you leant out and looked to your left, it would be at the southeast corner of the east wing. Hold on a jiffy. Look here."

"What's up?"

Alleyn was moving about, close to the window. He dodged his head and peered sideways through the glass.

"Turn off the lights, Jack, will you? There's something out there—yes, near the top of the fir. It's catching a stray gleam from somewhere. Take a look."

Mr. Wrayburn shaded his eyes and peered into the night. "I don't get anything," he said. "Unless you

mean a little sort of shiny wriggle. You can hardly
catch it."

"That's it. Quite close. In the fir."

"Might be anything. Bit of string."

"Or tinsel?"

"That's right. Blowing about."

"So what?"

"So nothing, I daresay. A passing fancy. We've still
got a hell of a lot to find out. About last night's
ongoings—the order of events and details of procedure
and so on."

"Mrs. Alleyn will be helpful, there, I make no doubt."

"You know," Alleyn said, austerely, "my views
under that heading, don't you?"

"That was before you took over, though."

"So it was. And now I'm in the delirious position of
having to use departmental tact and make routine
inquiries with my wife."

"Perhaps," Mr. Wrayburn dimly speculated, "she'll
think it funny."

Alleyn stared at him. "You know," he said at last,
"you've got something there. I wouldn't be at all surprised if she did." He thought for a moment. "And
I daresay," he said, "that in a macabre sort of way
she'll be, as usual, right. Come on. We'd better complete the survey. I'd like one more look at this blasted
padlock, though."

He was on his knees before it and Wrayburn was
peering over his shoulder when Colonel Forrester
said: "So you *have* found it. Good. Good. Good."

He had come in by the bathroom door behind their
backs. He was a little bit breathless but his eyes were
bright and he seemed to be quite excited.

"I didn't join the ladies," he explained. "I thought I'd
just pop up and see if I could be of any use. There
may be points you want to ask about. So here I am

and you must pack me off if I'm a nuisance. If one wasn't so worried it would be awfully interesting to see the real thing. Oh— and by the way—your wife tells me that you're George Alleyn's brother. He was in the Brigade in my day, you know. Junior to me, of course: an ensign. In the Kiddies, I remember. Coincidence, isn't it? Do tell me: what did he do after he went on the reserve? Took to the proconsular service, I seem to remember."

Alleyn answered this inquiry as shortly as, with civility, he could. The Colonel sat on the bed and beamed at him, still fetching his breath rather short but apparently enjoying himself. Alleyn introduced Mr. Wrayburn, whom the Colonel was clearly delighted to meet. "But I oughtn't to interrupt you both," he said. "There you are in the thick of it with your magnifying glass and everything. Do tell me: what do you make of my box?"

"I was going to ask you about that, sir," Alleyn said. "It's a clumsy attempt, isn't it?"

"Clumsy? Well, yes. But one couldn't be anything else but clumsy with a thing like a poker, could one?"

"You know about the poker?"

"Oh rather! Hilary told us."

"What, exactly, did he tell you?"

"That he'd found one in the fir tree out there. Now, that was a pretty outlandish sort of place for it to be, wasn't it?"

"Did he describe it?"

The Colonel looked steadily at Alleyn for some seconds. "Not in detail," he said, and after a further pause: "But in any case when we found the marks on the box we thought: 'poker,' B and I, as soon as we saw them."

"Why did you think 'poker,' sir?"

"I don't know. We just did. 'Poker,' we thought.

Or B did, which comes to much the same thing. Poker."

"Had you noticed that the one belonging to this room had disappeared?"

"Oh dear me, no. Not a bit of it. Not at the time."

"Colonel Forrester, Troy tells me that you didn't see Moult after he had put on your Druid's robe."

"Oh, but I did," he said, opening his eyes very wide. "I *saw* him."

"You did?"

"Well—'saw,' you may call it. I was lying down in our bedroom, you know, dozing, and he came to the bathroom door. He had the robe and the wig on and he held the beard up to show me. I think he said he'd come back before he went down. I think I reminded him about the window and then I did go to sleep, and so I suppose he just looked in and went off without waking me. That's what Mrs. Alleyn was referring to. I rather *fancy,* although I may be wrong her, but I rather *fancy* I heard him look out."

"Heard him? Look out?"

"Yes. I told him to look out of the dressing-room window for Vincent with the sledge at the corner. Because when Vincent was there it would be time to go down. That was how we laid it on. Dead on the stroke of half-past seven it was to be, by the stable clock. And so it was."

"What!" Alleyn exclaimed. "You mean—?"

"I like to run an exercise to a strict timetable and so, I'm glad to say, does Hilary. All our watches and clocks were set to synchronize. And I've just recollected: I *did* hear him open the window and I heard the stable clock strike the half-hour immediately afterwards. So, you see, at that very moment Vincent would signal from the corner and Moult would go down to have his beard put on, and—and there you are. That was, you might say, phase one of the exercise, what?"

"Yes, I see. And—forgive me for pressing it, but it is important—he didn't present himself on his return?"

"No. He didn't. I'm sure he didn't," said the Colonel very doubtfully.

"I mean—could you have still been asleep?"

"Yes!" cried the Colonel as if the Heavens had opened upon supreme enlightenment. "I could! Easily, I could. Of course!"

Alleyn heard Mr. Wrayburn fetch a sigh.

"You see," the Colonel explained, "I do drop off after my Turns. I think it must be something in the stuff the quack gives me."

"Yes, I see. Tell me—those fur-lined boots. Would he have put them on up here or in the cloakroom?"

"In the cloakroom. He'd put them all ready down there for me. I wanted to dress up here because of the big looking-glass, but the boots didn't matter and they're clumsy things to tramp about the house in."

"Yes, I see."

"You do think, don't you," asked the Colonel, "that you'll find him?"

"I expect we will. I hope so."

"I tell you what, Alleyn," said the Colonel, and his face became as dolorous as a clown's. "I'm afraid the poor fellow's dead."

"Are you, sir?"

"One shouldn't say so, of course, at this stage. But— I don't know—I'm very much afraid my poor old Moult's dead. He was an awful ass in many ways but we suited each other, he and I. What do you think about it?"

"There's one possibility," Alleyn said cautiously.

"I know what you're going to say. Amnesia. Aren't you?"

"Something, at any rate, that caused him to leave the clockroom by the outer door and wander off into the night. Miss Tottenham says he did smell pretty strongly of liquour."

"Did he? Did he? Yes, well, perhaps in the excitement he may have been silly. In fact—In fact, I'm afraid he was."

"Why do you say that?"

"Because when he found me all tied up in my robe and having a Turn, he helped me out and put me to bed and I must say he smelt most awfully strong of whisky. Reeked. But, if that was the way of it," the Colonel asked, "where is he? Out on those moors like somebody in a play? On such a night, poor feller? If he's out there," said the Colonel with great energy, "he must be found. That should come first. He must be found."

Alleyn explained that there was a search party on the way. When he said Major Marchbanks was providing police dogs and handlers, the Colonel nodded crisply, rather as if he had ordered this to be done. More and more the impression grew upon Alleyn that here was no ninny. Eccentric in his domestic arrangements Colonel Forrester might be, and unexpected in his conversation, but he hadn't said anything really foolish about the case. And now when Alleyn broached the matter of the tin box and the dressing-room, the Colonel cut him short.

"You'll want to lock the place up, no doubt," he said. "You fellers always lock places up. I'll tell Moult—" he stopped short and made a nervous movement of his hands. "Force of habit," he said. "Silly of me. I'll put my things in the bedroom."

"Please don't bother. We'll attend to it. There's one

thing, though: would you mind telling me what is in the uniform box?"

"*In* it? Well. Let me see. Papers, for one thing. My commission. Diaries. My Will." The Colonel caught himself up. "One of them," he amended. "My investments, scrip or whatever they call them." Again, there followed one of the Colonel's brief meditations. "Deeds," he said. "That kind of thing. B's money: some of it. She likes to keep a certain amount handy. Ladies do, I'm told. And the jewels she isn't wearing. Those sorts of things. Yes."

Alleyn explained that he would want to test the box for fingerprints, and the Colonel instantly asked if he might watch. "It would interest me no end," he said. "Insufflators and latent ones and all that. I read a lot of detective stories: awful rot, but they lead you on. B reads them backwards but I won't let her tell me."

Alleyn managed to steer him away from this theme and it was finally agreed that they would place the box, intact, in the dressing-room wardrobe pending the arrival of the party from London. The Colonel's effects having been removed to the bedroom, the wardrobe and the dressing-room itself would then be locked and Alleyn would keep the keys.

Before these measures were completed, Mrs. Forrester came tramping in.

"I thought as much," she said to her husband.

"I'm all right, B. It's getting jolly serious, but I'm all right. Really."

"What are you doing with the box? Good evening," Mrs. Forrester added, nodding to Mr. Wrayburn.

Alleyn explained. Mrs. Forrester fixed him with an embarrassing glare but heard him through.

"I see," she said. "And is Moult supposed to have been interrupted trying to open it with the poker, when he had the key in his pocket?"

"Of course not, B. We all agree that would be a silly idea."

"Perhaps you think he's murdered and his body's locked up in the box."

"Really, my dear!"

"The one notion's as silly as the other."

"We don't entertain either of them, B. Do we, Alleyn?"

"Mrs. Forrester," Alleyn said, "what do you think has happened? Have you a theory?"

"No," said Mrs. Forrester. "It's not my business to have theories. Any more than it's yours, Fred," she tossed as an aside to her husband. "But I do throw this observation out, as a matter you may like to remember, that Moult and Hilary's murderers were at loggerheads."

"Why?"

"Why! Why, because Moult's the sort of person to object to them. Old soldier-servant. Service in the Far East. Seen plenty of the seamy side and likes things done according to the Queen's regulations. Regimental snobbery. Goes right through the ranks. Thinks this lot a gang of riffraff and lets them know it."

"I tried," said the Colonel, "to get him to take a more enlightened view but he couldn't see it, poor feller, he couldn't see it."

"Was he married?"

"No," they both said and Mrs. Forrester added: "Why?"

"There's a snapshot in his pocket-book—"

"You've found him!" she ejaculated with a violence that seemed to shock herself as well as her hearers.

Alleyn explained.

"I daresay," the Colonel said, "it's some little girl in the married quarters. One of his brother-soldiers' children. He's fond of children."

"Come to bed, Fred."

"It isn't time, B."

"Yes, it is. For you."

Mr. Wrayburn, who from the time Mrs. Forrester appeared had gone quietly about the business of removing the Colonel's effects to the bedroom, now returned to say he hoped they'd find everything in order. With an air that suggested they'd better or else, Mrs. Forrester withdrew her husband, leaving both doors into the bathroom open, presumably with the object of keeping herself informed of their proceedings.

Alleyn and Wrayburn lifted the box by its end handles into the wardrobe, which they locked. Alleyn walked over to the window, stood on a Victorian footstool, and peered for some time through Hilary's glass at the junction of the two sashes. "*This* hasn't been dusted, at least," he muttered, "but much good will that be to us, I don't mind betting." He prowled disconsolately.

Colonel Forrester appeared in the bathroom door in his pyjamas and dressing-gown. He made apologetic faces at them, motioned with his head in the direction of his wife, bit his underlip, shut the door, and could be heard brushing his teeth.

"He's a caution, isn't he?" Mr. Wrayburn murmured.

Alleyn moved alongside his colleague and pointed to the window.

Rain still drove violently against the pane, splayed out and ran down in sheets. The frame rattled intermittently. Allen turned out the lights, and at once the scene outside became partly visible. The top of the fir tree thrashed about dementedly against an oncoming multitude of glistening rods across which, in the distance, distorted beams of light swept and turned.

"Chaps from the Vale. Or my lot."

"Look at that sapling fir."

"Whipping about like mad, isn't it? That's the Buster. Boughs broken. Snow blown out of it. It's a proper shocker, the Buster is."

"There *is* something caught up in it. Do you see? A tatter of something shiny?"

"Anything might be blown into it in this gale."

"It's on the lee side. Still—I suppose you're right. We'd better go down. You go first, will you, Jack? I'll lock up here. By the way, they'll want that shoe of Moult's to lay the dogs on. But what a hope!"

"What about one of his fur-lined boots in the cloakroom?"

Alleyn hesitated and then said: "Yes. All right. Yes."

"See you downstairs then."

"O.K."

Wrayburn went out. Alleyn pulled the curtains across the window. He waited for a moment in the dark room and was about to cross it when the door into the bathroom opened and admitted a patch of reflected light. He stood where he was. A voice, scarcely articulate, without character, breathed: "Oh," and the door closed.

He waited. Presently he heard a tap turned on and sundry other sounds of activity.

He locked the bathroom door, went out by the door into the corridor, locked it, pocketed both keys, took a turn to his left, and was in time to see Troy going into her bedroom.

He slipped in after her and found her standing in front of her fire.

"You dodge down passages like Alice's rabbit," he said. "Don't look doubtfully at me. Don't worry. You aren't here, my love. We can't help this. You aren't here."

"I know."

"It's silly. It's ludicrous."

"I'm falling about, laughing."

"Troy?"

"Yes. All right. I'll expect you when I see you."
"And that won't be—"

Troy had lifted her hand. "What?" he asked, and she pointed to her built-in wardrobe. "You can hear the Forresters," she said, "if you go in there and if they've left their wardrobe door open. I don't suppose they have and I don't suppose you want to. Why should you? But you can."

He walked over to the wardrobe and stuck his head inside. The sound of voices in tranquil conversation reached him, the Colonel's near at hand, Mrs. Forrester's very distant. She's still in the bathroom, Alleyn thought. Suddenly there was a rattle of coat hangers and the Colonel, startlingly close at hand, said, "—jolly difficult to replace—" and a few seconds later: "Yes, all right, I know. Don't *fuss* me."

Silence: Alleyn turned back into the room.

"On Christmas morning," Troy said, "just after midnight, when I hung my dress in there, I heard them having what sounded like a row."

"Oh?"

"Well—just one remark from the Colonel. He said something was absolutely final and if *she* didn't *he* would. He sounded very unlike himself. And then she banged a door—their bathroom door, I suppose, and I could hear her barking her way into bed. I remembered my manners with an effort and wrenched myself away."

"Curious," Alleyn said and after a moment's consideration: "I must be off."

He was halfway across the room when Mrs. Forrester screamed.

Seven – House Work

Colonel Forrester lay in a little heap face down under the window. He looked small and accidental. His wife, in her red dressing gown, knelt beside him, and as Troy and Alleyn entered the room, was in the act of raising him to a sitting position. Alleyn helped her.

Troy said, "He takes something, doesn't he?"

"Tablets. Bedside table. And water."

He was leaning back in his wife's arms now, his eyes wide open and terrified and his head moving very slightly in time with his breathing. Her thin plait of hair dangled over him.

"It's not here," Troy said.

"Must be. Pill things. Capsules. He put them there. Be quick."

Alleyn said: "Try his dressing gown pocket, if you can reach it. Wait. I will." It was empty.

"I saw them. I reminded him. You haven't looked. Fred! Fred, you're all right, old man. I'm here."

"Truly," said Troy. "They're not anywhere here. How about brandy?"

"Yes. His flask's in the middle drawer. Dressing table."

It was there. Troy unscrewed the top and gave it to her. Alleyn began casting about the room.

"That'll be better. Won't it, Fred? Better?"

Troy brought a glass of water but was ignored. Mrs. Forrester held the mouth of the flask between her husband's lips. "Take it, Fred," she said. "Just a sip. Take it. You must. That's right. Another."

Alleyn said: "Here we are!"

He was beside them with a capsule in his palm. He held it out to Mrs. Forrester. Then he took the flask from her and put it beside a glass phial on the dressing table.

"Fred, look. Your pill. Come on, old boy."

The delay seemed interminable. Into the silence came a tiny rhythmic sound: "Ah—ah—ah," of the Colonel's breathing. Presently Mrs. Forrester said: "*That's* better. Isn't it? *That's* better, old boy."

He was better. The look of extreme anxiety passed. He made plaintive little noises and at last murmured something.

"What? What is it?"

"Moult," whispered the Colonel.

Mrs. Forrester made an inarticulate exclamation. She brushed her husband's thin hair back and kissed his forehead.

"Turn," said the Colonel, "wasn't it?"

"Yes."

"All right soon."

"Of course you will be."

"Up."

"Not yet, Fred."

"Yes. Get up."

He began very feebly to scrabble with his feet on the carpet. Mrs. Forrester, with a look of helplessness of which Troy would have thought her totally incapable, turned to Alleyn.

"Yes, of course," he said, answering it. "He shouldn't lie flat, should he?"

She shook her head.

Alleyn leant over the Colonel. "Will you let me put you to bed, sir?" he asked.

"Very kind. Shouldn't bother."

Troy heaped up the pillows on the bed and opened it back. When she looked about her she found Alleyn with the Colonel in his arms.

"Here we go," said Alleyn and gently deposited his burden.

The Colonel looked up at him. *"Collapse,"* he said, *"of Old Party,"* and the wraith of his mischievous look visited his face.

"You old fool," said his wife.

Alleyn chuckled. "You'll do," he said. "You'll do splendidly."

"Oh yes. I expect so."

Mrs. Forrester chafed his hands between her two elderly ones.

Alleyn picked up the phial delicately between finger and thumb and held it up to the light.

"Where was it?" Troy asked.

He motioned with his head towards a lacquered leather wastepaper bin under the dressing table. The gesture was not so light that it escaped Mrs. Forrester.

"In *there*?" she said, "In there?"

"Is there something I can put the capsules in? I'd like to keep the phial if I may?"

"Anything. There's a pin box on the dressing table. Take that."

He did so. He spread his handkerchief out and gingerly wrapped up the phial and its stopper.

"The stable door bit," he muttered and put them in his pocket.

"What's that supposed to mean?" snapped Mrs. Forrester, who was rapidly returning to form.

"It means mischief," said Alleyn.

The Colonel in a stronger voice said, "Could there be some air?"

The curtain was not drawn across the window under which they had found him. The rain still beat against it. Alleyn said, "Are you sure?"

Mrs. Forrester said, "We always have it open at the top. Moult does it before he goes to bed. Two inches from the top. Always."

Alleyn found that it was unlatched. He put the heels of his hands under the top sash in the lower frame and couldn't budge it. He tried to raise it by the two brass loops at the base but with no success.

"You must push up the bottom in order to lower the top," Mrs. Forrester observed.

"That's what I'm trying to do."

"You can't be. It works perfectly well."

"It doesn't, you know."

"Fiddle," said Mrs. Forrester.

The ejaculation was intended contemptuously, but he followed it like an instruction. He fiddled. His fingers explored the catch and ran along the junction of the two sashes.

"It's wedged," he said.

"What?"

"There's a wedge between the sashes."

"Take it out."

"Wait a bit," Alleyn said, "Mrs. Forrester. You just wait a bit."

"Why!"

"Because I say," he replied and the astounded Troy saw that Mrs. Forrester relished this treatment.

"I suppose," she snapped, "you think you know what you're about."

"What is it, B?" asked her husband. "Is something wrong with the window?"

"It's being attended to."

"It's awfully stiff. Awfully stiff."

Alleyn returned to the bed. "Colonel Forrester," he said. "Did you wrestle with the window? With your hands above your head? Straining and shoving?"

"You needn't rub it in," said the Colonel.

"Fred!" cried his wife, "what *am* I to do with you! I said—"

"Sorry, B."

"I'll open the other window," Alleyn said. "I want this one left as it is. Please. It's important. You do understand, don't you? Both of you? No touching?"

"Of course, of course, of course," the Colonel drawled. His eyes were shut. His voice was drowsy. "When he isn't the White Knight," Troy thought, "he's the Dormouse."

His wife put his hands under the bedclothes, gave him a sharp look, and joined Alleyn and Troy at the far end of the room.

"What's all this about wedges?" she demanded.

"The houseman or whatever he is—"

"Yes. Very well. Nigel."

"Nigel. He may have wedged the sashes to stop the windows rattling in the storm."

"I daresay."

"If so, he only wedged one."

As if in confirmation, the second window in the Forresters' bedroom suddenly beat a tattoo.

"Ours haven't been wedged," said Troy.

"Nor has the dressing-room. May I borrow those scissors on your table? Thank you."

He pulled a chair up to the window, took off his shoes, stood on it, and by gentle manipulation eased a closely folded cardboard wedge from between the sashes. Holding it by the extreme tip he carried it to the dressing table.

"It looks like a chemist's carton," he said. "Do you recognize it? Please don't touch."

"It's the thing his pills come in. It was a new bottle."

Alleyn fetched an envelope from the writing table, slid the wedge into it and pocketed it.

He put on his shoes and replaced the chair. "Remember," he said, "don't touch the window and don't let Nigel touch it. Mrs. Forrester, will you be all right, now? Is there anything we can do?"

She sat down at her dressing table and leant her head on her hand. With her thin grey plait dangling and bald patches showing on her scalp she looked old and very tired.

"Thank you," she said. "Nothing. We shall be perfectly all right."

"Are you sure?" Troy asked and touched her shoulder.

"Yes, my dear," she said. "I'm quite sure. You've been very kind." She roused herself sufficiently to give Alleyn one of her looks. "So have you," she said, "as far as that goes. Very."

"Do you know," he said, "if I were you I'd turn the keys in the doors. You don't want to be disturbed, do you?"

She looked steadily at him, and after a moment, shook her head. "And I know perfectly well what you're thinking," she said.

2.

When Alleyn arrived downstairs it was to a scene of activity. Superintendent Wrayburn, now dressed in regulation waterproofs, was giving instructions to five equally waterproofed constables. Two prison warders and two dogs of supercaninely sharp aspect waited inside the main entrance. Hilary stood in front of one of the fires looking immensely perturbed.

"Ah!" he cried on seeing Alleyn. "Here you are! We were beginning to wonder—?"

Alleyn said that there had been one or two things to attend to upstairs, that the Colonel had been unwell but was all right again, and that he and Mrs. Forrester had retired for the night.

"Oh, *Lor'!*" Hilary said. "That too! Are you sure he's all right? Poor Uncle Flea, but how awkward."

"He's all right."

Alleyn joined Wrayburn, who made quite a thing of, as it were, presenting the troops for inspection. He then drew Alleyn aside and in a portentous murmur, said that conditions out-of-doors were now so appalling that an exhaustive search of the grounds was virtually impossible. He suggested, however, that they should make a systematic exploration of the area surrounding the house and extend it as far beyond as seemed feasible. As for the dogs and their handlers, Wrayburn said, did Alleyn think that there was anything to be got out of laying them on with one of the boots in the cloakroom and seeing if anything came of it? Not, he added, that he could for the life of him believe that anything would.

Alleyn agreed to this. "You've got a filthy night for it," he said to the men. "Make what you can of a bad job. You do understand the position, of course. The man's missing. He may be injured. He may be dead. There may be a capital charge involved, there may not. In any case it's urgent. If we could have afforded to leave it till daylight we would have done so. As it is—do your best. Mr. Wrayburn will give you your instructions. Thank you in advance for carrying out a foul assignment."

To the handlers he made suitable acknowledgments and was at some pains to put them in the picture.

"On present evidence," he said, "the missing man

was last seen in that cloakroom over there. He may
have gone outdoors, he may have gone upstairs. We
don't know where he went. Or how. Or in what state.
I realize, of course, that under these conditions, as
far as the open ground is concerned there can be
nothing for the dogs to pick up, but there may be
something in the entrance porch. If, for instance, you
can find more than two separate tracks, that would
be something, and you might cast round the front and
sides of the east wing, especially about the broken
conservatory area. I'll join you when you do that. In
the meantime Mr. Wrayburn will show you the ropes.
All right?"

"Very good, sir," they said.

"All right, Jack," Alleyn said. "Over to you."

Wrayburn produced the fur-lined boot—an incongruous and somehow rather piteous object—from under his cape and consulted with the handlers. The front
doors were opened, letting in the uproar of the
Nor'east Buster and letting out the search parties.
Fractured torch beams zigzagged across the rain. Alleyn
shut out the scene and said to Hilary, "And now, if you
please, I'll talk to the staff."

"Yes. All right. I'll ring—"

"Are they in their own quarters—the staff common-
room, you call it, don't you?"

"Yes. I think so. Yes, yes, they are."

"I'll see them there."

"Shall I come?"

"No need. Better not, I think."

"Alleyn: I do beg that you won't—won't—"

"I shall talk to them exactly as I shall talk to any
one of you. With no foregone conclusions and without
prejudice."

"Oh. Oh, I see. Yes. Well, good. But—look here,

don't let's beat about the bush. I mean, you do think—
don't you?—that there's been—violence?"

"When one finds blood and hair on the business end
of a poker, the thought does occur, doesn't it?"

"Oh Lord!" said Hilary. "Oh Lord, Lord, Lord,
what a *bore* it all is! What a disgusting, devastating
bore!"

"That's one way of putting it. The staff-room's at the
back through there, isn't it? I'll find my own way."

"I'll wait in the study, then."

"Do."

Beyond the traditional green baize door was a passage running behind the hall, from the chapel, at the
rear of the east wing, to the serveries and kitchen at
the rear of the dining room in the west wing. Alleyn,
guided by a subdued murmur of voices, tapped on a
central door and opened it.

"May I come in?" he asked.

It was a large, comfortable room with an open fire,
a television and a radio. On the walls hung reproduc-
tions of postimpressionist paintings, chosen, Alleyn
felt sure, by Hilary. There were bookshelves lined
with reading matter that proclaimed Hilary's hopes for
the intellectual stimulation of his employees. On a
central table was scattered a heterogeneous company
of magazines that perhaps reflected, more accurately,
their natural inclination.

The apple-cheeked boy was watching television, the
five members of the regular staff sat round the fire,
their chairs close together. As Alleyn came in they
got to their feet with the air of men who have been
caught offside. Blore moved towards him and then
stood still.

Alleyn said, "I thought it would be easier if we
talked this business over here where we won't be interrupted. May we sit down?"

Blore, with a quick look at the others, pulled back the central chair. Alleyn thanked him and took it. The men shuffled their feet. A slightly distorted voice at the other end of the room shouted, "What you guys waitin' for? Less go."

"Turn that off," Blore commanded in his great voice, "and come over here."

The rosy boy switched off the television set and slouched, blushing, towards them.

"Sit down, all of you," Alleyn said. "I won't keep you long."

They sat down and he got a square look at them. At Blore: once a headwaiter, who had knifed his wife's lover in the hanging days and narrowly escaped the rope, swarthy, fattish, baldish and with an air of consequence about him. At Mervyn, the ex-signwriter, booby-trap expert, a dark, pale man who stooped and looked sidelong. At Cooke, nicknamed Kittiwee, whose mouth wore the shadow of a smirk, who loved cats and had bashed a warder to death. At Slyboots and Smartypants, who lay along his ample thighs, fast asleep. At Nigel, pallid as uncooked pastry, almost an albino, possibly a lapsed religious maniac, who had done a sinful lady. Finally at Vincent, now seen by Alleyn for the first time at Halberds and instantly recognized since he himself had arrested him when, as gardener to an offensive old lady, he had shut her up in a greenhouse heavy with arsenical spray. His appeal, based on the argument that she had been concealed by a date palm and that he was unaware of her presence, was successful and he was released. At the time Alleyn had been rather glad of it. Vincent was a bit ferrety in the face and gnarled as to the hands.

They none of them looked at Alleyn.

"The first thing I have to say," he said, "is this.

You know that I know who you are and that you've all been inside and what the convictions were. You," he said to Vincent, "may say you're in a different position from the others, having been put in the clear, but where this business is concerned and at this stage of the inquiry, you're *all* in the clear. By this I mean that your past records, as far as I can see at the moment, are of no interest and they'll go on being uninteresting unless anything crops up to make me think otherwise. A man has disappeared. We don't know why, how, when or where and we've got to find him. To use the stock phrase, alive or dead. If I say I hope one or more of all of you can help us, I don't mean, repeat *don't* mean, that one or more of all of you is or are suspected of having had anything to do with his disappearance. I mean what I say: I'm here to see if you can think of anything at all, however trivial, that will give us a lead, however slight. In this respect you're on an equal footing with every other member of the household. Is that understood?"

The silence was long enough to make him wonder if there was to be no response. At last Blore said, "It's *understood,* sir, I suppose, by all of us."

"But not necessarily believed? Is that it?"

This time the silence was unbroken. "Well," he said, "I can't blame you. It's a natural reaction. I can only hope you will come to accept the proposition."

He turned to the boy, who stood apart looking guarded. "You're a local chap, aren't you?" Alleyn said.

He extracted with some difficulty that the boy, whose name was Thomas Appleby, was a farmer's son engaged for the festive season. He had never spoken to Moult, had with the other servants come into the drawing-room for the Christmas tree, had had no idea who the Druid was, had received his present, and had returned to his kitchen and outhouse duties as soon as the ceremony ended and had nothing whatever to offer in the way of information. Alleyn said he could go off to bed, an invitation he seemed to accept with some reluctance.

When he had gone Alleyn told the men what he had learnt about their movements at the time of the Christmas tree: that they too had seen the Druid, failed to recognize him, received their gifts, and returned to their duties. "I understand," he said, "that you, Cooke, with the extra women helpers, completed the arrangements for the children's supper and that you saw Miss Tottenham return to the drawing-room but didn't see anything of Moult. Is that right?"

"Yes, it is," said Kittiwee, setting his dimples. "And I was concerned with my own business, if I may put it that way, sir, and couldn't be expected to be anything else."

"Quite so. And you," Alleyn said to Vincent, "did exactly what it had been arranged you should do in respect of the tree. At half-past seven you stationed yourself round the corner of the east wing. Right?"

Vincent nodded.

"Tell me, while you were there did anyone throw open a window in the east frontage and look out? Do you remember?"

" 'Course I remember," said Vincent, who had an indeterminate accent and a bronchial voice. "He did. To see if I was there like he said he would. At seven-thirty."

"The Colonel? Or Moult?"

"I wouldn't know, would I? I took him for the Colonel because I expected him to be the Colonel, see?"

"Was he wearing his beard?"

"I never took no notice. He was black-like against the light."

"Did he wave or signal in any way?"

"I waved according, giving him the office to come down. According. Now they was all in the drawing-room. And he wove back, see, and I went round to the front. According."

"Good. Your next move was to tow the sledge round the corner and across the courtyard, where you were met by Moult, whom you took to be Colonel Forrester. Where exactly did you meet him?"

Behind Nigel's effigy, it appeared. There, Vincent said, he relieved that Druid of his umbrella and handed over the sledge, and there he waited until the Druid returned.

"So you missed the fun?" Alleyn remarked.

"I wouldn't of bothered anyway," said Vincent.

"You waited for him to come out and then you took over the sledge and he made off through the porch and the door into the cloakroom? Right."

"That's what I told Mr. Bill-Tasman and that's what I tell everyone else who keeps on about it, don't I?"

"Did you give him back the umbrella?"

"No. He scarpered off smartly."

"Where were you exactly when you saw him go into the cloakroom?"

"Where was I? Where would I be? Out in the bloody snow, that's where."

"Behind the effigy?"

"Hey!" said Vincent flaring up. "You trying to be funny? You trying to make a monkey outa me? You said no funny business, that's what you said."

"I'm not making the slightest attempt to be funny. I'm simply trying to get the picture."

"How could I see him if I was be'ind the bloody statcher?"

Blore, in his great voice, said, "Choose your words," and Kittiwee said, "Language!"

"You could have looked round the corner, I imagine, or even peered over the top," Alleyn suggested.

Vincent, in a tremulous sulk, finally revealed that he saw Moult go through the cloakroom door as he, Vincent, was about to conceal the sledge round the corner of the east wing.

Alleyn asked when the Christmas tree was demolished and Blore said this was effected by Vincent, Nigel and the boy while the party was at dinner. The children had finished their supper and had been let loose, with their presents, in the library. The ornaments were stripped from the tree, packed into their boxes and removed. The tree itself, on its movable base, was wheeled out through the french windows, and the curtains were drawn to conceal it.

"And there it remained, I suppose. Until when?" Another long silence.

"Well," Alleyn said cheerfully, "it's not there now. It's round the corner under the east wing. Who put it there? Did you, Vincent?"

He hung fire but finally conceded that he had moved the tree. "When?" Alleyn asked, remembering Troy's midnight observation from her window. Vincent couldn't say exactly when. It emerged that after the dining-room had been cleared, the mammoth washing-up disposed of and the rest of the exhaustive chores completed, the staff, with the outside help, had sat down to a late supper. Vincent, upon whose forehead a thread of minute sweat-beads had come into being, said that he'd been ordered by Mr. Bill-Tasman to clear away the tree because, Alleyn gathered, the sight of it, denuded and disreputable, would be too anticlimactic. In all the fuss Vincent had forgotten to do so until he was going to bed.

He had put on his oilskins, fetched a wheelbarrow from the woodshed, collected the tree, and dumped it in the wreckage of the old conservatory.

"Why there?" Alleyn asked.

With an air strangely compounded of truculence and something that might be fear, Vincent asked at large where he was expected to take it in the dead of night.

It would be shifted anyway, he said, when the bulldozers got round to making a clean sweep of all that glass and muck, which they were due to do any day now, for filling in their excavations.

Alleyn said, "I'm sure you know, all of you, don't you, why you were asked to search the area where the tree lies? It was because it was thought that Moult might have wandered there and collapsed or even, for some reason, leant too far out of an upstairs window and fallen."

"What an idea!" said Kittiwee and tittered nervously.

Vincent said that half-a-dozen bloody Moults might have fallen in that lot and he wouldn't have seen them. He had tipped the tree out and slung his hook.

"Tell me," Alleyn said, looking round the circle, "you must have seen quite a lot of Moult off and on? All of you?"

If they had been so many oysters and he had poked them, they couldn't have shut up more smartly. They looked anywhere but at him and they said nothing.

"Come—" he began and was interrupted by Nigel, who suddenly proclaimed in a high nasal twang: "He was a sinner before the Lord."

"Shut up," said Mervyn savagely.

"He was given to all manner of mockery and abomination."

"Oh, *do* stop him, somebody!" Kittiwee implored. He struck out with his legs and the cats, indignant, sprang to the ground. Kittiwee made faces at Alleyn to indicate that Nigel was not in full possession of his wits.

"In what way," Alleyn asked Nigel, "was Moult an abomination?"

"He was filled with malice," muttered Nigel, who appeared to be at a slight loss for anathemas. "To the brim," he added.

"Against whom?"

"Against the righteous," Nigel said quickly.

"Meaning you," said Mervyn. "Belt up, will you?"

Blore said, "That's quite enough, Nigel. You're exciting yourself and you know what it leads to." He turned to Alleyn. "I'm sure, sir," he boomed, "you can see how it is, here. We've been overstimulated and we're a little above ourselves."

"We're all abominations before the Lord," Nigel suddenly announced. "And I'm the worst of the lot." His lips trembled. "Sin lies bitter in my belly," he said.

"Stuff it!" Mervyn shouted and then, with profound disgust: "Oh Gawd, now he's going to cry!"

And cry poor Nigel did, noisily, into a handkerchief held to the lower half of his face like a yashmak. Over this he gazed dolorously at Alleyn through wet, white eyelashes.

"Now, look here," Alleyn said, "Nigel. Listen to me. No," he added quickly, anticipating a further demonstration. "Listen. You say you're a sinner. All right. So you may be. Do you want to cleanse your bosom or your belly or whatever it is, of its burden? Well, come on, man. Do you?"

Without removing the handkerchief, Nigel nodded repeatedly.

"Very well, then. Instead of all this nonsense, how

about helping us save another sinner who, for all you
know, may be out there dying of exposure?"

Nigel blew his nose and dabbed at his eyes.

"Come on," Alleyn pressed. "How about it?"

Nigel seemed to take council with himself. He gazed
mournfully at Alleyn for some moments and then
said: "It's a judgment."

"On Moult? Why?"

There was no marked—there was scarcely any discernible—movement among the other four men: it
was more as if they jointly held their breath and barely
saved themselves from leaning forward.

"He was a wine-bibber," Nigel shouted. "Wine is a
mocker. Strong drink is raging."

And now there was a distinct reaction: an easing
of tension, a shifting of feet, a leaning back in chairs,
a clearing of throats.

"Is that the case?" Alleyn asked at large. "What
do you say? Blore? Do you agree?"

"Allowing for the extravagant style of expression,
sir," Blore conceded, "I would say it is the case."

"He tippled?"

"He did, sir, yes. Heavily."

"Have you any reason to think, any of you, that he
had taken more than was good for him yesterday
afternoon?"

Suddenly they were loquacious. Moult, they said,
had undoubtedly been tippling all day. Mervyn volun-
teered that he had seen Moult sneak out of the dining-
room and had subsequently discovered that the whisky
decanter on the sideboard which he had only lately
filled had been half-emptied. Kittiwee had an unclear
story about the total disappearance of a bottle of cooking brandy from the pantry. Vincent unpersuasively
recollected that when Moult met him, in druidical

array, he had smelt very strongly of alcohol. Blore
adopted a patronizing and olympic attitude. He said
that while this abrupt spate of witness to Mr. Moult's
inebriety was substantially correct, he thought it only
proper to add that while Mr. Moult habitually took
rather more than was good for him, yesterday's ex-
cesses were abnormal.

"Do you think," Alleyn said, "that Colonel and Mrs.
Forrester know of this failing?"

"Oh, really, sir," Blore said with a confidential
deference that clearly derived from his headwaiter
days, "you know how it is. If I may say so, the Colonel
is very unworldly gentleman."

"And Mrs. Forrester?"

Blore spread his hands and smirked. "Well, sir," he
said. "The ladies!" which seemed to suggest, if it
suggested anything, that the ladies were quicker at
spotting secret drinkers than the gentlemen.

"While I think of it," Alleyn said. "Colonel Forrester has had another attack. Something to do with
his heart, I understand. It seems he really brought it
upon himself trying to open their bedroom window.
He didn't," Alleyn said to Nigel, who had left off crying,
"notice the wedge, and tried to force it. He's better,
but it was a severe attack."

Nigel's lips formed the word "wedge." He looked
utterly bewildered.

"Didn't you wedge it, then? To stop it rattling in
the storm? When you shut up their room for the
night?"

He shook his head. "I never!" he said. "I shut it,
but I never used no wedge." He seemed in two minds:
whether to cut up rough again or go into an aimless
stare. "You see me," he muttered, "when you come
in."

"So I did. You were wet. The window came down with a crash, didn't it, as I walked in."

Nigel stared at him and nodded.

"Why?" Alleyn asked.

Again, a feeling of general consternation.

Nigel said, "To see."

"To see what?"

"They don't tell me anything!" Nigel burst out. "I seen them talking, I heard."

"What?"

"Things," he said and became sulky and uncommunicative.

"Odd!" Alleyn said without emphasis. "I suppose none of you knows who wedged the Colonel's window? No? Ah, well, it'll no doubt emerge in due course. There's only one other thing I'd like to ask you. All of you. And before I ask it I want to remind you of what I said at the beginning. I do most earnestly beg you not to think I'm setting a trap for you, not to believe I'm influenced in the smallest degree by your past histories. All right. Now, I expect you all know about the booby-trap that was set for my wife. Did you tell them about it, Cox?"

After a considerable pause, Mervyn said: "I mentioned it, sir," and then burst out: "Madam knows I didn't do it. Madam believes me. I wouldn't of done it, not to her, I wouldn't. What would I do it to her for? You ask madam, sir. She'll tell you."

"All right, all right, nobody's said you did it. But if you didn't, and I accept for the sake of argument that you didn't, who did? Any ideas?"

Before Mervyn could reply, Nigel came roaring back into action.

"With malice aforethought, he done it," Nigel shouted.

"Who?"

The other four men all began to talk at once: their object very clearly being to shut Nigel up. They raised quite a clamour between them. Alleyn stopped it by standing up: if he had yelled at the top of his voice it would have been less effective.

"Who," he asked Nigel, "did it with malice aforethought?"

"You leave me alone, Mr. Blore. Come not between the avenger and his wrath, Mr. Blore, or it'll be the worse for all of us."

"Nobody's interrupting you," Alleyn said and indeed it was true. They were turned off like taps.

"Come on, Nigel," Alleyn said. "Who was it?"

"Him. Him that the wrath of the Almighty has removed from the midst."

"Moult?"

"That's perfectly correct," said Nigel with one of his plummet-like descents into the commonplace.

From this point, the interview took on a different complexion. Nigel withdrew into a sort of omniscient gloom, the others into a mulish determination to dissociate themselves from any opinion upon any matter that Alleyn might raise. Blore, emerging as a reluctant spokesman, said there was proof—and he emphasized the word—that Moult had set the booby-trap, and upon Nigel uttering in a loud voice the word "spite," merely repeated his former pantomime to indicate Nigel's total irresponsibility. Alleyn asked if Moult was, in fact, a spiteful or vindictive character and they all behaved as if they didn't know what he was talking about. He decided to take a risk. He said that no doubt they all knew about the anonymous and insulting messages that had been left in the Forresters' and Cressida Tottenham's rooms and the lacing of Mr. Smith's barley water with soap.

They would have liked, he thought, to deny all knowledge of these matters, but he pressed them and gradually collected that Cressida had talked within hearing of Blore, that Mr. Smith had roundly tackled Nigel, and that Moult himself had "mentioned" the incidents.

"When?" Alleyn asked.

Nobody seemed exactly to remember when.

"Where?"

They were uncertain where.

"Was it here, in the staff common-room, yesterday morning?"

This, he saw, had alarmed and bewildered them. Nigel said "How—?" and stopped short. They glared at him.

"How did I know, were you going to say?" said Alleyn. "It seems the conversation was rather noisy. It was overheard. And Moult was seen leaving by that door over there. You'd accused him, hadn't you, of playing these tricks with the deliberate intention of getting you into trouble?"

"We've no call to answer that," Vincent said. "That's what you say. It's not what we say. We don't say nothing."

"Come," Alleyn said, "you all disliked him, didn't you? It was perfectly apparent. You disliked him, and his general attitude gave you some cause to do so."

"Be that as it may, sir," said Blore, "it is no reason for supposing the staff had anything to do with—" His enormous voice trembled. He made a violent dismissive gesture. "—with whatever he's done or wherever he's gone."

"I agree. It doesn't follow."

"We went our way, sir, and Mr. Moult went his."

"Quite. Where to? What was Mr. Moult's way and where did it take him? That's the question, isn't it?"

"If you'll excuse the liberty," Kittiwee said, "that's your business, sir. Not ours."

"Of course it's my business," Alleyn cheerfully rejoined. "Otherwise, you know, I shouldn't waste half an hour butting my head against a concrete wall. To sum up. None of you knows anything about or is prepared to discuss, the matter of the insulting messages, booby-trap, soapy barley water or wedged window. Nor is anyone prepared to enlarge upon the row that took place in this room yesterday morning. Apart from Nigel's view that Moult was steeped in sin and, more specifically, alcohol (which you support), you've nothing to offer. You've no theories about his disappearance and you don't appear to care whether he's alive or dead. Correct?"

Silence.

"Right. Not only is this all my eye and Betty Martin but it's extremely damaging to what I'd hoped would be a sensible relationship between us. And on top of all that, it's so bloody silly that I wonder you've got the faces to go on with it. Good-night to you."

3.

Mr. Wrayburn was in the hall, pregnant with intelligence of police dogs and fur-lined boots. The dog Buck, who sat grinning competently beside his handler, had picked up two separate tracks from the cloakroom and across the sheltered porch, agreeing in direction with the druidical progress. "There and back," said Wrayburn, "I suppose." But there had been no other rewarding scents. An attempt within doors had been unproductive owing, Alleyn supposed, to a sort of canine *embarras de richesses*. All that could be taken from this, Mr. Wrayburn complained, was the fact, known already, that Moult left the cloakroom and returned to it and that unless he was carried out or changed his boots, he didn't leave by the porch door a second time.

Alleyn said, "Try one of the slippers from Moult's room: see what comes of that."

"I don't get you."

Alleyn explained. Wrayburn stared at him. "I see," he said. "Yes, I see."

The slipper was fetched and introduced to the dog Buck, who made a dutiful response. He was then taken to the porch and courtyard where he nosed to and fro, swinging his tail but obviously at a loss. The second dog, Mack, was equally disinterested. When taken to the cloakroom, however, they both produced positive and energetic reactions over the main area, but ignored the fellow of the fur-lined boot and the floor under the makeup bench.

"Well," Wrayburn said, "we know he was in here, don't we? Not only when he was being got up for the party but earlier when he was fixing the room for the Colonel. Still—it looks as if you're right, by gum it does. What next?"

"I'm afraid we'll have to tackle that mess that was once a convervatory, Jack. How's the search over the grounds going?"

"As badly as could be expected under these conditions. The chaps are doing their best but—if he's lying out in that lot they could miss him over and over again. Didn't this bunch of homicides have a go at the conservatory wreckage?"

"So we're told. With forks and spades. Thundering over the terrain like a herd of dinosaurs, I daresay. I think we must have a go. After all we can't rule out the possibility that he was hit on the head and stunned."

"And wandered away? And collapsed?"

"You name it. Hold on while I get my mackintosh."

"You'll need gum boots."

"See if there are any stray pairs in the other cloak-room, will you? I won't be long."

When Alleyn had collected his mackintosh and a futile hat from his dressing-room, he called on his wife.

He was surprised and not overdelighted to find Cressida Tottenham there, clothed in a sea-green garment that stuck to her like a limpet where it was most explicit and elsewhere erupted in superfluous frills.

"Look who's here!" Cressida said, raising her arm to a vertical position and flapping her hand. "My Favourite Man! Hullo, Heart-throb!"

"Hullo, Liar," he mildly returned.

"Rory!" Troy protested.

"Sorry."

"Manners, Jungle Cat," said Cressida. "Not that I object. It all ties in with the groovy image. The ruder they are, the nearer your undoing."

Troy burst out laughing. "Do you often," she asked, "make these frontal attacks?"

"Darling: only when aroused by a Gorgeous Brute. Do you mind?"

"Not a bit."

Alleyn said, "Gorgeous brute or not, I'm on the wing, Troy."

"So I see."

"Think nothing of it if you notice a commotion under your windows."

"Right."

"We've been brushing our hair," Cressida offered, "and emptying our bosoms. Ever so cosy."

"Have you, indeed. By the way, Miss Tottenham, while I think of it: what did you wear on your feet when you made Moult up in the cloakroom?"

"On my *feet*?" she asked and showed him one of them in a bejewelled slipper. "I wore golden open-toed sandals, Mr. Alleyn, and golden toenalls to go with my handsome gold dress."

"Chilly," he remarked.

"My dear—arctic! So much so, I may tell you, that I thrust my ten little pigs into Uncle Flea's fur-lined trotters."

"Damn!"

"Really? But why?" She reflected for a moment. "My dear!" Cressida repeated, making eyes at Troy. "It's the smell! Isn't it? Those wolfish dogs! I've mucked up poor Mr. Moult's footwork for them. Admit!"

"Presumably you swapped for the performance?"

"But, of course. And I'm sure his feet will have triumphed over mine or does my skin scent beat him to the post?"

Ignoring this, Alleyn made for the door and then stopped short. "I almost forgot," he said. "When did you come upstairs?"

Cressida blew out her cheeks and pushed up the tip of her nose with one finger. The effect was of an extremely cheeky Zephyr.

"Come on," Alleyn said, "When? How long ago?"

"*Well. Now.* When did I?"

"You came in here ten minutes ago, if it's any guide," Troy said. "I'd just wound my watch."

"And you'd been in your room," Alleyn said. "How long?" He glanced at her. "Long enough anyway to change your clothes."

"Which is no slight matter," Cressida said. "Say twenty minutes. It was getting a bit of a drag in the library. Hilly's lost his cool over the sleuthing scene and Uncle Bert Smith doesn't exactly send one. So I came up."

"Did you meet anybody on the way?"

"I certainly did. I met that ass Nigel at the head of the stairs, bellowing away about sin. I suppose you've heard how he pushed a sexy note under my door. About me being a sinful lady?"

"You feel certain he wrote it?"

"Who else would?" Cressida reasoned. "Whatever they might think? It's his theme song, isn't it—the sinful lady bit?"

"Very much so. When did you go down to dinner?"

"I don't know. Last, as usual, I expect."

"Did you at any stage meet anybody going into or coming out of the Forresters' rooms?"

Cressida helplessly flapped her arms. "Yes," she said. "Nigel again. Coming out. He'd been doing his turning down the bed lot. This time he only shrank back against the wall as if I had infective hepatitis."

"Thank you," Alleyn said. "I must be off." He looked at his wife.

"All right?" he asked.

"All right."

When he had gone Cressida said, "Let's face it, darling. I'm wasting my powder."

Eight – Moult

Before he went out into the night, Alleyn visited the study and found it deserted. He turned on all the lights, opened the window curtains, and left, locking the door behind him and putting the key in his pocket. He listened for a moment or two outside the library door and heard the dronc of two male voices topped by Mr. Smith's characteristic short bark of laughter. Then he joined Wrayburn, who waited in the great porch with four of his men and the two handlers with their dogs. They moved out into the open courtyard.

"Rain's lifted," Wrayburn shouted. It had spun itself into a thin, stinging drive. The noise out-of-doors was immense: a roar without definition as if all the trees at Halberds had been given voices with which to send themselves frantic. A confused sound of water mingled with this. There were whistles and occasional clashes as of metal objects that had been blown out of their places and clattered about wildly on their own account.

Nigel's monument was dissolving into oblivion. The recumbent figure, still recognizable, was horridly mutilated.

They rounded the front of the east wing, and turned right into the full venom of the wind.

The library windows were curtained and emitted only thin blades of light, and the breakfast-room was in darkness. But from the study a flood of lamplight caught the sapling fir, lashing itself to and fro distractedly, and the heaps of indeterminate rubble that surrounded it. Broken glass, cleaned by the rain, refracted the light confusedly.

Their faces were whipped by the wind, intermittent shafts of rain, and pieces of blown litter. The men had powerful search-lamps and played them over the area. They met at the discarded Christmas tree from which tatters of golden tinsel madly streamed. They searched the great heaps of rubble and patches of nettle and docks. They found, all over the place, evidence of Hilary's men with their forks and shovels and trampling boots. They explored the sapling fir and remained, focussed on it, while Alleyn with his back to the wind peered up into the branches. He saw, as he had already seen from the dressing-room window, that the tender ones were bent into uncouth positions. He actually found, in a patch of loamy earth beneath the study window, prints of Hilary's smart shoes where he had climbed over the sill to retrieve the poker.

He took a light, moved up to the tree, and searched its inward parts. After a minute or two he called to one of the men and asked him to hold the light steady as it was. He had to yell into the man's ear, so boisterous was the roar of the wind.

The man took the light and Alleyn began to climb the tree. He kept as close as he could to the trunk where the young boughs were strongest. Wet pine needles brushed his face. Cascades of snow fell about his neck and shoulders. Branches slapped at him and he felt resin sticking to his hands. As he climbed, the

tree swayed, he with it, and the light moved. He
shifted round the trunk and hauled himself upward.

Suddenly an oblong sliver of fresh light appeared
below and to his right. There was Hilary Bill-Tasman's
face, upturned and staring at Alleyn. He had come to
the library window.

Cursing, Alleyn grasped the now slender trunk with
his left hand, leant outward, and looked up. Dislodged
snow fell into his face.

There it was. He reached up with his right hand,
touched it, made a final effort and secured it. His
fingers were so cold that he could scarcely feel sure
of his capture. He put it in his mouth, and slithering,
swaying and scrambling, came down to earth.

He moved round until the tree was between him and
the library window and warmed his hands at the
lamp. Wrayburn, standing close by, said something
Alleyn could not catch and jerked his thumb in the
direction of the library. Alleyn nodded, groped in
his mouth and extracted a slender strip of metallic
gold. He opened his mackintosh and tucked it away
in the breast pocket of his jacket.

"Come indoors," he signalled.

They had moved away and were heading back to
the front of the house when they were caught in the
beams of two lights. Above the general racket and
clamour they heard themselves hailed.

The lights jerked, swayed and intensified as they approached. The men behind them suddenly plunged
into the group. Alleyn shone his torch into their
excited faces.

"What's up?" Wrayburn shouted. "Here? What's all
the excitement?"

"We've found 'im, Mr. Wrayburn, we've seen 'im!
We've got 'im."

"Where?"

"Laying on the hillside, up yonder. I left my mate to see to 'im."

"Which hillside?" Alleyn bawled.

"Acrost there, sir. On the way to the Vale road."

"Come on, then," said Wrayburn excitedly.

The whole party set off along the cinder path that Troy so often had taken on her afternoon walks.

They had not gone far before they saw a stationary light and a recumbent figure clearly visible spread-eagled and face down in the snow. Someone was stopping over it. As they drew near the stooping figure rose and began to kick the recumbent one.

"My God!" Wrayburn roared out, "what's he doing! My *God!* Is he mad! Stop him."

He turned to Alleyn and found him doubled up.

The man on the hillside, caught in his own torch-light, gave two or three more tentative kicks to the prostrate form and then, with an obvious effort, ad-ministered a brief and mighty punt that sent it career-ing into the gale. It gesticulated wildly and disinte-grated. Wisps of rank, wet straw were blown into their faces.

Hilary would have to find another scarecrow.

2.

A further ill-tempered, protracted and exhaustive search turned out to be useless, and at five minutes past twelve they returned to the house.

The rest of the search party had come in with nothing to report. They all piled up a shining heap of wet gear and lamps in the porch, left the two dogs in the unfurnished east-wing cloakroom, and in their stockinged feet entered the hall. The overefficient cen-tral heating of Halberds received them like a Turkish bath.

Hilary, under a hard drive of hospitality, came fussing out from the direction of the library. He was full of commiseration and gazed anxiously into one frozen face after another, constantly turning to Alleyn as if to call witness to his own distress.

"Into the dining-room! Everybody. Do do do do," cried Hilary, dodging about like a sheepdog. And, rather sheepishly, the search party allowed itself to be mustered.

The dining-room table displayed a cold collation that would have done honour to Dingley Dell. On a side table was ranked an assembly of bottles: whisky, rum, brandy, Alleyn saw, and a steaming kettle. If Hilary had known how, Alleyn felt, he would have set about brewing a punch bowl. As it was, he implored Wrayburn to superintend the drinks and set himself to piling up a wild selection of cold meats on plates.

None of the servants appeared at this feast.

Mr. Smith came in, however, and looked on with his customary air of sardonic amusement and sharp appraisal. Particularly, Alleyn thought, did Mr. Smith observe his adopted nephew. What did he make of Hilary and his antics? Was there a kind of ironic affection, an exasperation at Hilary's mannerisms and—surely?—an underlying anxiety? Hilary made a particularly effusive foray upon Wrayburn and a group of disconcerted subordinates, who stopped chewing and stared at their socks. Mr. Smith caught Alleyn's eye and winked.

The dining-room became redolent of exotic smells.

Presently Wrayburn made his way to Alleyn.

"Will it be all right, now," he asked, "if I get these chaps moving? The stream's coming down very fresh and we don't want to be marooned, do we?"

"Of course you don't. I hope my lot get through all right."

"When do you expect them?"

"I should think by daylight. They're driving through the night. They'll look in at the station."

"If they're short on waders," said Wrayburn, "we can fix them up. They may need them." He cleared his throat and addressed his troops: "Well, now. Chaps."

Hilary was effusive in farewells, and at one moment seemed to totter on the brink of a speech but caught sight of Mr. Smith and refrained.

Alleyn saw the men off. He thanked them for their work and told them he'd have been very happy to have carried on with their help and might even be obliged to call on them again though he was sure they hoped not. They made embarrassed but gratified noises, and he watched them climb into their shining gear and file off in the direction of the vans that had brought them.

Wrayburn lingered. "Well," he said. "So long, then. Been quite a pleasure."

"Of a sort?"

"Well—"

"I'll keep in touch."

"Hope things work out," Wrayburn said, "I used to think at one time of getting out of the uniformed branch but—I dunno—it didn't pan out that way. But I've enjoyed this opportunity. Know what I mean?"

"I think so."

"Look. Before I go. Do you mind telling me what it was you fished out of that tree?"

"Of course I don't mind, Jack. There just hasn't been the opportunity."

Alleyn reached into his breast pocket and produced, between finger and thumb, the golden strand. Wrayburn peered at it. "We saw it from the dressing room window," Alleyn said.

"Metallic," Wrayburn said. "But not tinsel. Now what would that be? A bit of some ornamental stuff blown off the Christmas tree into the fir?"

"It was on the wrong side of the fir for that. It looks more like a shred of dress material to me."

"It may have been there for some time."

"Yes, of course. What does it remind you of?"

"By gum!" Wrayburn said. "Yes—by gum. Here! Are you going to look?"

"Care to keep your troops waiting?"

"What do you think!"

"Come on, then."

They unlocked the cloakroom door and went in. Again the smell of makeup, the wig on its improvised stand, the furtopped boot, the marks on the carpet, the cardboard carton with the poker inside and, on its coat hanger against the wall, the golden lamé robe of the Druid.

Alleyn turned it on its coat hanger and once again displayed the wet and frayed back of the collar. He held his shred of material against it.

"Might be," he said. "It's so small one can't say. It's a laboratory job. But could be."

He began to explore the robe, inch by inch. He hunted back and front and then turned it inside out.

"It's damp, of course, and wet at the bottom edge. As one would expect, from galloping about in the open courtyard. The hem's come unstitched here and ravelled out. Zips right down the back. Hullo! The collar's come slightly adrift. Frayed. Might be. Could be."

"Yes, but—look, it'd be ridiculous. It doesn't add up. Not by any reckoning. The thing's *here*. In the cloakroom. When he was knocked off, if he *was* knocked off, he wasn't wearing it. He couldn't have been. Unless," said Wrayburn, "it was taken off his body and returned to this room, but that's absurd. What a muck it'd be in!"

"Yes," Alleyn agreed absently. "It would, wouldn't it?"

He had stooped down and was peering under the makeup bench. He pulled out a cardboard box that had been used for rubbish and put it on the bench.

"Absorbent tissues," he said, exploring the contents. "A chunk of rag. Wrapping paper and—hullo, what's this."

Very gingerly he lifted out two pads of cotton wool about the shape of a medium-sized mushroom.

"Wet," he said and bent over them. "No smell. Pulled off that roll there by the powder box. But what for? What the devil for?"

"Clean off the makeup?" Wrayburn hazarded.

"They're not discoloured. Only wettish. Odd!"

"I'd better not keep those chaps waiting," Wrayburn said wistfully. "It's been a pleasure, by and large. Made a change. Back to routine, now. Good luck, anyway."

They shook hands and he left. Alleyn cut himself a sample of gold lamé from the hem of the robe.

He had a final look round and then locked the cloakroom. Reminded by this action of the study, he crossed the hall into the east-wing corridor, unlocked the door, and turned out the lights.

As he returned, the library door at the far end of the corridor opened and Mr. Smith came out. He checked for a moment on seeing Alleyn, and then made an arresting gesture with the palm of his hand as if he were on point duty.

Alleyn waited for him by the double doors into the hall. Mr. Smith took him by the elbow and piloted him through. The hall was lit by two dying fires and a single standard lamp below the gallery and near the foot of the right-hand stairway.

"You're up late," Alleyn said.

"What about yourself?" he rejoined. "Matter of fact, I thought I'd like a word with you if that's in order. 'Illy's gone up to bed. How about a nightcap?"

"Thanks very much, but no. Don't let me stop you, though."

"I won't bother. I've had my lot and there's still my barley water to come. Though after that little how-d'ye-do the other night the mere idea tends to turn me up in advance."

"There's been no more soap?"

"I should bloody well hope not," said Mr. Smith.

He walked up to the nearest hearth and kicked its smouldering logs together. "Spare a moment?" he asked.

"Yes, of course."

"If I was to ask you what's your opinion of this turn-up," he said. "I suppose I'd get what they call a dusty answer, would'n I?"

"In the sense that I haven't yet formed an opinion, I suppose you would."

"You telling me you don't know what to think?"

"Pretty much. I'm collecting."

"What's that mean?"

"You've been a collector and a very successful one, haven't you, Mr. Smith?"

"What of it?"

"There must have been times in your early days, when you had a mass of objects in stock on which you couldn't put a knowledgeable value. Some of them might be rubbish and some might be important. In all the clutter of a job lot there might be one or two authentic pieces. But in those days I daresay you couldn't for the life of you tell which was which."

"All right. All right. You've made your point, chum."

"Rather pompously, I'm afraid."

"I wouldn't say so. But I tell you what. I pretty soon learned in my trade to take a shine on the buyer and seller even when I only had a instinct for good stuff. And I always had that, I always had a flare. You ask 'Illy. Even then I could pick if I was having a stroke pulled on me."

Alleyn had taken out his pipe and was filling it. "Is that what you want to tell me, Mr. Smith?" he asked. "Do you think someone's pulling a stroke on me?"

"I don't say that. They may be, but I don't say so. No, my idea is that it must come in handy in your job to know what sort of characters you're dealing with. Right?"

"Are you offering," Alleyn said lightly, "to give me a breakdown on the inhabitants of Halberds?"

"That's your definition, not mine. All right, I'm thinking of personalities. Like I said. Character. I'd of thought in your line, character would be a big consideration."

Alleyn fished out a glowing clinker with the fire-tongs. "It depends," he said, lighting his pipe. "We deal in hard, bumpy facts and they can be stumbling blocks in the path of apparent character. People, to coin a bromide, can be amazingly contradictory," He looked at Mr. Smith. "All the same, if you're going to give me an expert's opinion on—" he waved his hand "—on the collection here assembled, I'll be very interested."

There was no immediate answer. Alleyn looked at Mr. Smith and wondered if he were to define his impression in one word, what that word would be. "Sharp"? "Cagey"? "Inscrutable"? In the bald head with streaks of black hair trained across it, the small bright eyes and compressed lips, he found a predatory character. A hard man. But was that hindsight? What would he have made of Mr. Smith if he'd known nothing about him?

"I assure you," he repeated, "I'll be very interested," and sat down in one of two great porter's chairs that flanked the fireplace.

Mr. Smith stared at him pretty fixedly. He took out his cigar case, helped himself, and sat in the other chair. To anyone coming into the hall and seeing them, they would have looked like subjects for a Christmas Annual illustration called "The Cronies."

Mr. Smith cut his cigar, removed the band, employed a gold lighter, emitted smoke, and contemplated it.

"For a start," he said. "I was fond of Alf Moult."

3.

It was a curious little story of an odd acquaintanceship. Mr. Smith knew Moult when Hilary was a young man living with the Forresters in Hans Place. The old feud had long ago died out and Mr. Smith made regular visits to luncheon on Sundays. Sometimes he would arrive early before the Forresters had returned from church, and Moult would show him into the Colonel's study. At first Moult was very standoffish, having a profound mistrust of persons of his own class who had hauled themselves up by their bootstraps. Gradually, however, this prejudice was watered down if never entirely obliterated, and an alliance was formed: grudging, Alleyn gathered, on Moult's part but cordial on Mr. Smith's. He became somebody with whom Moult could gossip. And gossip he did, though never about the Colonel, to whom he was perfectly devoted.

He would talk darkly about unnamed persons who

exploited the Colonel, about tradesmen's perfidy and the beastliness of female servants of whom he was palpably jealous.

"By and large," said Mr. Smith, "he *was* a jealous kind of bloke." And waited for comment.

"Did he object to the adopted nephew under that heading?"

"To 'Illy? Well—kind of sniffy on personal lines, like he made work about the place and was late for meals. That style of thing."

"He didn't resent him?"

Mr. Smith said quickly, "No more than he did anybody else that interfered with routine. He was a caution on routine, was Alf. 'Course he knew I wouldn't—" He hesitated.

"Wouldn't?" Alleyn prompted.

"Wouldn't listen to anything against the boy," said Mr. Smith shortly.

"How about Miss Tottenham? How did she fit in with Moult's temperament?"

"The glamour girl? I'm talking about twenty years ago. She was—what?—three? I never see 'er, but they talked about 'er. She was being brought up by some posh family what was down on its uppers and needed the cash. Proper class lot. Alf used to rave about 'er and I will say the result bears 'im out." The unelevating shadow of a leer slipped over Mr. Smith's face and slid away again. "Bit of all right," he said.

"Has Moult ever expressed an opinion about the engagement?"

"He's human. Or was, which ever it is, poor bloke. He made out 'Illy was a very, very lucky man. Raved about 'er, Alf did, like I said, and wouldn't hear a word to the contrary. That was because the Colonel took an interest in 'er and nothing the Colonel did was wrong in Alf's book. And it seems 'er old pot was killed saving the Colonel's life, which would make 'im a bleedin' 'ero. So there you were."

"You approve of the engagement?"

"It's not official yet, is it? Oh, yes. 'Illy's a good picker. You know. In the trade or out of it. Knows a nice piece when 'e sees one. She may be pushing the spoilt beauty bit now but he knows the answers to that one and no error. Oh, yes," Mr. Smith repeated, quizzing the top of his cigar. "I know about the Bill-Tasman image. Funny. Vague. Eccentric. Comes in nice and handy that lot, more ways than one. But 'e won't stand for any funny business, don't worry, in work *or* pleasure. She'll 'ave to be a good girl and I reckon she knows it."

Alleyn waited for a moment and then said: "I see no reason why I shouldn't tell you this. There's a theory in circulation that Moult was responsible for the practical jokes, if they can be so called."

Mr. Smith became vociferous. "Don't give me that one, chum," he said. "That's just silly, that is. Alf Moult put soap in my barley water? Not on your nelly. Him and me was pals, wasn't we? Right? Well, then: arst yourself."

"He didn't like the staff here, did he?"

" 'Course 'e didn't. Thought they was shockers and so they are. That lot! But that's not to say 'e'd try to put their pot on, writing silly messages and playing daft tricks. Alf Moult! Do me a favour!"

"You may not have heard," Alleyn said, "of all the other incidents. A booby-trap, in the Mervyn manner, set for my wife."

"Hullo-ullo! I thought there was something there."

"Did you? There was a much nastier performance this evening. After Nigel went his rounds and before

Colonel Forrester went to bed, somebody wedged the window in their room. The strain of trying to open it brought on an attack."

"There you are! Poor old Colonel. Another turn! And *that* wasn't done by Alf Moult, was it!"

"Who would you think was responsible?"

"Nigel. Simple."

"No. Not Nigel, Mr. Smith. Nigel shut the window when I was in the room and then ran downstairs bellowing about his own troubles."

"Came back, then."

"I don't think so. There's too narrow a margin in time. Of course we'll want to know who was in that part of the house just then. And if anyone can—"

" 'Help the police,' " Mr. Smith nastily suggested, " 'in the execution of their duty.' "

"Quite so."

"I can't. I was in the library with 'Illy."

"All the evening?"

"All the evening."

"I see."

"Look! This carry-on—notes and soap and booby-traps—brainless, innit? Nobody at home where it come from. Right? So where's the type that fits—? Only one in this establishment and he's the one with the opportunity? Never mind the wedge. That may be different. It's obvious."

"Nigel?"

"That's right! Must be. Mr. Flippin' Nigel. In and out of the princely apart-e-mongs all day. Dropping notes and mixing soapy nightcaps."

"We'll find out about the wedge."

"You will?"

"Oh, yes."

"Here! You think you know who done it? Don't you? Well—do you?"

"I've got an idea."

"Innit marvellous?" said Mr. Smith. "Blimey, innit blinkin' marvellous?"

"Mr. Smith," Alleyn said, "tell me something. Why do you go to such pains to preserve your original turn of speech? If it is your original style. Or is it— I hope you'll excuse this—a sort of embellishment? To show us there's no nonsense about Bert Smith? Do forgive me—it's nothing whatever to do with the matter in hand. I've no right to ask you, but it puzzles me."

"Look," said Mr. Smith, "you're a peculiar kind of copper, aren't you? What's your game. What are you on about? Christ, you're peculiar!"

"There! You *are* offended. I'm sorry."

"Who says I'm offended? I never said so, did I? All right, all right, Professor 'Iggins, you got it second time. Put it like this. I see plenty of fakes in our business, don't I? Junk tarted up to look like class? And I see plenty of characters who've got to the top same way as I did: from the bottom. But with them it's putting on the class. Talking posh. Plums in their gullets. Deceiving nobody but themselves. 'Educated privately' in *Who's Who* and coming a gutser when they loose their cool and forget themselves. Not for mine. I'm me. Born Deptford. Ejjercation, where I could pick it up. Out of the gutter mostly. Me." He waited for a moment and then, with an indescribably sly glance at Alleyn, said ruefully, "Trouble is, I've lost touch. I'm not contemp'ry. I'm mixing with the wrong sort and it's a kind of struggle to keep the old flag flying, if you can understand. P'raps I'm what they call an inverted snob. Right?"

"Yes," Alleyn said. "That may be it. It's an understandable foible. And we all have our affectations, don't we?"

"It's not a bloody affection," Mr. Smith shouted and then with another of his terribly prescient glances: "And it works," he said. "It rings the bell, don' it? They tell you George V took a shiner to Jimmy Thomas, don't they? Why? Because he *was* Jimmy Thomas and no beg yer pardons. If 'e forgot 'imself and left an aitch in, 'e went back and dropped it. Fact!" Mr. Smith stood up and yawned like a chasm. "Well, if you've finished putting the screws on me," he said, "I think I'll toddle. I intended going back tomorrow, but if this weather keeps up I might alter me plans. So long as the telephone lines are in business, so am I."

He moved to the foot of the stairs and looked back at Alleyn. "Save you the trouble of keeping obbo on me, if I stay put. Right?"

"Were you ever in the Force, Mr. Smith?"

"Me! A copper! Do me a favor!" said Mr. Smith and went chuckling up to bed.

Alone, Alleyn stood for a minute or two, staring at the moribund fire and listening to the night sounds of a great house. The outer doors were shut and barred and the curtains closed. The voice of the storm was transmitted only through vague soughing noises, distant rattling of shutters and an ambiguous mumbling that broke out intermittently in the chimneys. There were characteristic creaks and percussion-like cracks from the old woodwork and, a long way off, a sudden banging that Alleyn took to be a bout of indigestion in Hilary's central-heating system. Then a passage of quiet.

He was accustomed and conditioned to irregular hours, frustrations, changes of plan and lack of sleep, but it did seem an unconscionable time since he landed in England that morning. Troy would be sound asleep, he expected, when he went upstairs.

Some change in the background of small noises caught his attention. A footfall in the gallery upstairs? What? He listened. Nothing. The gallery was in darkness but he remembered there was a time-button at the foot of each stairway and a number of switches controlling the lights in the hall. He moved away from the fireplace and towards the standard lamp near the right-hand flight of stairs and just under the gallery.

He paused, looking to see where the lamp could be switched off. He reached out his left arm towards it.

A totally unexpected blow can bring about a momentary dislocation of time. Alleyn, for a split second, was a boy of sixteen, hit on the right upper arm by the edge of a cricket bat. His brother George, having lost his temper, had taken a swipe at him. The blunted thump was as familiar as it was shocking.

With his right hand clapped to his arm, he looked down and saw at his feet, shards of pale green porcelain gaily patterned.

His arm, from being numb, began to hurt abominably. He thought, no, not broken, that would be *too* much, and found that with an effort he could close and open his hand and then, very painfully, slightly flex his elbow. He peered at the shards scattered round his feet and recognized the remains of the vase that stood on a little table in the gallery: a big and, he was sure, extremely valuable vase. No joy for Bill-Tasman, thought Alleyn.

The pain was setting into a sort of rhythm, horrid but endurable. He tried supporting his forearm inside his jacket as if in a sling. That would do for the present. He moved to the foot of the stairs. Something bolted down them, brushed past him, and shot into the shadows under the gallery. He heard a feline exclamation, a scratching and a thud. That was the green baize door, he thought.

A second later, from somewhere distant and above him, a woman screamed. He switched on the gallery lights and ran upstairs. His arm pounded with every step.

Cressida came galloping full tilt and flung herself at him. She grabbed his arms and he gave a yelp of pain.

"No!" Cressida babbled. "No! I can't stand it. I won't take it! I hate it. No, no, no!"

"For the love of Mike!" he said. "What is it? Pull yourself together."

"Cats! They're doing it on purpose. They want to get rid of me."

He held her off with his right hand and felt her shake as if gripped by a rigor. She laughed and cried and clung to him most desperately.

"On my bed," she gabbled. "It was on my bed. I woke up and touched it. By my face. They know! They hate me! You've got to help."

He managed agonizingly to get hold of her wrists with both his hands and thought, "Well, no bones broken, I suppose, if I can do this."

"All right," he said. "Pipe down. It's gone. It's bolted. Now, please. No!" he added as she made a sort of abortive dive at his chest. "There isn't time and it hurts. I'm sorry but you'd better just sit on the step and get hold of yourself. Good. That's right. Now, please stay there."

She crouched on the top step. She was clad in a short, diaphanous nightgown and looked like a pin-up girl adapted to some kind of sick comedy.

"I'm cold," she chattered.

The check system on the stair lights cut out and they were in near darkness. Alleyn swore and groped for a wall-switch. At the same moment, like a well-timed cue in a French farce, the doors at the far ends of the gallery opened simultaneously, admitting a flood of light. Out came Troy, on the left hand, and Hilary on the right. A row of wall-lamps sprang to life.

"What in the name of Heaven——" Hilary began but Alleyn cut him short. "Cover her up," he said, indicating Cressida. "She's cold."

"Cressida! Darling! But what with?" Hilary cried. He sat beside his fiancée on the top step and made an ineffectual attempt to enclose her within the folds of his own dressing gown. Troy ran back into the guest-room corridor and returned with an eiderdown counterpane. Voices and the closure of doors could be heard. Alleyn was briefly reminded of the arousing of the guests at Forres.

Mr. Smith and Mrs. Forrester arrived in that order, the former in trousers, shirt, braces and stocking feet, the latter in her sensible dressing gown and a woolen cap rather like a baby's.

"Hilary!" she said on a rising note. "Your uncle and I are getting very tired of this sort of thing. It's bad for your uncle. You will put a stop to it."

"Auntie Bed, I assure you——"

"Missus!" said Mr. Smith, "you're dead right. I'm with you all the way. Now! What about it, 'Illy?"

"I don't know," Hilary snapped, "anything. I don't know what's occurred or why Cressida's sitting here in her nighty. And I don't know why you all turn on me. I don't like these upsets any more than you do. And how the devil, if you'll forgive me, Aunt Bed, you can have the cheek to expect *me* to do something about anything when everything's out of my hands, I do not comprehend."

Upon this they all four looked indignantly at Alleyn.

"They're as rum a job lot as I've picked up in many a long day's night," he thought and addressed himself to them.

"Please stay where you are," he said. "I shan't, I hope, keep you long. As you suggest, this incident must be cleared up, and I propose to do it. Miss Tottenham, are you feeling better? Do you want a drink?"

("Darling! *Do* you?" urged Hilary.)

Cressida shuddered and shook her head.

"Right," Alleyn said. "Then please tell me exactly what happened. You woke up, did you and found a cat on your bed?"

"Its *eyes!* Two inches away! It was making that awful rumbling noise and doing its ghastly pounding bit. On me! On *me!* I smelt its fur. Like straw."

"Yes. What did you do?"

"*Do!* I screamed."

"After that?"

After that, it transpired, all hell was let loose. Cressida's reaction set up an equally frenzied response. Her visitor tore round her room and cursed her. At some stage she turned on her bedside lamp, and revealed the cat glaring out from under the petticoats of her dressing table.

"Black-and-white?" Hilary asked. "Or tabby?"

"What the hell does it matter?"

"No, of course. No. I just wondered."

"Black-and-white."

"Smartypants, then," Hilary muttered.

After the confrontation, it seemed, Cressida, on the verge of hysteria, had got off her bed, sidled to the door, opened it, and then thrown a pillow at Smartypants, who fled from the room. Cressida, greatly shaken, slammed the door, turned back to her bed, and was softly caressed round her ankles and shins.

She looked down and saw the second cat, Slyboots, the tabby, performing the tails-up brushing ceremony by which his species make themselves known.

Cressida had again screamed, this time at the top of

her voice. She bolted down the corridor and into the gallery and Alleyn's reluctant embrace.

Closely wrapped in her eiderdown, inadequately solaced by the distracted Hilary, she nodded her head up and down, her eyes like great damp pansies and her teeth still inclined to chatter.

"All right," Alleyn said. "Two questions. How do you think the cats got into your room? When you visited Troy, did you leave your door open?"

Cressida had no idea.

"You do leave doors open, rather, my darling," Hilary said, "don't you?"

"That queen in the kitchen put them there. Out of spite. I know it."

"Now, *Cressida!* Really!"

"Yes, he did! He's got a thing about me. They all have. They're jealous. They're afraid I'm going to make changes. They're trying to frighten me off."

"Where," Alleyn asked before Hilary could launch his protests, "is the second cat, now? Slyboots?"

"He was walking about the corridor," Troy began and Cressida immediately began a sort of internal fight with her eiderdown cocoon. "It's all right," Troy said quickly. "He came into my room and I've shut the doors."

"Do you swear that?"

"Yes, I do."

"In Heaven's name!" Mrs. Forrester ejaculated, "Why don't you take her to bed, Hilary?"

"Really, Aunt B! Well, all right. Well, I will."

"Give her a pill. She takes pills, of course. They all do. Your uncle mustn't have any more upsets. I'm going back to him. Unless," she said to Alleyn, "you want me."

"No, do go. I hope he's all right. *Was* he upset?"

"He woke up and said something about a fire engine.

Good-morning to you all," snorted Mrs. Forrester and left them.

She had scarcely gone when Hilary himself uttered a stifled scream. He had risen and was leaning over the bannister. He pointed downwards like an accusing deity at a heap of broken porcelain lying near a standard lamp.

"God damn it!" Hilary said, "that's my K'ang Hsi vase. Who the hell's broken my K'ang Hsi vase!"

"Your K'ang Hsi vase," Alleyn said mildly, "missed my head by a couple of inches."

"What do you mean? Why do you stand there saying things with your arm in your chest like Napoleon Bonaparte?"

"My arm's in my chest because the vase damn' nearly broke it. It's all right," Alleyn said, catching Troy's eye. "It didn't."

"Very choice piece, that," Mr. Smith observed. "*Famille verte*. You bought it from Eichelbaum, didn't you? Pity."

"I should bloody well think it is a pity."

"Insurance O.K.?"

"Naturally. And cold comfort *that* is, as you well know. The point is, who did it? Who knocked it over." Hilary positively turned on his beloved. "Did you?" he demanded.

"I did not!" she shouted. "And don't talk to me like that. It must have been the cat."

"The cat! How the hell——"

"I must say," Alleyn intervened, "a cat did come belting downstairs immediately afterwards."

Hilary opened his mouth and shut it again. He looked at Cressida, who angrily confronted him, clutching her eiderdown. "I'm sorry," he said. "My darling. Forgive me. It was the shock. And it *was* one of our treasures."

"I want to go to bed."

"Yes, yes. Very well. I'll take you."

They left, Cressida waddling inside her coverlet.

"Oh dear!" said Mr. Smith. "The little rift what makes the music mute," and pulled a dolorous face.

"Your room's next to hers, isn't it?" Alleyn said. "Did you hear any of this rumpus?"

"There's her bathroom between. She's got the class job on the northeast corner. Yes, I heard a bit of a how-d'yer-do but I thought she might be having the old slap-and-tickle with 'Illy. You know."

"Quite."

"But when she come screeching down the passage, I though Hullo-ullo. So I come out. Gawd love us," said Mr. Smith, "it's a right balmy turn-out though, and no error. Good-night again."

When he had gone Alleyn said, "Come out of retirement," and Troy emerged from the background. "Your arm," she said. "Rory, I'm not interfering, but your arm?"

With a creditable imitation of the Colonel, Alleyn said: "Don't fuss me, my dear," and put his right arm round his wife. "It's a dirty great bruise, that's all," he said.

"Did somebody—?"

"I'll have to look into the Pussyfoot theory and then, by Heaven, come hell or high water, we'll go to bed."

"I'll leave you to it, shall I?"

"Please, my love. Before you do, though, there's a question. From your bedroom window, after the party, and at midnight, you looked out and you saw Vincent come round the northeast corner of the house. He was wheeling a barrow and in the barrow was the Christmas tree. He dumped the tree under the Colonel's dressing-room window. You saw him do it?"

"No. There was an inky-black shadow. I saw him coming, all right, along the path. It's wide, you know. More like a rough drive. The shadow didn't cover it. So along he came, clear as clear in the moonlight. Against the snowy background. And then he entered the shadow and I heard him tip the tree out. And then I came away from the window."

"You didn't see him leave?"

"No. It was chilly. I didn't stay."

" 'Clear as clear in the moonlight.' From that window you can see all those earthworks and ongoings where they're making a lake and a hillock?"

"Yes. Just out to the left."

"Did you look, particularly, in that direction?"

"Yes. It was very beautiful. One could have abstracted something from it. The shapes were exciting."

"Like a track across the snow leading into the distance?"

"Nothing as obvious as that. The whole field of snow—all the foreground—was quite unbroken."

"Sure?"

"Quite sure. That's what made it good as a subject."

"Nothing like a wheel track and footprints anywhere to be seen? For instance?"

"Certainly not. Vincent had trundled round the house by the track and that was already tramped over."

"Did you look out of your window again in the morning?"

"Yes, darling, I did. And there were no tracks anywhere across the snow. And I may add after our telephone conversation, I went out of doors. I had a look at Nigel's sculpture. It had been blurred by weathering, particularly on its windward side. Otherwise it was still in recognizable shape. I walked round the house past the drawing-room windows and had a look at last night's 'subject' from that angle. No tracks anywhere on the snow. The paths round the house and the courtyard and driveway were trampled and muddy. The courtyard had been swept."

"So nobody, during the night or morning, had gone near the earthworks."

"Unless from the far side. Even then one would still have seen their tracks on the hillside."

"And there had been no snowfall after midnight."

"No. Only the north wind. The sky was still cloudless in the morning."

"Yes. The Buster only blew up tonight. Thank you, my love. Leave me, now. I shan't be long."

"There isn't—?"

"Well?"

"I suppose there isn't anything I can do? Only stand and wait like those sickening angels?"

"I'll tell you what you can do. You can fetch my small suitcase and go downstairs and collect every last bloody bit of Bill-Tasman's *famille verte*. Don't handle it any more than you can help. Hold the pieces by the edges, put them in the case, and bring them upstairs. I'll be here. Will you do that?"

"Watch me."

When she was established at her task he went to the table in the gallery where the vase had stood. He looked down and there, in aerial perspective, was the top of a standard lamp, a pool of light surrounding it, and within the pool, a pattern of porcelain shards, the top of Troy's head, her shoulders, her knees and her long, thin hands moving delicately about the floor. She was directly underneath him.

A little table, Chinese, elegant but solid, stood against the gallery railing. The ebony pedestal on which the vase had rested was still in position. It had brought the base of the vase up to the level of the balustrade. Alleyn guessed that Hilary wished people in the hall to look up and see his lovely piece of *famille verte* gently signalling from above. As indeed it had signalled to him, much earlier in this long night. Before, he thought, it had hit him on the arm and then killed itself.

He turned on all the lights in the gallery and used a pocket torch that Wrayburn had lent him. He inspected the table, inch by inch, so meticulously that he was still at it when Troy, having finished her task, switched off the downstairs lamp and joined him.

"I suppose," she said, "you're looking for claw-marks."

"Yes."

"Found any?"

"Not yet. You go along. I've almost finished here. I'll bring the case."

And when, finally, just after Troy heard the stable clock strike one, he came to her, she knew it was not advisable to ask him if he had found any traces of Smartypants's claws on the Chinese table.

Because clearly he had not.

4.

Alleyn obeyed his own instructions to wake at three. He left Troy fast asleep and found his way through their bedroom, darkling, to his dressing-room, where he shaved and dipped his head in cold water. He looked out of his window. The moon was down but there were stars to be seen, raked across by flying cloud. The wind was still high but there was no rain. The Buster was clearing. He dressed painfully, dragging on thick sweaters and stuffing a cloth cap in his pocket.

He found his way by torchlight along the corridor,

out to the gallery and downstairs. The hall was a lightless void except for widely separated red eyes where embers still glowed on the twin hearths. He moved from the foot of the stairs to the opening into the east-wing corridor and, turning left, walked along it till he came to the library.

The library, too, was virtually in darkness. The familiar reek of oil and turpentine made Alleyn feel as if he had walked into his wife's studio. Had the portrait been taken out of seclusion and returned to the library?

He moved away from the door and was startled, as Troy had been before him, by the click of the latch as it reopened itself. He shut it again and gave it a hard shove.

His torchlight dodged about the room. Books, lamps, chairbacks, pictures, ornaments, showed up and vanished. Then he found the workbench and, at last, near it, Troy's easel.

And now, Hilary started up out of the dark and stared at him.

As he came nearer to the portrait his beam of torchlight intensified and so did the liveliness of the painting. Troy was far from being a "representational" portrait painter. Rather she abstracted the essence of her subjects as if, Alleyn thought, she had worked with the elements of Hilary's personality for her raw material and laid them out directly on the canvas.

What were those elements? What had she seen?

Well, of course, there was the slightly supercilious air which she had compared to that of a "good-looking camel." And in addition elegance, fastidiousness, a certain insolence, a certain quirkiness. But, unexpectedly, in the emphasis on a groove running from his nostrils to the corner of his faunish mouth and in the surprising heaviness of the mouth itself, Troy had unveiled a hedonist in Hilary.

The library was the foremost room in the east wing and had three outside walls. Its windows on the left as one entered it, looked on to the great courtyard. Alleyn made his way to them. He knew they were curtained and shuttered.

He opened the curtains, exposed a window and opened that. It crossed his mind that windows played a major role in whatever drama was unfolding at Halberds. Now his torchlight shone on the inside aspect of the shutters. This was the lee side of the east wing, but they rattled slightly and let in blades of cold air. Not strong enough, he thought, to make a great disturbance in the room, but he returned to the easel and gingerly pushed it into a sheltered position.

Then he operated the sliding mechanism in the shutters. The louvres turned and admitted the outside world, its noise and its cold. Alleyn peered through one of the slits. There were no clouds left in the sky. Starlight made a non-darkness of the great courtyard and he could discern, quite close at hand, Nigel's catafalque, denuded of all but a fragment of its effigy, a thin pock-marked mantle of snow.

He put on his cap, turned up the double collar of his sweater, like a beaver, over his mouth and ears, settled himself on the window-seat, and put out his torch.

"Keeping obbo," he thought and wondered if Fox and his lot were well on their way. He could have done with a radio link. They might arrive at precisely the wrong moment. Not that, ultimately, it would make any difference.

When did the staff get up at Halberds? Sixish? Was he completely, ludicrously at fault? Waiting, as so often on the job, for a non-event?

After all, his theory, if it could be called a theory, was based on a single tenuous thread of evidence. Guesswork, almost. And he could have proved it right or wrong as soon as it entered his head. But then— no confrontation, no surprise element.

He went over the whole field of information as he had received it piecemeal from Troy, from the guests, from Hilary and from the staff. As far as motive went, a clotted mess of non-sequiturs, he thought. But as far as procedure went: that was another story. And the evidence in hand? A collection of imbecile pranks that might be threats. A disappearance. A man in a wig. A hair of the wig and probably the blood of the man on a poker. A scrap of gold in a discarded Christmas tree. A silly attempt upon a padlock. A wedge in a window-sash. A broken vase of great price and his own left arm biceps now thrumming away like fun. Mr. Smith's junk yard in his horse-and-barrow days could scarcely have offered a more heterogeneous collection, thought Alleyn.

He reversed his position, turned up the collar of his jacket, and continued to peer through the open louvre. Icy blades of air made his eyes stream.

Over years of that soul-destroying non-activity known to the Force as keeping obbo, when the facility for razor-sharp perception must cut through the drag of bodily discomfort and boredom, Alleyn had developed a technique of self-discipline. He hunted through his memory for odd bits from his favourite author that, in however cockeyed a fashion, could be said to refer to his job. As: "O me! what eyes hath Love put in my head / which have no correspondence with true sight." And: "Mad slanderers by mad ears believed be." And : "Hence, thou suborn'd informer," which came in very handy when some unreliable snout let the police-side down.

This frivolous pastime had led indirectly to the memorizing of certain sonnets. Now, when, with his eyes streaming and his arm giving him hell, he had embarked upon "The expense of spirit in a waste of shame," he saw, through his peephole, a faint light.

It came jouncing across the courtyard and darted like a moth about the catafalque of Nigel's fancy.

"Here, after all, we go," thought Alleyn.

For a split second the light shone directly into his eyes and made him feel ludicrously exposed. It darted away to its original object and then to a slowly oncoming group out of some genre picture that had become blackened almost to oblivion by time. Two figures bent against the wind dragging at an invisible load.

It was a sledge. The torchlight concentrated on the ground beside the catafalque and into this area gloved hands and heavy boots shoved and manoeuvred a large, flat-topped sledge.

Alleyn changed his position on the window-seat. He squatted. He slid up the fastening device on the shutters and held them against the wind almost together but leaving a gap for observation.

Three men. The wind still made a great to-do, howling about the courtyard, but he could catch the sound of their voices. The torch, apparently with some bother, was planted where it shone on the side of the packing case. A figure moved across in the field of light: a man with a long-handled shovel.

Two pairs of hands grasped the top of the packing case. A voice said: "Heave."

Alleyn let go the shutters. They swung in the wind and banged open against the outside wall. He stepped over the sill and flashed his own light.

Into the faces of Kittiwee and Mervyn and, across the top of the packing case, Vincent.

"You're early to work," said Alleyn.

There was no answer and no human movement. It was as if the living men were held inanimate at the centre of a boisterous void.

Kittiwee's alto voice was heard. "Vince," it said, "asked us to give him a hand, like. To clear."

Silence. "That's right," said Vincent at last.

Mervyn said: "It's no good now. Sir. Ruined. By the storm."

"Quite an eyesore," said Kittiwee.

"Nigel's not giving a hand?" Alleyn said.

"We didn't want to upset him," Mervyn explained. "He's easy upset."

They had to shout these ridiculous observations against the noise of the gale. Alleyn moved round the group until he gently collided with something he recognized as one of the pillars supporting the entrance porch. He remembered that when Wrayburn's men collected their gear from the porch, one of them had switched on the converted lanterns that adorned the pillars.

Alleyn kept his torchlight on the men. They turned to follow his progress, screwing up their eyes and sticking close together. His hand reached out to the end pillar and groped round it. He backed away and felt for the wall of the house.

"Why," he called out, "didn't you wait for the light for this job?"

They all began to shout at once and very confusedly. Scraps of unlikely information were offered: Hilary's dislike of litter, Nigel's extreme sensitivity about the fate of his masterpiece. It petered out.

Vince said: "Come on. Get moving," and the pairs of gloved hands returned to the packing case.

Alleyn had found a switch. Suddenly the porch and

the courtyard were there to be seen: all lit up as they had been for Hilary's party.

The drama of darkness, flashing lights and half-seen ambiguous figures was gone. Three heavily clad men stood round a packing case and glowered at a fourth man.

Alleyn said: "Before you take it away, I want to see inside that thing."

"There's nothing in it," Kittiwee shrilly announced, and at the same time Vincent said, "It's nailed up. You can't."

Mervyn said: "It's just an old packing case, sir. The pianna come in it. It's got a lot of rubbish inside thrown out for disposal."

"Fair enough," Alleyn said. "I want to look at it, if you please."

He walked up to them. The three men crowded together in front of the case. "God!" he thought. "How irremediably pitiable and squalid."

He saw that each of them was using the others, hopelessly, as some sort of protection for himself. They had a need to touch each other, to lose their separate identities, to congeal.

He said, "This is no good, you know. You'll only harm yourselves if you take this line. I must see inside the case."

Like a frightened child making a show of defiance, Kittiwee said, "We won't let you. We're three to one. You better watch out."

Mervyn said, "Look, sir, *don't*. It won't do you any good. Don't."

And Vincent, visibly trembling: "You're asking for trouble. You better not. You didn't ought to take us on." His voice skipped a register. "I'm warning you," he squeaked. "See? I'm warning you."

"Vince!" Kittiwee said. "Shut up."

Alleyn walked up to them and in unison they bent their knees and hunched their shoulders in a travesty of squaring up to him.

"The very worst thing you could do," he said, "would be to attack me. Think!"

"Oh Gawd!" Kittiwee said, "Oh Gawd, Gawd, Gawd."

"Stand aside, now. And if you knock me over the head and try the same game with another job, you'll come to worse grief. You must know that. Come, now."

Vincent made an indeterminate gesture with his shovel. Alleyn took three steps forward and ducked. The shovel whistled over his head and was transfixed in the side of the packing case.

Vincent stared at him with his mouth open and his fingers at his lips. "My oath, you're quick!" he said.

"Lucky for you, I am," Alleyn said. "You bloody fool, man! Why do you want to pile up trouble for yourself? Now stand away, the lot of you. Go on, stand back."

"*Vincey!*" Kittiwee said in scandalized tones. "You might of cut his head off!"

"I'm that upset."

"Come on," Mervyn ordered them. "Do like 'e says. It's no good."

They stood clear.

The case was not nailed up. It was hinged at the foot and fastened with hook-and-eye catches at the top. They were very stiff and Alleyn could use only one hand. He wrenched the shovel from its anchorage and saying, "Don't you try that again," dropped it to the ground at his feet.

He forced open the first two catches and the side gaped a little, putting a strain on the remaining one. He struck at it with the heel of his hand. It resisted and then flew up.

The side of the case fell against him. He stepped back and it crashed on the paved courtyard.

Moult, having laid against it, rolled over and turned his sightless gaze on Alleyn.

Nine – Post Mortem

Moult, dead on the flagstones, seemed by his grotesque entry to inject a spasm of activity into his audience.

For a second or two after he rolled into view, the three servants were motionless. And then, without a word, they bolted. They ran out of the courtyard and were swallowed up by the night.

Alleyn had taken half-a-dozen steps after them when they returned as wildly as they had gone, running and waving their arms like characters in some kind of extravaganza. To make the resemblance more vivid, they were now bathed in light as if from an offstage spot. They turned to face it, made prohibitive gestures, shielded their eyes, and huddled together.

The field of light contracted and intensified as a police car moved into the courtyard and stopped. Vincent turned and ran straight into Alleyn's arms. His companions dithered too long, made as if to bolt, and were taken by four large men who had quitted the car with remarkable expertise.

They were Detective-Sergeants Bailey and Thompson, fingerprint and photography experts, respectively; the driver, and Detective-Inspector Fox.

"Now then!" said Mr. Fox, the largest of the four men, "what's all the hurry?"

Kittiwee burst into tears.

"All right, all right," Alleyn said. "Pipe down, the lot of you. Where d'you think you're going. Over the hill to the Vale? Good-morning, Fox."

" 'Morning, Mr. Alleyn. You've been busy."

"As you see."

"What do we do with this lot?"

"Well may you ask! They've been making a disgusting nuisance of themselves."

"We never done a thing. We never touched him," Kittiwee bawled. "It's all a bloody misunderstanding."

"Touched who?" Inspector Fox asked.

Alleyn, whose arm had been excruciatingly stirred up by Vincent, jerked his head towards the packing case. "Him," he said.

"Well, well!" Fox observed. "A body, eh?"

"A body."

"Would this be the missing individual?"

"It would."

"Do we charge these chaps then?"

"We get them indoors, for Heaven's sake," said Alleyn crossly. "Bring them in. It'll have to be through the windows over there. I'll go ahead and switch on the lights. They'd better be taken to their own quarters. And *keep quiet,* all of you. We don't want to rouse the household. Cooke—what's your name?—Kittiwee—for the love of decency—*shut up*."

Fox said, "What about the remains?"

"One thing at a time. Before he's moved, the Divisional Surgeon will have to take a look. Bailey—Thompson."

"Sir?"

"You get cracking with this setup. As it lies. Dabs. Outside and inside the packing case. The sledge. All

surfaces. And the body, of course. Complete job."
Alleyn walked to the body and stooped over it. It was
rigid and all askew. It lay on its back, the head at a
grotesque angle to the trunk. One arm was raised.
The eyes and the mouth were open. Old, ugly scars
on jaw and fattish cheek and across the upper lip,
started out lividly.

"But the beard and moustache and wig would have
covered those," Alleyn thought. "There's nothing in
that."

His hands were busy for a moment. He extracted an
empty flat half-pint bottle from a jacket in the coat
and sniffed at it. Whisky. From the waistcoat pocket
he took a key. Finding nothing more, he then turned
away from the body and contemplated Vincent and
his associates.

"Are you lot coming quietly?" he asked. "You'll
be mad if you don't."

They made affirmative noises.

"Good. You," Alleyn said to the driver of the police
car, "come with us. You," to Bailey and Thompson,
"get on with it. I'll call up the Div. Surgeon. When
you've all finished wait for instructions. Where's your
second car, Fox?"

"Puncture. They'll be here."

"When they come," Alleyn said to Bailey, "stick
them along the entrances. We don't want people barg-
ing out of the house before you've cleared up here.
It's getting on for six. Come on, Fox. Come on, you
lot."

Alleyn led the way through the library window,
down the corridor, across the hall, through the green
baize door, and into the servants' common-room. Here
they surprised the Boy in the act of lighting the fire.
Alleyn sent him with his compliments to Mr. Blore,
whom he would be pleased to see. "Is Nigel up?"

he asked. The Boy, all eyes, nodded. Nigel, it appeared, was getting out early-morning tea trays in the servery.

"Tell him we're using this room and don't want to be disturbed for the moment. Got that? All right. Chuck some coal on the fire and then off you cut, there's a good chap."

When the boy had gone Alleyn rang up Wrayburn on the staff telephone, told him of the discovery, and asked him to lay on the Divisional Surgeon as soon as possible. He then returned to the common-room, where he nodded to the Yard car-driver, who took up a position in front of the door.

Mervyn, Kittiwee and Vincent stood in a wet, dismal and shivering group in the middle of the room. Kittiwee mopped his great dimpled face and every now and then, like a baby, caught his breath in a belated sob.

"Now then," Alleyn said. "I suppose you three know what you've done, don't you? You've tried to obstruct the police in the execution of their duty, which is an extremely serious offence."

They broke into a concerted gabble.

"Pipe down," he said. "Stop telling me you didn't do him. Nobody's said anything to the contrary. So far. You could be charged as accessories after the fact, if you know what that means."

Mervyn, with some show of dignity, said: "Naturally."

"All right. In the meantime I'm going to tell you what I think is the answer to your cockeyed behaviour. Get in front of the fire, for pity's sake. I don't want to talk to a set of castanets."

They moved to the hearthrug. Pools formed round their boots, and presently they began to smell and steam. They were a strongly contrasted group: Kittiwee with his fat, as it were, gone soggy; Vincent, ferret-like with the weathered hide of his calling; and Mcrvyn, dark about the jaws, black-browed and white-faced. They looked at nobody. They waited.

Alleyn eased his throbbing arm a little further into his chest and sat on the edge of the table. Mr. Fox cleared his throat, retired into a sort of self-made obscurity, and produced a notebook.

"If I've got this all wrong," Alleyn said, "the best thing you can do is to put me right, whatever the result. And I mean that. Really. You won't believe me, but *really*. Best for yourselves on all counts. Now. Go back to the Christmas tree. The party. The end of the evening. At about midnight, you," he looked at Vincent, "wheeled the dismantled tree in a barrow to the glasshouse wreckage under the east wing. You tipped it off under Colonel Forrester's dressing-room window near a sapling fir. Right?"

Vincent's lips moved inaudibly.

"You made a discovery. Moult's body, lying at the foot of the tree. I can only guess at your first reaction. I don't know how closely you examined it, but I think you saw enough to convince you he'd been murdered. You panicked in a big way. Then and there, or later, after you'd consulted your mates—"

There was an involuntary shuffling movement, instantly repressed.

"I see," Alleyn said. "All right. You came indoors and told Blore and these two what you'd found. Right?"

Vincent ran his tongue round his lips and spoke.

"What say I did? I'm not giving the O.K. to nothing. I'm not concurring, mind. But what say I did? That'd be c'rrect procedure, wouldn't it? Report what I seen? Wouldn't it?"

"Certainly. It's the subsequent ongoings that are not so hot."

"A chap reports what he seen to the authorities. Over to them."

"Wouldn't you call Mr. Bill-Tasman the authority in this case?"

"A chap puts it through the right channels. *If. If.* See? I'm not saying—"

"I think we've all taken the point about what you're not saying. Let's press on, shall we, and arrive at what you *do* say. Let's suppose you did come indoors and report your find to Mr. Blore. And to these two. But not to Nigel, he being a bit tricky in his reactions. Let's suppose you four came to a joint decision. Here was the body of a man you all heartily disliked and whom you had jointly threatened and abused that very morning. It looked as if he'd been done to death. This you felt to be an acute embarrassment. For several reasons. Because of your records. And because of singular incidents occurring over the last few days: booby-traps, anonymous messages, soap in the barley water, and so on. And all in your several styles."

"We never—" Mervyn began.

"I don't for a moment suggest you did. I do suggest you all believed Moult had perpetrated these unlovely tricks in order to discredit you, and you thought that this circumstance, too, when it came to light, would incriminate you. So I suggest you panicked and decided to get rid of the corpse."

At this juncture Blore came in. He wore a lush dressing gown over silk pyjamas. So would he have looked, Alleyn thought, if nocturnally disturbed in his restaurant period before the advent of the amorous busboy.

"I understand," he said to Alleyn, "sir, that you wished to see me."

"I did and do," Alleyn rejoined. "For your information, Blore, Alfred Moult's body has been found in the packing case, supporting Nigel's version of the Bill-Tasman effigy. These men were about to remove the whole shooting box on a sledge. The idea, I think, was to transfer it to an appropriate sphere of activity where, with the unwitting aid of bulldozers, it would help to form an artificial hillock overlooking an artificial lake. End result, an artifact known, appropriately, as a folly. I've been trying to persuade them that their best course—and yours, by the way—is to give me a factual account of the whole affair."

Blore looked fixedly at the men, who did not look at him.

"So: first," Alleyn said, "did Vincent come to you and report his finding of the body on Christmas night? Or, rather, at about ten past midnight, yesterday morning?"

Blore dragged at his jaw and was silent.

Vincent suddenly blurted out. "We never said a thing, Mr. Blore. Not a thing."

"You did, too, Vince," Kittiwee burst out. "You opened your great silly trap. Didn't he, Merv?"

"I never. I said 'if.' "

"If what?" Blore asked.

"I said supposing. Supposing what he says was right it'd be the c'rrect and proper procedure. To report to you. Which I done. I mean—"

"Shut up," Mervyn and Kittiwee said in unison.

"My contention," Alleyn said to Blore, "is that you decided, among you, to transfer the body to the packing case there and then. You couldn't take it straight to the dumping ground because in doing so you would leave your tracks over a field of unbroken snow for all to see in the morning and also because any effort you made to cover it at the earthworks would be extremely difficult in the dark and would stand out like a sore thumb by the light of day. ·

"So one of you was taken with the very bright notion of transferring it to the packing case, which was destined for the earthworks anyway. I suppose Vincent wheeled it round in his barrow and one or more of you gave him a hand to remove the built-up box steps, to open the side of the case, stow away the body, and replace and re-cover the steps. It was noticed next morning that the northern aspect appeared to have been damaged by wind and rain but there had been a further fall of snow which did something to restore them."

Alleyn waited for a moment. Kittiwee heaved a deep sigh. His associates shuffled their feet.

"I really think we'd all better sit down," Alleyn said. "Don't you?"

They sat in the same order as in yesterday's assembly. Mr. Fox, after his habit, remained unobtrusively in the background, and the driver kept his station in front of the door.

"I wonder," Alleyn said, "why you decided to shift the case at five o'clock this morning? Had you lost your collective nerve? Had its presence out there become a bit more than some of you could take? Couldn't you quite face the prospect of dragging it away in the full light of morning and leaving it to the bulldozers to cover? What were you going to do with it? Has the storm produced some morass in the earthworks or the lake site into which it could be depended upon to sink out of sight?"

They shifted their feet and darted sidelong glances at him and at each other. "I see. That's it. Come," Alleyn said quietly, "don't you think you'd better face up to the situation? It looks like a fair cop, doesn't it? There you were and there's the body. You may not believe me when I tell you I don't think any of you killed him, but I certainly don't intend, at this point, to charge any of you with doing so. You've conspired to defeat the ends of justice, though, and whether you'll have to face that one is another matter. Our immediate concern is to find the killer. If you're helpful rather than obstructive and behave sensibly we'll take it into consideration. I'm not offering you a bribe," Alleyn said. "I'm trying to put the situation in perspective. If you all want a word together in private you may have it, but you'll be silly if you use the opportunity to cook up a dish of cod's wallop. What do you say? Blore?"

Blore tilted his head and stared into the fire. His right hand, thick and darkly hirsute, hung between his knees. Alleyn reflected that it had once wielded a lethal carving knife.

Blore heaved a sigh. "I don't know," he boomed in his great voice, "that it will serve any purpose to talk. I don't know, I'm sure."

None of his friends seemed inclined to help him in his predicament.

"You don't by any chance feel," Alleyn said, "that you rather owe it to Mr. Bill-Tasman to clear things up? After all, he's done quite a lot for you, hasn't he?"

Kittiwee suddenly revealed himself as a person of intelligence.

"Mr. Bill-Tasman," he said, "suited himself. He'd never have persuaded the kind of staff he wanted to come to this dump. Not in the ordinary way. He's got what he wanted. He's got value and he knows it. If he likes to talk a lot of crap about rehabilitation, that's his affair. If we hadn't given the service, you wouldn't have heard so much about rehabilitation."

The shadow of a grin visited all their faces.

"*Owe* it to him!" Kittiwee said and his moon face, still blotted with tears, dimpled into its widest smile. "You'll be saying next we ought to show our gratitude. We're always being told we ought to be grateful. Grateful for what? Fair payment for fair services? After eleven years in stir, Mr. Alleyn, you get funny ideas under that heading."

Alleyn said: "Yes. Yes, I've no doubt you do." He looked round the group. "The truth is," he said, "that when you come out of stir it's into another kind of prison and it's heavy going for the outsider who tries to break in."

They looked at him with something like astonishment.

"It's no good keeping on about this," he said, "I've a job to do and so have you. If you agree with the account I've put to you about your part in this affair, it'll be satisfactory to me and I believe the best thing for you. But I can't wait any longer for the answer. You must please yourselves."

A long pause.

Mervyn got to his feet, moved to the fireplace, and savagely kicked a log into the flames.

"We got no choice," he said. "All right. Like you said."

"Speak for yourself," Vincent mumbled but without much conviction.

Blore said, "People don't think."

"How do you mean?"

"They don't know. For us, each of us, it was what you might call as isolated act. Like a single outbreak—an abscess that doesn't spread. Comes to a head and bursts and that's it. It's out of the system. We're no more likely to go violent than anyone else. Less. We know what it's like afterwards. We're oncers. People don't think."

"Is that true of Nigel?"

They looked quickly at each other.

"He's a bit touched," Blore said. "He gets put out. He doesn't understand."

"Is he dangerous?"

"I'll go with what you've put to us, sir," Blore said, exactly as if he hadn't heard Alleyn's question. "I'll agree it's substantially the case. Vince found the body and came in and told us and we reached a decision. I daresay it was stupid but the way we looked at it we couldn't afford for him to be found."

"Who actually moved the body into the packing case?"

Blore said, "I don't think we'll go into details," and Mervyn and Vincent looked eloquently relieved.

"And Nigel knows nothing about it?"

"That's right. He's settled that Mr. Moult was struck down by a sense of sin for mocking us and went off somewhere to repent."

"I see." Alleyn glanced at Fox, who put up his notebook and cleared his throat. "I'll have a short statement written out and will ask you all to sign it if you find it correct."

"We haven't said we'll sign anything," Blore interjected in a hurry and the others made sounds of agreement.

"Quite so," Alleyn said, "It'll be your decision."

He walked out followed by Fox and the driver.

"Do you reckon," Fox asked, "there'll be any attempt to scarper?"

"I don't think so. They're not a stupid lot: the stowing of the body was idiotic but they'd panicked."

Fox said heavily, "This type of chap: you know, the oncer. He always bothers me. There's something in what they said: you can't really call him a villain. Not in the accepted sense. He's funny." Fox meditated.

"That flabby job. The cook. What was it you call him?"

" 'Kittiwee.' "

"I thought that was what you said."

"He's keen on cats. *A propos,* cats come into my complicated story. I'd better put you in the picture, Br'er Fox. Step into the hall."

2.

Alleyn finished his recital, to which Mr. Fox had listened with his customary air: raised brows, pursed lips and a hint of catarrhal breathing. He made an occasional note and when Alleyn had finished remarked that the case was "unusual" as if a new sartorial feature had been introduced by a conservative tailor.

All this took a considerable time. When it was over, seven o'clock had struck. Curtains were still drawn across the hall windows, but on looking through Alleyn found that they were guarded on the outside by Fox's reinforcements and that Bailey and Thompson held powerful lights to the body of Albert Moult while a heavily overcoated person stooped over it.

"The Div. Surgeon," Alleyn said. "Here's the key of the cloakroom, Fox. Have a shiner at it while I talk to him. Go easy. We'll want the full treatment in there."

The Divisional Surgeon, Dr. Moore, said that Moult had either been stunned or killed outright by a blow on the nape of the neck and that the neck had subsequently been broken, presumably by a fall. When Alleyn fetched the poker and they laid it by the horrid wound, the stained portion was found to coincide and the phenomenon duly photographed. Dr. Moore, a weathered man with a good keen eye, was then taken to see the wig, and in the wet patch Alleyn found a tiny skein of hair that had not been washed perfectly clean. It was agreed that this and the poker should be subjected to the sophisticated attention of the Yard's pathological experts.

"He's been thumped all right," said Dr. Moore. "I suppose you'll talk to Sir James." Sir James Curtis was Consultant Pathologist to the Yard. "I wouldn't think," Dr. Moore added, "there'd be much point in leaving the body there. It's been rolled about all over the shop, it seems, since he was thumped. But thumped he was."

And he drove himself back to Downlow where he practiced. The time was now seven-thirty.

Alleyn said, "He's about right, you know, Fox. I'll get through to Curtis but I think he'll say we can move the body. There are some empty rooms in the stables under the clock tower. You chaps can take him round in the car. Lay him out decently, of course. Colonel Forrester will have to identify."

Alleyn telephoned Sir James Curtis and was given rather grudging permission to remove Moult from Hilary's doorstep. Sir James liked bodies to be *in situ* but conceded that as this one had been, as he put it, rattled about like dice in a box, the objection was academic. Alleyn rejoined Fox in the hall. "We can't leave Bill-Tasman uninformed much longer," he said, "I suppose. Worse luck. I must say I don't relish the prospect of coming reactions."

"If we exclude the servants, and I take it we do, we've got a limited field of possibilities, haven't we, Mr. Alleyn?"

"Six, if you also exclude thirty-odd guests and Troy."

"A point being," said Mr. Fox, pursuing after his fashion, his own line of thought, "whether or not it was a case of mistaken identity. Taking into consideration the wig and whiskers."

"Quite so. In which case the field is reduced to five."

"Anyone with a scunner on the Colonel, would you say?"

"I'd have thought it a psychological impossibility. He's walked straight out of *Winnie-the-Pooh*."

"Anybody profit by his demise?"

"I've no idea. I understand his will's in the tin box."

"Is that a fact?"

"Together with the crown jewels and various personal documents. We'll have to see."

"What beats me," said Mr. Fox, "on what you've told me, is this. The man Moult finishes his act. He comes back to the cloakroom. The young lady takes off his wig and whiskers and leaves him there. She takes them *off*. Unless," Fox said carefully, "she's lying, of course. But suppose she is? Where does that lead you?"

"All right, Br'er Fox, where does it lead you?"

"To a nonsense," Fox said warmly. "That's where. To some sort of notion that she went upstairs and got the poker and came back and hit him with it, Gawd knows why, and then dragged him upstairs under the noses of the servants and kids and all and removed the wig and pitched him and the poker out of the window. Or walked upstairs with him alive when we know the servants saw her go through this hall on her own and into the drawing room and anyway there wasn't time and—Well," said Fox, "why go on with it? It's silly."

"Very."

"Rule her out, then. So we're left with? What? This bit of material from his robe, now. If that's what it was. That was caught up in the tree? So he was wearing the robe when he pitched out of the window. So why isn't it torn and wet and generally mucked up and who put it back in the cloakroom?"

"Don't you rather feel that the scrap of material might have been stuck to the poker. Which *was* in the tree."

"Damn!" said Fox. "Yes. Damn. All right. Well now. Sometime or another he falls out of the upstairs window, having been hit on the back of his head with the upstairs poker. *Wearing the wig?*"

"Go on, Br'er Fox."

"Well—presumably wearing the wig. On evidence, wearing the wig. We don't know about the whiskers."

"No."

"No. So we waive them. Never mind the whiskers. But the wig—the wig turns up in the cloakroom same as the robe, just where they left it, only with all the signs of having been washed where the blow fell and not so efficiently but that there's a trace of something that might be blood. So what do we get? The corpse falling through the window, replacing the wig, washing it and the robe clean, and going back and lying down again."

"A droll conceit."

"All right. And where does it leave us? With Mr. Bill-Tasman, the Colonel and his lady and this Bert Smith. Can we eliminate any of them?"

"I think we can."

"You tell me how. Now, then."

"In response to your cordial invitation, Br'er Fox. I shall attempt to do so."

The men outside, having been given the office, lifted the frozen body of Alfred Moult into their car and drove away to the rear of the great house. The effigy of Hilary Bill-Tasman's ancestor, reduced to a ghastly storm-pocked wraith, dwindled on the top of the packing case. And Alleyn, watching through the windows, laid out for Fox, piece by piece, his assemblage of events fitting each until a picture was completed.

When he had done, his colleague drew one of his heavy sighs and wiped his great hand across his mouth.

"That's startling and it's clever," he said. "It's very clever indeed. It'll be a job to make a dead bird of it, though."

"Yes."

"No motive, you see. That's always awkward. Well —no apparent motive. Unless there's one locked up somewhere behind the evidence."

Alleyn felt in his breast pocket, drew out his handkerchief, unfolded it and exposed a key: a commonplace barrel-key such as would fit a commonplace padlock.

"This may help us," he said, "to break in."

"I only need one guess," said Mr. Fox.

Before Alleyn went to tell Hilary of the latest development, he and Fox visited Nigel in the servery, where they found him sitting an an apparent trance with an assembly of early morning tea trays as his background. Troy would have found this a paintable subject, thought Alleyn.

At first, when told that Moult was dead, Nigel looked sideways at Alleyn as if he thought he might be lying. But finally he nodded portentously several times. "Vengeance is Mine, saith the Lord," he said.

"Not in this instance," Alleyn remarked. "He's been murdered."

Nigel put his head on one side and stared at Alleyn through his white eyelashes. Alleyn began to wonder if his wits had quite turned or if, by any chance, he was putting it on.

"How?" Nigel asked.

"He was hit with a poker."

Nigel sighed heavily: "Like Fox," Alleyn thought irrelevantly.

"Everywhere you turn," Nigel generalized, "sinful ongoings! Fornication galore. Such is the vice and depravity of these licentious times."

"The body," Alleyn pressed on, "was found in the packing case under your effigy."

"Well," Nigel snapped, "if you think I put it there you're making a very big mistake." He gazed at Alleyn for some seconds. "Though it's well known to the Lord God of Hosts," he added in a rising voice, "that I'm a sinner. A sinner!" he repeated loudly and now he really did look demented. "I smote a shameless lady in the face of the Heavens and they opened and poured down their phials of wrath upon me. Because such had not been their intention. My mistake." And as usual when recalling his crime, he burst into tears.

Alleyn and Fox withdrew into the hall.

"That chap's certifiable," said Fox, looking very put out. "I mean to say, he's certifiable."

"I'm told he only cuts up rough occasionally."

"Does he cart those trays round the bedrooms?"

"At eight-thirty, Troy says."

"I wouldn't fancy the tea."

"Troy says it's all right. It's Vincent who's the arsenic expert, remember, not Nigel."

"I don't like it," Fox said.

"Damn it all, Br'er Fox, nor do I. I don't like Troy being within a hundred miles of a case, as you very well know. I don't like—well, never mind all that. Look. Here are the keys of Colonel Forrester's dressing-room. I want Thompson and Bailey to give it the full treatment. Window-sashes. All surfaces and objects. That's the wardrobe key. It's highly probable that there are duplicates of the whole lot but never mind. In the wardrobe, standing on its end, is this damned tin uniform box. Particular attention to that. Tell him to report to me when they've finished. I'm going to stir up Bill-Tasman."

"For God's sake!" cried Hilary from the top of the stairs. *"What now!"*

He was leaning over the gallery in his crimson dressing gown. His hair rose in a crest above his startled countenance. He was extremely pale.

"What's happening in the stable yard?" he demanded. "What are they doing? You've found him? Haven't you? You've found him."

"Yes," said Alleyn. "I'm on my way to tell you. Will you wait? Join us, Fox, when you're free."

Hilary waited, biting his knuckles. "I should have been told," he began as soon as Alleyn reached him. "I should have been told at once."

"Can we go somewhere private?"

"Yes, yes, yes. All right. Come to my room. I don't like all this. One should be told."

He led the way round the gallery to his bedroom, a magnificent affair in the west wing corresponding, Alleyn supposed, with that occupied by Cressida in the east wing. It overlooked on one side the courtyard, on the other the approach from the main road, and in front, the parklands-to-be. A door stood open into a dressing-room and beyond that into a bathroom. The dominant feature was a fourposter on a dais, sumptuously canopied and counterpaned.

"I'm sorry," Hilary said, "if I was cross, but really the domestic scene in this house becomes positively quattrocento. I glance through my window," he gestured to the one that overlooked the courtyard, "and see something quite unspeakable being pushed into a car. I glance through the opposite window and the car is being driven round the house. I go to the far end of the corridor and look into the stable yard and there they are, at it again, extricating their hideous find. No!" Hilary cried. "It's too much. Admit. It's too much."

There was a tap on the door. Hilary answered it and disclosed Mr. Fox. "How do you do," Hilary said angrily.

Alleyn introduced them and proceeded, painstakingly, to rehearse the circumstances leading to the discovery of Moult. Hilary interrupted the recital with petulant interjections.

"Well, now you've found it," he said when he had allowed Alleyn to finish, "what happens? What is expected of me? My servants will no doubt be in an advanced state of hysteria, and I wouldn't be surprised if one and all they gave me notice. But command me. What must I do?"

Alleyn said, "I know what a bore it all is for you, but it really can't be helped. Can it? We'll trouble you as little as possible and, after all, if you don't mind a glimpse of the obvious, it's been an even greater bore for Moult."

Hilary turned slightly pink. "Now you're making me feel shabby," he said. "What an alarming man you are. One doesn't know where to have you. Well— what shall I do?"

"Colonel Forrester must be told that Moult has been found, that he's dead, that he's been murdered, and that we shall ask the Colonel to identify the body?"

"Oh *no!*" Hilary shouted. "How beastly for him! Poorest Uncle Flea! Well, I can't tell him. I'll come with you if you do," he added. "I mean if you tell him. Oh all *right,* then, I'll tell him but I'd like you to come."

He walked about the room, muttering disconsolately.

Alleyn said, "But of course I'll come. I'd rather be there."

"On the watch!" Hilary pounced. "That's it, isn't it? Looking out for the way we all behave?"

"See here," Alleyn said. "You manoeuvred me into taking this case. For more than one reason I tried to get out of it but here, in the event, I am, and very largely by your doing. Having played for me and got me, I'm afraid you'll have to lump me and that's the short of it."

Hilary stared at him for some seconds and then the odd face Troy had likened to that of a rather good-looking camel broke into a smile.

"How you do cut one down to size!" he said. "And of course you're right. I'm behaving badly. My dear man, do believe me, really I'm quite ashamed of myself and I *am,* indeed I am, more than thankful we are in your hands. *Peccavi, peccavi,*" cried Hilary, putting his hands together and after a moment, with a decisive air: "Well! The sooner it's over the better, no doubt. Shall we seek out Uncle Flea?"

But there was no need to seek him out. He was coming agitatedly along the corridor with his wife at his heels, both wearing their dressing gowns.

"There you are!" he said. "They've found him, haven't they? They've found poor Moult."

"Come in, Uncle," Hilary said. "Auntie—come in."

They came in, paused at the sight of Alleyn and Fox, said, "Good morning," and turned simultaneously on Hilary. "Speak up, do," said Mrs. Forrester. "He's been found?"

"How did you know? Yes," said Hilary. "He has."

"Is he—?"

"Yes, Uncle Flea, I'm afraid so. I'm awfully sorry."

"You'd better sit down, Fred. Hilary; your uncle had better sit down."

Colonel Forrester turned to Alleyn. "Please tell me exactly what has happened," he said. "I should like a full report."

"Shall we obey orders and sit down, sir? It'll take a little time."

The Colonel made a slight impatient gesture but he took the chair Hilary pushed forward. Mrs. Forrester walked over to the windows, folded her arms and throughout Alleyn's recital stared out at the landscape. Hilary sat on his grand bed and Fox performed his usual feat of self-effacement.

Alleyn gave a full account of the finding of Moult's body and, in answer to some surprisingly succinct and relevant questions from the Colonel, of the events that led up to it. As he went on he sensed a growing tension in his audience: in their stillness, in Mrs. Forrester's withdrawal, in her husband's extreme quietude and in Hilary's painful concentration.

When he had finished there was a long silence. And then, without turning away from the window or, indeed, making any movements, Mrs. Forrester said, "Well, Hilary, your experiment has ended as might have been predicted. In disaster."

Alleyn waited for an expostulation, if not from the Colonel, at least from Hilary. But Hilary sat mum on his magnificant bed and the Colonel, after a long pause, turned to look at him and said: "Sorry, old boy. But there it is. Bad luck. My poor old Moult," said the Colonel with a break in his voice. "Well—there it is."

Alleyn said: "Do I take it that you all suppose one of the servants is responsible?"

They moved just enough to look at him.

"We mustn't lose our common sense, you know,

Alleyn," said the Colonel. "A man's record is always the best guide. You may depend upon it."

"Uncle Flea, I wish I could think you're wrong."

"I know, old boy. I know you do."

"The question is," said Mrs. Forrester. "Which?" Hilary threw up his hands and then buried his face in them.

"Nonsense!" said his aunt glancing at him. "Don't play-act, Hilary."

"No. B! Not fair: He's not play-acting. It's a disappointment."

"A bitter one," said Hilary.

"Although," his aunt went on, pursuing her own line of thought, "It's more a matter of which *isn't* guilty. Personally, I would think it's a conspiracy involving the lot with the possible exception of the madman." She turned her head slightly. "Is that the view of the police?" she asked, over her shoulder.

"No," Alleyn said mildly.

"*No!* What do you mean, 'No'?"

"No, I don't think the servants conspired to murder Moult. I think that with the exception of Nigel they conspired to get rid of the body because they knew they would be suspected. It seems they were not far wrong. But of course it was an idiotic thing to do."

"May I ask," said Mrs. Forrester very loudly, "if you realize what this extraordinary theory implies? May I ask you that?"

"But of course," Alleyn said politely. "Do, please. Ask."

"It implies—" she began on a high note and then appeared to boggle.

"There's no need to spell it out, Aunt B."

"—something perfectly ridiculous," she barked. "I said, something perfectly ridiculous."

Alleyn said, "I'm sorry to have to ask you this, sir, but there's the matter of formal identification."

Colonel Forrester said, "What? Oh! Oh, yes, of course. You—you want me to—to—"

"Unless there is a member of his family within call? There will presumably be relations who should be informed. Perhaps you can help us there? Who is the next-of-kin, do you know?"

This produced a strange reaction. For a moment Alleyn wondered if Colonel Forrester was going to have one of his "turns." He became white and then red in the face. He looked everywhere but at Alleyn. He opened his mouth and then shut it again, half rose and sank back in his chair.

"He had no people," he said at last, "that I know of. He—he has told me. There are none.

"I see. Then, as his employer—"

"I'll just get dressed," the Colonel said and rose to his feet.

"No!" Mrs. Forrester interjected. She left the window and joined him. "You can't, Fred. It'll upset you. I can do it, I said I can do it."

"Certainly not," he said with an edge to his voice that evidently startled his wife and Hilary. "Please don't interfere, B. I shall be ready in ten minutes, Alleyn."

"Thank you very much, sir. I'll join you in the hall."

He opened the door for the Colonel who squared his shoulders, lifted his chin and walked out.

Alleyn said to Mrs. Forrester. "It can wait a little. There's no need for him to come at once. If you think it will really upset him—"

"It doesn't in the least matter what I think. He's made up his mind," she said and followed him out.

3.

They hadn't been able to make what Mr. Fox called a nice job of Moult's body, owing to its being in an advanced state of rigor mortis. They had borrowed a sheet to cover it and had put it on a table in an old harness room. When Alleyn turned back the sheet Moult seemed to be frozen in the act of shaking his fist at the Colonel and uttering a soundless scream out of the head that was so grossly misplaced on its trunk.

Colonel Forrester said, "Yes," and turned away. He walked past the constable on duty, into the yard, and blew his nose. Alleyn gave him a few moments and then joined him.

"Long time," said the Colonel. "Twenty-five years. Quarter of a century. Long time."

"Yes," Alleyn said. "It's a rather special relationship—the officer, soldier-servant one—isn't it?"

"He had his faults but we understood each other's ways. We suited each other very well."

"Come indoors, sir. It's cold."

"Thank you."

Alleyn took him to the library where a fire had now been lit and sat him down by it.

"No need for it, really," said the Colonel, making tremulous conversation, "with all this central heating Hilly's put in, but it's cheerful, of course." He held his elderly veined hands to the fire and finding them unsteady, rubbed them together.

"Shall I get you a drink?"

"What? No, no. No, thanks. I'm perfectly all right. It's just—seeing him. Might have been killed in action. They often looked like that. Bit upsetting."

"Yes."

"I—there'll be things to see to. I mean—you'll want—formalities and all that."

"I'm afraid so. There'll be an inquest of course."

"Of course."

"Do you happen to know if he left a will?"

The hands were still and then, with a sudden jerk, the Colonel crossed his knees and clasped them in a travesty of ease.

"A will?" he said. "Not a great deal to leave, I daresay."

"Still—if he did."

"Yes, of course." He seemed to think this over very carefully.

"You don't know, then, if he did?"

"As a matter of fact," the Colonel said in a constrained voice, "he gave me a—an envelope to keep for him. It may contain his will."

"I think we shall probably ask to see it, Colonel. Of course if it's irrelevant—"

"Yes, yes, yes," he said. "I know. I know."

"Is it," Alleyn asked lightly, "perhaps in that famous uniform box?"

A long silence. "I—rather think so. It may be," said the Colonel and then: "He has—he had the key. I told you, didn't I? He looked after that sort of thing for us. Keys and things."

"You placed an enormous trust in him, didn't you?"

"Oh that?" said the Colonel dismissing it with a shaky wave of his hand. "Oh rather, yes. Absolutely."

"I think I've recovered the key of the padlock."

The Colonel gave Alleyn a long watery stare. "Have you?" he said at last. "From—him?"

"It was in his pocket."

"May I have it, Alleyn?"

"Of course. But if you don't mind we'll do our routine nonsense with it first."

"Fingerprints?" he asked faintly.

"Yes. It really is only routine. I expect to find none but his and your own, of course. We have to do these things."

"Of course."

"Colonel Forrester, what is it that's worrying you? There is something, isn't there?"

"Isn't it enough," he cried out with a kind of suppressed violence, "that I've lost an old and valued servant? Isn't that enough?"

"I'm sorry."

"So am I," said the Colonel at once. "My dear fellow, you must excuse me. I do apologize. I'm not quite myself."

"Shall I tell Mrs. Forrester you're in here?"

"No, no. No need for that. None in the world. Rather like to be by myself for a bit: that's all. Thank you very much, Alleyn. Very considerate."

"I'll leave you, then."

But before he could do so the door opened and in came Mr. Bert Smith, dressed but not shaved.

"I been talking to 'Illy," he said without preliminaries, "and I don't much fancy what I hear. You found 'im, then?"

"Yes."

"Been knocked off? Bashed? Right?"

"Right."

"And there was three of them convicted murderers trying to make away with the corpse. Right?"

"Right."

"And you make out they got nothing to do with it?"

"I don't think, at this stage, that it looks as if any of them killed him."

"You got to be joking."

"Have I?" said Alleyn.

Mr. Smith made a noise suggestive of contempt and disgust, and placed himself in front of the Colonel, who was leaning back in his chair frowning to himself.

"Glad to see you, Colonel," said Mr. Smith. "It's time we got together for a talk. 'Illy's coming down when he's broken the news to 'is loved one and collected 'is Auntie. Any objections?" he shot at Alleyn.

"Good Lord!" Alleyn said. "What possible objections could there be and how on earth could I enforce them? You can hold meetings all over the house if you feel so disposed. I only hope a bit of hog-sense comes out of them. If it does I'll be glad if you'll pass it on. We could do with it."

"Honestly," said Mr. Smith sourly, "you devastate me."

Hilary came in with Mrs. Forrester and Cressida, who was *en negligée* and looked beautiful but woebegone. The other two were dressed.

Mrs. Forrester gave her husband a sharp look and sat beside him. He nodded as if, Alleyn thought, to reassure her and stave off any conversation. Hilary glanced unhappily at Alleyn and stood before the fire. Cressida approached Alleyn, gazed into his face, made a complicated, piteous gesture and shook her lovely head slowly from side to side after the manner of a motion-picture star attempting the ineffable in close-up.

"I can't cope," she said. "I mean I just can't. You know?"

"You don't really have to," he said.

An expression that might have been the prelude to a grin dawned for a moment. "Well, actually I don't, do I?" said Cressida. "Still, admit—it's all a pretty good drag, isn't it?"

She gave him another extremely matey look and

then, in her usual fashion collapsed superbly into a chair.

Smith, Mrs. Forrester and even Hilary stared at her with unmistakable disfavour, Colonel Forrester with a kind of tender bewilderment.

"Cressy, my dear!" he mildly protested.

And at that an astonishing change came about in Cressida. Her eyes filled with tears, her mouth quivered and she beat with her pretty clenched fists on the arms of her chair. "All right, you lot," she stammered. "I know what you're thinking: how hard and mod and ghastly I'm being. All *right*. I don't drip round making sorry-he's-dead noises. That doesn't mean I don't mind. I do. I liked him—Moult. He was nice to me. You've all seen death, haven't you? I hadn't. Not ever. Not until I looked out of my window this morning and saw them putting it in a car, face up and awful. You needn't say anything, any of you. No, Hilly, not even you—not yet. You're old, *old*, all of you and don't *get* it. That's all. Crack ahead with your meeting, for God's sake."

They stared at each other in consternation. Cressida beat on the arms of her chair and said, "Damn! I *won't* bloody cry. I *won't*.

Hilary said, "*Darling*—" but she stamped with both feet and he stopped. Smith muttered something that sounded like "does you credit, love," and cleared his throat.

Mrs. Forrester said: "I collect, Smith, that ludicrous as it sounds, you wish to hold some sort of meeting. Why don't you do it?"

"Give us a chance," he said resentfully.

Alleyn said, "I'm afraid I'm the stumbling block. I'll leave you to it in a moment."

Colonel Forrester, with something of an effort, got to his feet.

"Ask you to excuse me," he said to Smith. "I'm not much good at meetings. Never have been. If you'll allow me, Hilly, I'll just sit in your study till breakfast."

"Fred—"

"No, B. I haven't got one of my Turns. I simply would like a moment or two to myself, my dear."

"I'll come with you."

"No," said the Colonel very firmly indeed. "Don't fuss me, B. I prefer to be alone." He went to the door, paused and looked at Cressida. She had her hand pressed to her mouth. "Unless," the Colonel said gently, "you would care to join me, Cressy, presently. I think perhaps we're both duffers at meetings, don't you?"

She lifted her hand from her lips, sketched the gesture of blowing him a kiss, and contrived a smile. "I'll come," said Cressida. The Colonel nodded and left them. Alleyn opened the door for him. Before he could shut it again Mr. Fox appeared. Alleyn went out to him, pulling the door to. According to its habit it clicked and opened a few inches.

Fox rumbled at some length. Isolated words reached the listeners round the fire. "Finished . . . dressing-room . . . nothing . . . latent . . . urgent."

Alleyn said, "Yes. All right. Tell the men to assemble in the stable yard. I want to speak to them. Tell Bailey and Thompson to leave the box out and the dressing-room unlocked. We've finished up there. Colonel Forrester will open the box when he's ready to do so."

"It's an urgent phone call, Mr. Alleyn."

"Yes. All right. I'll take it. Away you go."

He started off, clapped his hand to his waistcoat and said: "Damn, I forgot. The key of the box?"

"I've got it. Nothing for us, there."

"Let the Colonel have it, then, will you, Fox?"

"Very good, sir."

"I'll take this call in the drawing-room. I'll probably be some time over it. Carry on, Fox, will you? Collect the men outside at the back."

"Certainly, sir," Fox said.

Fox shut the library door and Alleyn went into the hall.

But he didn't speak on the drawing-room, or any other, telephone. He ran upstairs two steps at a time, jolting discomfort to his left arm, and sought out his wife in their room.

"My love," he said. "I want you to stay put. Here. And be a triple ape."

"What on earth's a triple ape?"

Alleyn rapidly touched her eyes, ears and lips.

"Oh," she said flatly. "I see. And I don't breathe either, I suppose."

"That's my girl. Now listen—"

He had not gone far with what he had to say before there was a knock on the door. At a nod from him, Troy called out, "Just a second. Who is it?"

The door opened a crack.

Fox whispered, "Me."

Alleyn went to him. "Well?"

"Like a lamb," said Fox, "to the slaughter."

Ten – Departure

"What I got to say," said Mr. Smith, "is important and I'll thank you to hear me out. When I've said it, I'll welcome comment, but hear me out first. It's a bit of luck for us that flipping door opens of itself. You heard. He's got a phone call and he's going to talk to his mob in the backyard. That gives us a breather. All right. He's made up his mind, Gawd knows why, that your lovely lot's out of it, 'Illy. That means—its got to mean—'e's settled for one of us. So what we say in the next confrontation is bloody important. No, Missus, don't butt in. Your turn's coming.

"Now. We know Alf Moult was alive when 'e finished 'is act and waltzed out of the drawing-room winder looking a proper charlie and all. We know 'e was alive when 'e 'ad 'is whiskers taken off. We know 'e was left, alive, in the cloakroom. And that's all we do know of our own observations. So. The important thing for us is to be able to account for ourselves, all of us, from the time we last see 'im. Right? Acourse it's right.

"Well then. As it appears, we all can answer for the fair sex in the person of Cressy Tottenham. Matter of a minute after Alf finished his act, Cressy come in, having removed his whiskers for 'im, and she certainly hadn't 'ad time to do 'im in and dispose of 'is body."

"Look here, Uncle Bert—"

"All right, all right, all right! I said she couldn't of, didn't I? So she couldn't of. This is important. From Cressy's point of view. Because she seems to of been the last to see 'im alive. Except of course, 'is slayer, and that puts 'er in a special category."

"It does nothing of the sort," Hilary said.

"Don't be silly, Hilary," said his aunt. "Go on, Smith."

"Ta. To resume. I was coming to you, Missus. Cressy come in an' mentioned to you it was Alf and not the Colonel done the Daddy Christmas act and you lit off. Where did you go?"

"To my husband. Naturally."

"Straight off? Direct?"

"Certainly. To our bedroom."

"You didn't look in on the dressing-room?"

"I did not."

"Can you prove it?"

Mrs. Forrester reddened angrily. "No," she said.

"That's unfortunate, innit?"

"Nonsense. Don't be impertinent."

"Ah, for Gawd's sake!"

"Aunt B, he's trying to help us."

"When I require help I'll ask for it."

"You require it now, you silly old bag," said Mr. Smith.

"How dare you speak to me like that!"

"Uncle Bert—*really*."

"And what about yourself, 'Illy? We'll be coming to you in a sec. Where was I? Oh, yes. With Cressy in the drawingroom. She tells you two about the job and one after another you leave the room. Where did you go?"

"I? I looked for Moult to thank him. I looked in the cloakroom and the library and I went upstairs to see if he was there. And I visited Uncle Flea and Aunt B was with him and finally I joined you all in the dining-room."

"There you are," said Mr. Smith. "So if Alf Moult went upstairs you or your auntie or (supposing 'e 'adn't 'ad one of 'is turns) your uncle, *could* of done 'im in."

"Well—my dear Uncle Bert—'could have'! Yes, I suppose so. But so could—" Hilary stopped short.

"So could who? I couldn't of. Mrs. Alleyn couldn't of. Cressy couldn't of. We was all sitting down to our Christmas dinner, good as gold, as anyone will bear us out."

Mrs. Forrester said, "Are we to take it, Smith, that your attitude is entirely altruistic? If you are persuaded that you are completely free of suspicion, why all this fuss?"

"Innit marvellous?" Mr. Smith apostrophized. "Innit bleeding marvellous? A man sees 'is friends, or what 'e thought was 'is friends, in a nasty situation and tries to give them the office. What does 'e get? You can't win, can you?"

"I'm sure," she said, "we're very much obliged to you, Smith. There's one aspect of this affair, however, that I think you have overlooked."

She paused, thrust her hands up the opposite sleeves of her magenta cardigan and rested them on her stomach. "Isn't it possible," she said, "that Moult was done away with much later in the evening? Your uncle, Hilary, will not care to admit it but Moult did, from time to time, indulge in drinking bouts. I think it extremely likely this was such an occasion. Cressida considers he had drink concealed about his person. He may well have taken it after his performance, hidden himself away somewhere, possibly in a car, and thus eluded the searchers and emerged later in the evening—to be murdered."

"You've thought it all out very nice and tidy, 'aven't you?" sneered Mr. Smith.

"And so, you may depend upon it, has Mr. Alleyn," she retorted.

"The search was very thorough, Aunt Bed."

"Did they look in the cars?"

Hilary was silent.

"In which case," Mrs. Forrester said exactly as if he had answered, "I cannot see that you, Smith, or Cressida or indeed you, Hilary, are to be excluded from the list of suspected persons."

"What about yourself?" Smith asked.

"I?" she said with her customary spirit. "No doubt I could have killed Moult. I had no conceivable motive for killing him but no doubt I could have done so."

"Nothing simpler. You go up to the Colonel, who's on 'is bed and asleep. You hear Alf Moult in the dressing-room. You go froo the barfroom into the dressing-room, pick up the poker and Bob's your uncle. You shove the corpse out of the winder." Mr. Smith caught himself up. "You did say Vince and Co. picked it up under the winder, didn't you, 'Illy?"

"I don't think I said anything about it. But according to Alleyn, yes, they did."

"The *modus operandi* you have outlined, Smith, could have been used by anybody if my theory is correct. You've talked a great deal but you've proved nothing, I said you've—"

"Don't you bawl me out as if I was your old man," Mr. Smith roared. "I been watching you, Missus. You been acting very peculiar. You got something up your sleeve you're not letting on about."

Hilary, with a wildish look, cried out, "I won't have this sort of thing!"

"Yes, you will. You can't help yourself. You want to watch your aunt. I did. When Alleyn was talking about that marvellous tin box. You didn't like that, Missus, did you?"

Mr. Smith advanced upon Mrs. Forrester. He jabbed at her with a fat forefinger. "Come on," he said. "What's it all about? What's in the ruddy tin box?"

Mrs. Forrester walked out of the room, slamming the door. When she had gone, it opened silently of its own accord.

2.

The key fitted. It turned easily. Now. The hoop was disengaged. The hasp was more difficult, it really needed a lever but there was none to hand. At the cost of a broken fingernail and in spite of a glove it was finally prised up from the staple.

The lid opened to a vertical position but tended to fall forward, so that it was necessary to prop it up with the head. This was irksome.

A cash box: locked. A map-case. Canvas bags, tied at the neck and red tape. Tubular cartons. Manila envelopes, labelled. "Correspondence: B to F.F. F.F. to B." He had kept all their letters.

"Receipts." "Correspondence, general." "Travel, etc." "Miscellaneous." A document in a grand envelope. "To our Trusty and Well-beloved—"

It was necessary to keep calm. To keep what Cressida called one's cool. Not to scrabble wildly in the welter of accumulated papers. To be methodical and workmanlike. Sensible.

A locked box that rattled. The jewels she hadn't taken out for the party. And at last a leather dispatch-case with an envelope flap: locked.

No panic but something rather like it when somebody walked past the door. The keys had been removed so one couldn't lock the door.

The impulse to get out at once with the case and deal with it in safety was almost irresistible, but it presented its own problems. If only one knew how to pick a lock! Perhaps they would think that Moult had burst it. It was a sliding mechanism with a metal hinged piece on the leather flap engaging with a lock on the case itself. Perhaps the slide could be knocked down? Or, better, force the hinged piece up? The poker, of course, had gone but there were the tongs with their little thin flat ends.

Yes. Between the metal flap and the lock there was just room. Shove. Shove hard and force it up.

There!

A diary. A large envelope. "My Will." Not sealed. A rapid look at it. Leave that. Put it back—quick. The thing itself: a reinforced envelope and inside it the document, printed in German, filled in and signed. The statement in Colonel Forrester's hand. The final words: "declare her to be my daughter," and the signature: "Alfred Moult."

Replace the dispatch-case, quick, quick, quick.

Relock the tin box. Back into the wardrobe with it. Now, the envelope. She must hide it under her cardigan and away.

She stood up, breathless.

The doors opened simultaneously and before she could cry out there were men in the room and Alleyn advancing upon her.

"I'm afraid," he said, "this is it."

And for the second time during their short acquaintance Cressida screamed at the top of her voice.

3.

"It's been a short cut," Alleyn said. "We left the library door open and let it be known the coast was clear. Fox displayed the key of the padlock, Cressida Tottenham said she was on her way to the study and would give it to the Colonel. We went upstairs, kept out of sight, and walked in on her. It was a gamble and it might never have come off. In which case we would have been landed with a most exhaustive routine investigation. We are, still, of course, but with the advantage of her first reaction. She was surprised and flabbergasted and she gave herself away in several most significant places."

"Rory—when did you first—?"

"Oh—that. Almost from the beginning, I think," said he with a callow smirk. "You see, there everybody was, accepting her story that Moult substituted for the Colonel, which put her ostensibly in the clear and made a squint-eyed nonsense of the evidence: the robe, the wig, the lot. Whereas if *she* had substituted for the Colonel there was no confusion.

"She hit Moult on the base of his skull with the poker in the dressing-room, probably when he was leaning out of the window looking for his signal from Vincent, who, by the way, saw him and, according to plan, at once hauled his sledge round to the front. At this point the bells started up. A deafening clamour. She removed the wig and the robe, which unzips completely down the back. If he was lolling over the sill, there'd be no trouble. Nor would it be all that difficult to tumble him out.

"The tricky bit, no doubt, was going downstairs but by that time, as she knew when she heard the bells, the whole household, including the staff, were

assembled in the library. Even if one of the servants
had seen her carrying the robe and all the other
gear, they'd have thought nothing of it at the time.
She went into the dressing-room, stuffed a couple of
cotton-wool pads in her cheeks and put on the wig,
the robe, the great golden beard and moustache and
the mistletoe crown. And the fur-lined boots. *And*
the Colonel's woolly gloves which you all thought he'd
forgotten. And away she went. She was met by the
unsuspecting Vincent. She waltzed round the Christmas
tree, returned to the cloakroom and offed with her
lendings. In five minutes she was asking you if Moult
did his act all right because she couldn't see very well
from the back of the room."

"Rory—where is she?"

"In her bedroom with a copper at the door. Why?"

"Is she—frightened?"

"When I left her she was furious. She tried to bite
me. Luckily I was on my guard so she didn't repeat
her success with the vase."

Alleyn looked at his wife. "I know, my love," he
said. "Your capacity for pity is on the Dostoevskian
scale." He put his arm round her. "You are such a
treat," he said. "Apart from being a bloody genius.
I can't get over you. After all these years. Odd, isn't
it?"

"Did she work it out beforehand?"

"No. Not the assault. It was an improvisation—a
toccata. Now, she's in for the fugue."

"But—those tricks—the booby-trap and all?"

"Designed to set Bill-Tasman against his cosy little
clutch of homicides. She would have preferred a
group of resentful Greeks in flight from the Colonels."

"Poor old Hilary."

"Well—yes. But she really is a horrid piece of
work. All the same there are extenuating circum-

stances. In my job one examines them, as you know, at one's peril."

"Go on."

"At one's peril," he repeated and then said, "I don't know at what stage Colonel Forrester felt he was, according to his code, obliged to step in. From the tenor of the documents in that infernal tin box, one gathers that she was Moult's daughter by a German girl who died in childbirth, that it was Moult who, with great courage, saved the Colonel's life and got a badly scarred face for his pains. That Moult had means comprising a tidy inheritance from a paternal tobacconist's shop, his savings, his pay and his wages. That the Colonel, poor dear, felt himself to be under a lifelong debt to Moult. All right. Now Moult, like many of his class, was an unrepentant snob. He wanted his natural daughter upon whom he doted to be 'brought up a lady.' He wanted the Colonel to organize this process. He wanted to watch the process, as it were, from well back in the pit, unidentified, completely anonymous. And so it fell out. Until the whirligig of time, according to its practice, brought in its revenges. Hilary Bill-Tasman, having encountered her at his uncle's and aunt's house, decided that she was just the chatelaine for Halberds and, incidentally, the desire of his heart. She seemed to fill the bill in every possible respect. 'Tottenham' for instance. A damn' good family."

"Is it?" said Troy. "Yes. Well *Tottenham*. Why Tottenham?"

"I'll ask the Colonel," said Alleyn.

4.

"Moult," said the Colonel, "was a keen follower of the Spurs. He chose it for that reason."

"We didn't care for it," said Mrs. Forrester. "After all there are—Fred tried to suggest Bolton or Wolverhampton but he wouldn't hear of them. She is Tottenham by deedpoll."

"How," Alleyn asked, "did it all come to a crisis?"

The Colonel stared dolefully into space. "You tell him, B," he said.

"With the engagement. Fred felt—we both felt—that we couldn't let Hilary marry under false pretence. She had told him all sorts of tarradiddles—"

"Wait a bit," Alleyn said. "Did she know—?"

They both cried out: no, of course she didn't. She had only been told that she had no parents, that there were no relatives.

"This was agreed upon with Moult," said the Colonel. "She grew up from infancy in this belief. Of course, when she visited us he saw her."

"Gloated," Mrs. Forrester interpolated. "Took her to the zoo."

"Peter Pan and all that," her husband agreed. " 'Fraid he forgot himself a bit and let her understand all sorts of fairytales—father's rank and all that."

But it emerged that on her own account Cressida had built up a magnificent fantasy for herself, and when she discovered that Hilary was steeped up to the teeth in armorial bearings went to all extremes to present herself in a complementary image.

"You see," the Colonel said unhappily, "Hilary sets such store by that sort of thing. She considered, and one can't say without cause, that if he learnt that she had been embroidering he would take a grave view. I blame myself, I blame myself entirely, but when she persisted I told her that she should put all that nonsense out of her head and I'm afraid I went further than that."

"He told her," said his wife, "without of course implicating Moult, that she came from a sound but not in the least grand sort of background, quite humble in fact, and she—from something he said—she's quick, you know—she realized that she'd been born out of wedlock. Fred told her it wouldn't be honourable to marry Hilary letting him think all this nonsense. Fred said that if Hilary loved her the truth wouldn't stop him."

"I—warned her—" the Colonel said and stopped.

"That if *she* didn't tell him, *you* would."

The Colonel opened his eyes as wide as saucers: "Yes. I did. How did you know?" he said.

"I guessed," Alleyn lied.

There was a long silence.

"Oh, yes?" said Mrs. Forrester with a gimlet glance at the wardrobe door.

The Colonel made a helpless gesture with his thin hands. "What is so dreadful," he said, "what I cannot reconcile myself to believe is that—that she—"

He got up and walked over to the windows. Mrs. Forrester made a portentous grimace at Alleyn.

"—that when she attacked Moult she mistook him for you?" Alleyn suggested.

He nodded.

"Believe me, Colonel," Alleyn said, going to him. "You need have no misgivings about that. She knew it was Moult. Believe me."

The Colonel gazed at him. "But—I—of course one is relieved in a way. Of course. One can't help it? But—Moult? Why my poor Moult? Why here? No!" he cried out. "No. I don't want to hear. Don't tell me."

5.

But Alleyn told Hilary.

He and Hilary and, at the latter's entreaty, Troy,

sat together in the study. The police, apart from
Alleyn's driver had gone and so had Cressida and so,
in a mortuary car, had her father, Alfred Moult.

As if to promote a kind of phony symbolism, the
sun had come out and the snow was melting.

Hilary said to Troy. "But you see she's so very
beautiful. That's what diddled me, I suppose. I mean,
all her ongoings and rather tedious conversation, for
me was filtered through her loveliness. It reached me
as something rather endearing—or, to be honest, didn't
reach me at all." He fell into a brief reverie. The look
that Troy had secured in her painting—the faint
smirk—crept into the corners of his mouth. "It's all
quite dreadful," he said, "and of course, in a way
I'm shattered. I promise you—shattered. But—I understand from Uncle Flea and Aunt Bed, she really
did tell me the most awful whoppers. I mean—
'Tottenham' and so on."

Troy said: "She knew you minded about things
like that."

"Of course I do. I'm the last of the howling snobs.
But—Moult? *Moult!* Her papa!"

"She didn't know," Alleyn said, "about Moult."

Hilary pounced: "When did she find out?" he
snapped. "Or did she? Has she—has she—confessed?"

"She's said enough," Alleyn said sparsely. And as
Hilary stared at him: "She knew that documents re-
lating to her parentage were in the uniform case.
The Colonel told her so when he said that you should
know of her background. When she thought that the
Colonel was downstairs in the cloakroom waiting for
her and when everybody else had assembled for the
tree, she tried to break into the case with the dressingroom poker. Moult, who had been showing himself
to the Colonel in his robe and wig, returned to the
dressing-room and caught her in the act. Climax. He'd

taken a lot to drink, he was excited and he told her. The bells had started up downstairs, he looked out of the window for Vincent, and she hit him with the poker."

"Unpremeditated, then," Hilary said quickly. "Not planned? A kind of reflex thing? Yes?"

"You may say so."

"At least one may be glad of that. And no designs upon poorest Uncle Flea. Thank Heaven for *that*."

Alleyn said nothing. There would not, he believed, be cause to produce the evidence of the wedge in the Colonel's window-sash nor of the concealment of his tablets.

"The defence," he said, "will probably seek to have the charge reduced to one of manslaughter."

"How long?"

"Difficult to say. She may get off."

Hilary looked alarmed.

"But not altogether, I fancy," said Alleyn.

"You might almost say," Hilary ventured after a pause, "that my poor creatures, Vincent and Co., collaborated."

"In a way, I suppose you might."

"Yes," Hilary said in a hurry, "but it's one thing to staff one's house with—er 'oncers'—but quite another to—" He stopped short and turned rather pink.

"I think we should be off, Rory," said Troy.

Hilary was effusive in thanks, ejaculations about his portrait, apologies and expressions of goodwill.

As they drove away in the thin sunshine he stood, manorially, on the steps of the great porch. Mervyn and Blore, having assisted with the luggage, were in the offing. At the last moment Hilary was joined by Mr. Smith and the Forresters. Troy waved to them.

"We might be going away from a jolly weekend party," she said.

"Do you know," her husband asked, "what Hilary very nearly said?"

"What?"

"That when she comes out she'll qualify for a job at Halberds. Not quite the one envisaged. Parlourmaid perhaps. With perks."

"Rory!"

"I bet you anything you like," said Alleyn.

are you missing out on some great Pyramid books?

You can have any title in print at Pyramid delivered right to your door! To receive your Pyramid Paperback Catalog, fill in the label below (use a ball point pen please) and mail to Pyramid...

PYRAMID PUBLICATIONS
Mail Order Department
9 Garden Street
Moonachie, New Jersey 07074

NAME_____

ADDRESS_____

CITY_____STATE_____

P-5   ZIP_____